S0-BAR-986

Warm Waves at the Beach House

Diamond Beach Book 6

MAGGIE MILLER

WARM WAVES AT THE BEACH HOUSE: Diamond Beach,
book 6
Copyright © 2023 Maggie Miller

All rights reserved. No part of this book may be reproduced in any
form or by any electronic or mechanical means, including
information storage and retrieval systems—except in the case of
brief quotations embodied in critical articles or reviews—without
permission in writing from the author.
This book is a work of fiction. The characters, events, and places
portrayed in this book are products of the author's imagination
and are either fictitious or are used fictitiously. Any similarity to
real person, living or dead, is purely coincidental and not intended
by the author.

All she wanted was one last summer at the beach house...

With the wedding behind them and life in Diamond Beach taking shape, everyone in the beach house seems to be doing just fine.

Claire's busy with all the last-minute details that go into opening a new business, something that brings her and Danny even closer together. For the first time in a long time, she's thinking about the future in a way she never has before.

Roxie isn't quite sure of where she fits in just yet, but she's confident she'll find her place. It's daughter Trina she's worried about. She's become the source of ire for another young woman in town and Roxie doesn't like it one bit. She just doesn't know how to help. Yet.

With new jobs, new opportunities, and new directions, the women of the Double Diamond beach house have come a long way since they first arrived. There's nothing but blue skies and warm waves ahead for them.

Chapter One

*W*illie and Miguel had checked out of the honeymoon suite at the Hamilton Arms later than anticipated after the hotel had surprised them with a complimentary late checkout of 4 p.m. Willie figured they must not have had any other newlyweds booked in. Whatever the reason, she was grateful for the extra time.

Because of that late checkout, she and Miguel had left their suitcases with the concierge and gone back to the poolside bar to enjoy one more drink and watch the sunset. Why not? They were getting an Uber back to their houses.

She was glad they'd had that little interlude by the pool.

Now, however, she wasn't quite as glad. She and Miguel stood at the front door of the Stewarts' house as the last light of sunset was leaving the sky. She'd thought about putting off this conversation until tomorrow, but Miguel had talked her out of it. She was nervous. But not because they were about to confront these people over their daughter's behavior toward Trina, Willie's granddaughter. Willie could handle confrontation.

What she *was* nervous about was word getting back to Trina that she and Miguel had talked to the Stewarts on Trina's behalf. Willie knew Trina wouldn't like that, but she couldn't sit idly by while Liz Stewart harassed Trina every time she saw her.

Miguel pushed the doorbell.

Willie studied the house. It was a big place. Stucco accented with stone, probably fake, because Florida didn't have a lot of stone like that, but it still looked nice. Two stories with lots of windows in an older section of Diamond Beach, where the lots were twice the size of the one she and Miguel had just bought in Dunes West.

The trees were old, too, and provided a lot of shade. It was a nice community with beautiful, colorful landscaping and well-maintained yards. Quiet in that way Old Money neighborhoods usually were.

The house sat on a big lake. Natural or man-made, Willie couldn't tell. She wondered if there were gators in it. Had to be, she thought. They said if a body of water in Florida was at least two feet deep, it probably had a gator.

The door opened and a woman in white pants and a pink gingham shirt, sleeves rolled up, answered, a beagle at her side. "Hello, there."

"Grace?" Miguel said. "I'm sure you don't remember me, but—"

"Miguel Rojas, right?" Grace smiled. "Of course I remember you. And not just from the Chamber of Commerce. I know it was years ago, but we had Eddie Jr.'s tenth birthday party at your popcorn store. The downtown location. Oh, he loved that. So did all his friends. Too bad they're not as easy to please when they grow up." She laughed. "What can I do for you?"

Miguel smiled. "I'm glad you remember me." He gestured toward Willie. "This is my new bride, Willie. We're sorry to bother you this evening, but we were wondering if we could have a few moments of your time."

"Absolutely. Come on in. And congratulations on your marriage." She bent down, took hold of the dog's collar and pulled him back as she stepped out of the way to let them through.

"Thank you," Willie said. The house was beautiful on the inside. Looked like something out of a fancy magazine about beach houses, even though the house wasn't that close to the beach. The back of the house had lots of glass. Tall windows and sliding doors. The view to the lake was pretty nice, even though it was mostly dark.

"If you were hoping to speak to Ed, I'm afraid he went to the driving range after dinner. I imagine he'll be home in an hour or so, though."

"That's all right," Miguel said. "We're happy to talk to you."

"Cute dog," Willie said.

Grace smiled. "Thank you. That's Trooper. He was a rescue. He's still in training but he's doing pretty well. Aren't you, boy?" She scratched the dog's head.

Trooper leaned into her hand. She motioned to Miguel and Willie. "Come on into the living room and we can talk there."

They followed her through the house and took seats on a couch upholstered in beautiful white and blue fabric patterned with shells. Willie couldn't imagine having a couch with a white background. It seemed like something that would get dirty so fast.

But it was gorgeous enough to make her rethink that impression.

"Your house is lovely," Willie said. "We're having a home built in Dunes West and your place is giving me all kinds of decorating ideas."

"Thank you," Grace said. She'd taken the chair, which was covered in a bold white and blue stripe that complimented the shells. Trooper settled down right beside her. "But I can't take the credit. I'd be happy to give you the name and number of the decorator we used. I've been very happy with what she did."

Willie nodded. "That would be great. Thanks." She'd never even considered using a decorator. Those were for people with money. But she had money now, so why not at least talk to the woman?

Miguel cleared his throat softly. "It was very kind of you to invite us in. I'm afraid what we want to speak to you about isn't as nice."

"Oh?" Grace's brows lifted.

Miguel nodded. "It's about Liz."

Grace let out a sigh. "What's she done now?"

Willie narrowed her eyes. "That sounds like you know she's been up to something."

"I don't, actually," Grace said. "But she hasn't been in a good place since her father and I had a long talk with her about making something of herself." She shook her head and looked perturbed. "Liz is a good girl, but in the last few years she's come to see our money as her birthright."

Miguel nodded. Willie stayed quiet, waiting to hear what came next.

Grace sat back. "I really don't know how that happened. How she got so spoiled and entitled. Her brother had the same upbringing and he's completely focused on school and his grades." She smiled. "He's going to be an orthodontist."

"Good profession," Willie said.

"I think so, too," Grace agreed. "But ever since Liz graduated from college she's just coasted through life. I guess her end game is living off our good will, but that's not a life. We told her as much about a month ago. Told her we were no longer going to be her bank, and that she needed to get a job and do something with her life. Things have gone downhill from there. Although she did finally get a job, thank goodness."

Willie exchanged a glance with Miguel.

"It's all right," Grace said, clearly interpreting their unspoken conversation. "You can tell me what she's done."

Miguel's brows lifted slightly as if asking Willie if

she wanted to be the one to explain.

She nodded and told Grace what had happened, starting with Trina turning an inexperienced and rude Liz down for a job at the salon.

Grace listened, the look on her face growing increasingly horrified. When Willie was done explaining the latest incident at Clipper's, Grace swallowed and blinked as if trying to digest everything Willie had told her. "I am...*so* sorry."

"The thing is," Willie continued. "We don't want Trina knowing we were here or that we talked to you. She wouldn't like it, I'm sure. She's a very independent young woman and currently focused on getting her new hair salon up and running. As her grandmother, I just couldn't sit by and watch this happen."

Miguel nodded. "In fact, I would consider it a personal favor if you would keep us out of it. If you need anything from me or my family, all you have to do is ask."

"I get it," Grace said. "And I understand. I'll have to tell Ed, of course, but we won't say a thing about who spoke to us. Although he might want to talk to you about sponsoring a foursome for his next fundraiser at the country club."

"Thank you," Miguel said. "And I'd be glad to."

Grace looked at Willie. "Trina sounds lovely, by the way. You must be very proud of her."

"I am." Willie smiled. Grace was a lot nicer than she'd imagined. "I'm sorry about Liz. I hate that we even had to have this conversation."

"I'm the one who's sorry," Grace said.

Miguel nodded. "Are you sure you can speak to her without letting her know we came to you?"

Grace responded immediately. "I don't plan on mentioning you at all, after I explain everything to my husband. But I promise he'll understand you not wanting to be involved further. I know my daughter. Sadly, one word that you were here, and she'll be even more laser focused on Trina." She exhaled, a vaguely hopeless sound.

"I really am sorry we had to bring this to your attention," Miguel said.

"Please, don't apologize. I'll speak to Ed as soon as I can, and we'll come up with something. It won't be hard. We're well known in the community. Could be just about anyone who saw their last interaction at Clipper's and mentioned it to us. In the meantime, if Liz bothers your granddaughter again, please let me know. This cannot continue."

Willie certainly agreed with that. "You've been

really understanding about this. Thank you for that."

Grace offered a weak smile. "You're welcome." Then her smile picked up a little. "Miguel, I heard you're adding to the Mrs. Butter's empire with a new shop. A bakery?"

He nodded. "That's right. We're hoping to open very soon."

"I think that's marvelous. Diamond Beach could use a great bakery and Publix could use the competition." She laughed. "They might not think so, but I do. I promise I'll be in to have a look once you open. Ed definitely has a sweet tooth and baking is not my thing."

"We'll take good care of you," Miguel said. "Thanks again for listening to us. We've taken up enough of your time this evening."

"Thank you for coming to me. Again, my apologies that Liz has caused Trina such a headache."

Willie and Miguel got to their feet as Grace did, too. Trooper immediately stood and accompanied Grace as she walked them out.

"Take care," Grace called after them as they headed to the car that was waiting on them.

"Have a good night." Miguel gave her a little wave over his shoulder.

He helped Willie into the backseat, where he joined her. He shut the door. "I hope offering to sponsor a team for Ed's next charity golf tournament was enough. I also hope we did the right thing."

"So do I," Willie said. "I'll guess we'll find out soon enough."

Chapter Two

Upon hearing the news that Conrad's meddling sister, Dinah, was planning on moving to Diamond Beach, Margo had gone momentarily speechless. Then she'd come to her senses and told Conrad to meet her at Digger's for breakfast the next morning. Without Dinah.

She'd then helped Claire get dinner ready and enjoyed an evening with her family, even if her thoughts had been mostly on this new game Dinah was now playing.

Margo had even dreamed about Dinah last night. In the dream, Margo and Conrad had been in his office, working on their thriller, *The Widow*. Dinah had repeatedly come in, distracted Conrad and, when he wasn't looking, she'd pressed the Delete key, erasing all the work they'd just done.

Needless to say, the dream had not put Margo in

the best of moods this morning. Now, as Margo pulled her car into the little diner's lot, she searched for Conrad's car. She hoped he was here already, even if it was ten minutes before they were due to meet.

He was.

She parked beside his vehicle and went in. She found him at a quiet booth near the back, two cups of coffee and menus on the table. "Morning."

His smile was tense. "Morning. Sorry about all this."

"It's not your fault." She sat. "Or is it?"

He frowned. "I don't honestly know what put this idea into her head."

"I think it's obvious. We put the idea into her head because we refused to go along with her trying to separate us. If anyone's to blame, it's both of us."

He reached across the table and took Margo's hand. "I promise you, I had no idea she was going to be this bad. I've never liked anyone as much as you, though. I've never really pushed back at her, either. I'm sure that's thrown her for a loop."

"Perhaps. But when do you think she's going to get it through her head that you're an *adult*?" Margo let go of his hand to fix her coffee. "It's ridiculous,

Conrad. She has no say over how you live your life. And who you live it with."

"I know that. I've told her that. But it makes no impact."

She stirred a splash of creamer in, then picked up the cup and took a long swallow. "So, she's going to move here to become a permanent thorn in your side?" Hers, too, but Margo wouldn't be around Dinah nearly as much as Conrad would be.

He nodded, looking rather bereft at the thought. "Apparently."

Margo shrugged. "Let's say she does move here. Is that going to change anything between us?"

He shook his head. "Not for me."

"Not for me, either. Will it affect our writing?"

"Not if I refuse to let her in." He drank his coffee. "We could also work at your house some days, too. Once you've moved in."

She nodded. "We should split our time between both places." She laced her fingers with his once he set his cup down. She smiled at him. "I say let her move."

His brow furrowed. "Seriously?"

She'd had a lot of time to think about this. "Yes. If she wants to uproot her life, sell the home she's lived in for decades, and come here, let her. I think she'll be miserable in no time flat, but maybe I'm wrong. I also think she's expecting you to protest her move. To really argue her out of it."

Margo lifted one shoulder and gave him a coy grin. "I also say call a realtor and book some showings, then get Dinah out to them as soon as possible. I'd be happy to come along and offer my opinion, as well."

Conrad stared at her for a moment before he laughed. "Call her bluff."

Margo nodded. "That's exactly what I'm saying."

Their server approached. "Morning. Are you ready to order?"

Margo glanced at the young woman. "I'm sorry, I haven't even opened the menu yet. Are there any specials we should know about?"

"That's okay," the server said. "We have two specials this morning: coconut pancakes and a broccoli, bacon and cheddar quiche served with a side of fruit salad or home fries."

Margo looked at Conrad. "I'm happy with the quiche and fruit salad. Do you need a minute?"

He shook his head and handed his menu to the server. "The quiche with fruit salad is fine for me."

"Perfect," Margo said, giving her menu to the young woman as well. As the server left, Margo looked at Conrad again. "Where does Dinah think you are this morning?"

"I have no idea. I left before I talked to her. She was up, but still pouting, so I just put a note on the counter saying I'd be back in about an hour."

Margo nodded. "So, do you know a realtor?"

"I do." He took out his phone. "If you don't mind, I'm going to call him right now and see if he can help me out."

"I don't mind at all."

Conrad's friend seemed to be eager, based on Conrad's side of the conversation. As the call was finishing up, their server returned with their plates.

She put one in front of each of them. "Enjoy. I'll be right back with more coffee."

They held off on resuming their conversation until their server had topped off their coffee. Then Conrad leaned in. "Jerry says he can probably get us into two to three places today, depending on what Dinah is interested in. House or condo, that sort of thing."

"Excellent."

"Come home with me after breakfast and help me sell the whole thing, would you? If she sees we're both in agreement that her moving to Diamond

Beach is a good idea, she might change her mind faster than you think."

"I'm willing to give it a try." Margo picked up her fork and ate, her appetite renewed at the possibility of thwarting Dinah at her own game.

Half an hour later, they were headed back to Conrad's. He pulled into the garage, and she parked behind him in the driveway. They walked in together.

"Dinah?" Conrad called out as they went into the kitchen.

She came out of the guest room, smiling—until she saw Margo. "Oh. Hello."

Margo smiled with sincerity. She wasn't happy to see Dinah, but she *was* happy that they might soon be rid of her. "Good morning, Dinah. Conrad told me all about your plans. I think it's marvelous."

"Plans?" Dinah's brow furrowed.

Margo nodded. "To move here."

Dinah's skepticism was obvious. "You think that's marvelous?"

"I do. Family is everything. Don't you agree?"

Dinah glanced at Conrad. "Of course. That's why I want to move here."

Sure, *that* was why she wanted to move here. Margo just played along. "What kind of place are you thinking about?" she asked. "A house? A condo? An apartment?"

"I..." Dinah didn't seem as though she'd thought that much about it.

Because she hadn't, Margo knew. "A condo would be easier to take care of. But a house is nice, too, especially if you want some yard space for gardening."

Conrad nodded. "I've often thought about condo living, but I like having some green space. Not sure I could live with wall-to-wall neighbors, either."

Dinah chewed on her bottom lip. "I don't know, a condo might not be so bad. I don't want to have to cut the grass. Or pay someone to do it."

"You'll have to share a pool," Margo countered. "If you have a house, you could have your own pool."

Dinah shook her head. "Just one more thing to look after."

"A condo it is," Conrad said. He took out his phone. "My friend Jerry is a realtor. I'm going to call him right now and see what he's got available." He grinned at his sister. "Exciting, huh?"

She smiled thinly. "Very."

"Jerry! It's Conrad Ballard. My sister's looking to move to Diamond Beach. What have you got in the way of condos?" He nodded. "Just a second, I'll ask her." He looked at Dinah. "Two-bedroom? Three?"

"Um…" Dinah took a breath. "Two would be fine, I suppose."

"Two-bedroom," Conrad said into the phone.

Margo went out to the living room and took a seat on the couch. Dinah drifted a few steps in that direction as well, but seemed reluctant to get too far away from Conrad.

Finally, Conrad hung up and faced both women. "Jerry's a good guy. He's got three condos he can show us in about an hour." He gave Dinah a big smile. "It's good to have connections."

"I see that," Dinah said. "Won't he want some sort of financial proof from my bank or something?"

Conrad shook his head. "Not for my sister. All of that can be dealt with later when you make an offer."

Dinah twisted her hands together. "This might be a bit premature. I still have to get my house ready to sell and put it on the market. There's a lot to do."

"Absolutely," Margo said. "But there's no reason you can't put a contingent offer on a place if you find something you like. Diamond Beach is a very popular place. It's a hot market. You'll have to act fast if you're serious." She looked to Conrad for confirmation.

He nodded. "Margo's right. Jerry was just saying the same thing about how inventory turns over so quickly." He looked at the time. "Maybe Margo and I can get a page or two written while you get ready to go, Dinah."

She frowned. "I am ready."

His brows lifted as he scanned her outfit of loose linen capris and matching short-sleeve shirt over a tank top. "Oh. All right then."

Margo almost laughed, only just managing to get the smirk off her face before Dinah saw it. She stood. "To the office?"

"To the office," Conrad said.

"You're actually going to work?" Dinah said.

"Yes," Conrad answered. "That's what we'd normally be doing today. And we're already going to be taking time off to go house hunting with you. Unless you've changed your mind?"

Dinah lifted her chin. "No, of course not. I'll just have another cup of tea until it's time to leave."

Margo slipped into Conrad's office and finally allowed herself a grin. This was going to be a very interesting day.

Chapter Three

*R*oxie was up and out the door early, hitting the beach for her workout within minutes of waking. She hadn't even made coffee, something she'd probably regret when she got back, but it could brew while she showered.

There was no other reason for her to get moving so early other than she was really motivated by how good it made her feel. And how good she'd been feeling about focusing more on her fitness. The motivation for that had mostly come from Ethan and his sweet attention. She wanted to look good for herself, but for him, too.

Unfortunately, the good feeling exercise gave her didn't extend to the still unanswered question of what Roxie was going to do with her life. She had to do *something*. She pushed herself to walk faster.

She had no great desire to return to her nursing

career. It was a worthwhile profession, but it didn't always have the best hours and it was incredibly hard at times. Especially when you worked in hospice, as she had. Hard physically, just like any nursing job, but also hard emotionally and mentally, because in hospice there was no chance of anyone getting better and going home to their family.

Truth was, with her own mom getting older, Roxie didn't think she could handle being around people of the same age who were making their exit from this life. It underscored the reality that her time with Willie was limited. Roxie was already well aware of that. She didn't want to be reminded of it so clearly on a daily basis.

Granted, Willie was a stubborn woman and might very well live long enough to set some kind of record. All the same, Roxie wanted to go in a different direction, workwise. She just wasn't sure what direction that might be.

She dug her heels into the sand. It bothered her to feel so...untethered. So aimless. Everyone around her had a new path or a big project. Willie had the house in Dunes West she and Miguel were building. Trina had the hair salon. Claire had the bakery. Jules had her album. Margo was writing a book. Kat had a new job with a great charity. Even Paulina had a baby to take care of.

Roxie had...nothing.

A trickle of sweat dripped down the back of her neck. She launched into a quick sprint, pushing herself to go as fast as she could, then slowing down when her lungs felt ready to burst. Even with that shot of adrenaline, her good mood was starting to fade. What did she want out of life?

Well, that was the million-dollar question, wasn't it? And not one she had a real answer for. She had some general answers. She wanted to be happy. She wanted to feel like she was using her time in a valuable way. She wanted to feel needed. And to feel like she was making a difference.

But what did that actually translate into?

She didn't have a clue. And that frustrated her more than she could say.

She went a little farther down the beach, then turned around and headed back toward the house, interspersing her powerwalking with some more sprints.

As she finally slowed to a normal pace to cool down, it occurred to her that her sudden focus on working out and getting into shape might be because of that frustration. She didn't feel very much in control of her life at the moment, but working out was something she could control. How much she did, how often, how hard.

It was giving her something to go after when the rest of her life felt like one giant question mark.

But getting into shape wasn't the worst thing she could be doing with her time, so she wasn't going to worry about it.

On the final trek back to the house, she did some walking lunges. Then, in the shade of the house, she added some body weight squats and pushups off the back of the outdoor couch. Maybe she should join a gym. Maybe she should work at a gym? No. That didn't feel like the thing she was supposed to be doing.

Sweaty and ready for a shower and coffee, she trudged up the spiral steps to the back deck so she could go in the same way she'd come out. Taking the elevator one flight up after working out would feel like cheating. She left her sandy sneakers by the door and slipped through the sliding doors, the A/C raising goosebumps on her skin. With a little shiver, she went straight to the kitchen.

She got the coffee brewing then headed off to shower. The water felt great, even if she was too hot to crank up the temperature past lukewarm. She washed her hair with the color-safe shampoo Trina had gotten her, then rinsed and added conditioner, which she let sit while she soaped up.

Working at the salon and helping Trina would be great, but Roxie suspected her daughter was only giving her the job because she was Trina's mother. Roxie knew there were more capable people Trina could hire. People who actually knew the beauty business. Roxie was going to have to be taught. She'd never worked in a salon before. How much help was she actually going to be?

She sighed as she finished her shower and got out. She wrapped her hair in a towel, dried off, and got dressed in denim shorts and a cute T-shirt. She figured she'd go over to the salon with Trina today and do whatever needed to be done, just like she had before.

The delicious aroma of coffee led her back to the kitchen. Trina was already out there, sitting on the couch with her laptop and a cup of coffee in one hand. She looked up. "Morning, Ma."

"Morning, Trina."

"Mimi's still sleeping. Thanks for making coffee."

"You're welcome. You're headed to the shop today, right?"

Trina nodded. "I have a few more interviews to

do, although I'm pretty close to being all hired up. I still need a part-time stylist to cover the hours when the rest of the stylists are having their day off."

"I'll work on more organizing while you do that."

"Excellent."

Roxie got her coffee and carried it over, taking her usual seat in one of the side chairs. "There is something I want to ask you. And I want you to answer me honestly."

Trina nodded and sat up straighter. "Of course."

"Wouldn't you rather have someone in the salon who knows what they're doing instead of me? You know I don't know anything about running a salon. Won't I just take up more of your time? You're going to have to teach me everything."

Trina smiled. "I don't mind that, Ma. I think it'll be nice having you there. And I know you'll pick it up quickly. You were a nurse. Nurses are super smart people. Running a salon isn't even half as hard as what you used to do."

"That's nice of you to say, but you're still going to have to teach me how to do everything. Is that really the best way for you to spend your time?"

"In the beginning, I'm going to have all kinds of time." Trina set her laptop on the coffee table. "Salons don't open up fully booked. People in this town are going to have to get to know me and the way I do hair before I get busy. That means word of mouth has to spread, too. That's not an overnight thing. I'd much rather be teaching you the booking software or how to do inventory than sitting around, twiddling my thumbs."

"Really?"

Trina nodded. "There is every chance the stylists I'm hiring will be busier than me, because most of them are bringing some clientele with them. I'm not. No one's going to drive from Port St. Rosa to Diamond Beach just to get their hair done."

"They might," Roxie said. "You are that good."

Trina laughed. "Thanks, but it's a pretty slim chance."

Roxie was feeling better. "Do you promise you're not giving me the job just because I'm your mother and you feel sorry for me?"

Trina made a face. "Yes and no."

"What's that mean?"

"It means I am definitely giving you the job because you're my mother. When it comes to stuff like inventory and payroll and dealing with clients, I totally want someone I can trust and who do I trust more than my mom?" Trina snorted. "As for feeling sorry for you? That's a fat no. I have no reason to feel sorry for you. Why would you even think that?"

Roxie sipped her coffee and shrugged. "I just...I don't know. I'm in a strange place, Trina. With your dad gone and the rest of my life ahead of me, I've been feeling a little lost lately. Figuring out what to do with myself hasn't been easy. I want to do something that matters."

Trina blinked a few times. "Do you feel like working at the salon doesn't matter? I mean, in the way that working as a nurse did? Because it doesn't. I get that. But it's still about making people look and feel their best. And that makes people happy. That's one of the things I've always loved about it. And to be really honest, you'll be helping me."

Roxie nodded as she thought about that.

Trina went on. "Opening a brand new salon is a big thing to take on, Ma. I'd feel so much better with you there beside me."

Roxie smiled. That was all she needed to hear. "I will definitely be beside you, sweetheart. And you make a really good point about the salon being another way of helping people. I probably just need to get into the job and once I start to learn what needs to be done, I'll be fine."

Trina crossed her legs and sat back. "You could

also look into volunteering for some of the groups at church in your free time. That might help you find something that makes you feel fulfilled."

"Fulfilled," Roxie repeated. "That's exactly what I want." It really was. "Thanks, Trina. I'm going to call the church and see what sorts of things they have going on."

Maybe it wasn't nursing, but volunteering for some outreach programs would be a great way of helping people. When she wasn't helping her daughter.

Roxie felt better already.

Chapter Four

*J*ules woke up to the sound of Toby's snoring and her phone vibrating with an incoming text. She glanced over to see her mother's bed empty and already made.

She checked the time and groaned. She'd slept in later than she'd meant to, but then she'd been up very late last night texting with her agent, Billy Grimm. He was in a different time zone, too, which had only made it later for her.

He'd started the conversation when he'd texted by letting her know that her new song, *Dixie's Got Her Boots On*, had been uploaded to the online streaming services and sent out to all of the various places where he'd been hyping it up. That included music magazines, radio stations, and social media influencers who were big in the music scene.

She was equal parts excited and nervous about

that, but there was nothing she could do now except hope and pray the song was well received.

After a yawn, she picked up her phone and looked at the text that had come in. It was from Jesse, asking if she and Toby wanted to meet him and Shiloh, his golden retriever, for a walk on the beach.

Jules already knew what Toby's answer would be. She texted Jesse back. *15 mins okay?*

Perfect, came his response.

She nudged Toby with her foot. "Hey, sleepy-head. Wake up. It's time to go see your girlfriend."

One of his ears twitched.

"Come on, Tobes. You want to go to the beach? Go see Shiloh?"

That got him up. Jules wasn't sure if it was the mention of the beach or Shiloh but the combination had him off the bed in no time.

Jules got up, went to the bathroom, brushed her teeth, wound her hair up into a messy bun that would have to do, then pulled on shorts and a thin, long-sleeved tee. She stuck her sunglasses on her face, her phone in her pocket, then slid her feet into flipflops and went to get Toby's leash.

The house was quiet and seemed empty. Apparently, everyone else had already started their day.

Toby danced around her feet, eager to go. Probably because he had to pee just as much as he was excited to see Shiloh and chase seagulls.

"Okay, hang on, you silly thing." She hooked his leash to his collar, and they got in the elevator.

About thirty seconds after they reached the ground floor, he found a patch of grass to do his business on. Then they were off to the beach. She sent Jesse a quick text. *On our way.*

She saw him as she was tucking her phone away. He was straight out from the beach house, standing near the waterline. Shiloh was sniffing at something.

Jules waved. "Jesse. *Jesse!*"

He looked in her direction and waved back.

Toby saw Shiloh and took off, tugging at the end of the leash and barking. Jules laughed and shook her head. She picked up her pace so Toby didn't strangle himself trying to get to his girlfriend. "Hold on, crazy man."

When they joined Jesse and Shiloh, much butt sniffing took place.

Jesse kissed her. "Morning. How's my favorite superstar doing today?"

She smiled. "Good. Nervous. But good. Billy got the song uploaded and sent out everywhere last night. I think he's as excited as I am."

"No doubt. It's exciting stuff. I know you're nervous, but it's going to be great."

She nodded. "I hope so. How are you?"

"Excited. Happy. Ready to watch *Dixie* fly up the charts."

She could only hope that was actually what happened. "Come on, let's walk or these two are going to try to drag us into the water." Toby's feet were already wet and the rest of him would be, too, if the right wave came along.

Jules really didn't want to have to give him a bath. Washing his feet was no big deal, but bathing all of him was a lot less fun. As much as he liked water, getting bathed was *not* his favorite thing.

Jesse nodded and clicked his tongue at Shiloh. "Come on, girl. Let's go."

The four of them started down the beach.

"So, what's the plan going forward?" Jesse asked.

"The plan is to get back in the studio and work on the rest of the album. I've got all the songs I need, although the last two need to be finished, because while I'm mostly happy with the lyrics, I don't have the music down yet. Thankfully, *Folsom Prison Blues* is one everybody should know, so we can probably knock that out right away. Oh, and I need to get everyone on the payroll, too."

"You need a business manager. They should be handling all of that back-end stuff for you."

She sighed. "I know. I had one, but he retired after my last tour and, frankly, I wasn't sure when I'd tour again, so I never found another one."

"You'd better start looking. In fact, I have a suggestion."

She glanced at him. "It's not that you take the job, is it? Because that's too much. You're already stretched thin with the club. And until you find a manager to replace you, I don't think you should take on anything else."

"I agree. I wasn't about to suggest myself." He smiled. "But I do have an idea about someone."

"Who?"

He wrapped Shiloh's leash around his hand once to shorten it and bring her closer. "Cash."

She thought about that, nodding slowly. "It's not a bad suggestion. I just don't know if it would be something he'd really want to do. Or if he could handle it. Might be too much work for him."

"It's not that much work. And you won't know until you give him a shot at doing it. He's a smart guy. Seems to me he'd be capable. He went to college, right?"

"He did. He's got a bachelor's in music. I think

there were some business classes in there somewhere, but I'm not entirely sure."

"I can probably teach him some of it. If he wants
me to. But I bet he'd figure a lot of it out on his own."

"I'll ask him. See what he thinks," Jules said. She
liked the idea of giving Cash that kind of responsibility. It would be good for him and it would make
him feel like an even bigger part of what was going
on. Not only that, but it would allow her to pay him
more. She liked that part of it a lot. "There's something else I've been meaning to talk to you about."

"I'm all ears."

Toby barked at a seagull a few yards ahead of
them. The seagull responded by glaring back. Jules
smiled. "The video for *Dixie*. I think I need one. I just
have never done anything that's more than just clips
of me playing and singing. Cash and Sierra have a
whole script worked up. They've centered the whole
thing around the rodeo lifestyle. Buckle bunnies,
RVs, cowboys, and horses."

"I like that," he said. "I like that a lot. I know
some people that would probably love to get on
board with this. They did the commercial for the
Dolphin Club years ago. I was their first big job and
we've stayed friends. Let me reach out to them and
see what they think about a project of this scope."

"Okay."

He glanced at her. "Won't be cheap, as we've discussed."

"I know. I'm all right with that. So long as I get something good in exchange for all that money."

He nodded. "I'll make sure you do." He took her hand. "I want this song and this album to be the biggest thing you've ever done. I want it to take off like a rocket."

"Thanks." She smiled. "Is that because you really, really, *really* want to go on tour with me?"

He laughed. "That's part of it. But it's also because I want to see the woman I've fallen for do phenomenally well. You deserve it, Jules. You really do." He shrugged. "And I really deserve to go on tour with you."

She chuckled and moved closer so that they bumped against each other. "Then let's see if we can't make this video happen."

Chapter Five

*T*rina drove herself and her mom to A Cut Above, making one short detour to get coffees on the way. Trina had dressed in black capris, a turquoise and black leopard print top, and black wedge sandals. Not the best outfit for getting stuff done, but she was interviewing people today and wanted to look nice.

She'd also brought a pair of cutoffs, a tank top, and some flipflops to change into afterwards. Those, she wouldn't mind getting dirty in, and if there was more work than her mom could handle, Trina planned on doing her part.

She really hoped her mom felt better about the job situation. She hated that her mom felt so lost at the moment. That couldn't be a good feeling. Trina tried to fill the silence so that her mom wouldn't focus on feeling bad. "I can't believe Mimi was only just getting up as we were leaving."

Roxie nodded. "Married life has ruined her."

Trina laughed. "She was in a good mood, though."

Roxie smiled. "Who wouldn't be? She and Miguel are headed out to do some furniture shopping today. You know how she loves to spend money. And now that she has it to spend, there's no stopping her."

"That would be fun. Having a whole house to decorate? I'm excited for her."

"So am I. I hope the building goes smoothly and doesn't take longer than expected. I want them to be able to get moved in and enjoy their life." She glanced over at Trina. "Just like I want the salon to get open so you can get things underway."

"Same. Which reminds me—I got an email notice that there's a Chamber of Commerce cocktail thing next week at a place called Blue Wave downtown. It's a modern bistro, according to the description. Do you want to go with me?" She glanced over at her mom. "Please say yes. I really don't want to go alone."

"Sure, I'll go with you." Roxie sipped her skinny mocha latte. "Would you mind if I asked Ethan along? I think we'd do better to have him with us. He knows everyone. Plus, it would give us someone to talk to if it's boring."

"That would be great. I really want to start spreading the word about the salon. In fact, once we have a better idea of our opening date, I'm going to start visiting businesses in town and handing out flyers and cards. I might even start sooner. I don't care where the business comes from, so long as it comes."

"That's not a bad idea. Everyone needs their hair done."

"Thankfully," Trina said. She pulled into the parking lot and found a space near the door. Ethan's truck was in the lot, as were a few others. Down by the bakery, she saw Danny's truck. Claire was probably with him. They'd been working as hard at getting the bakery ready to open as Trina and her mom had been at the salon.

Trina turned the engine off, then she and Roxie grabbed their drinks and purses. Trina had her laptop, too. She locked the car, and they went toward the shop.

Her mom veered toward the left. "I'm sure Ethan's down at the photography studio working. I'm going to ask him about the Chamber of Commerce meeting, then I'll be in."

"Okay," Trina said. She went into the salon. There were several big boxes blocking her view of most of the interior. "Hello?"

Ethan appeared from behind one of them. "Hey, good morning. Guess what arrived early? Actually, it arrived after you guys left yesterday, but that was definitely earlier than expected."

She shook her head. There was nothing on the boxes to indicate what was inside. "I have no idea."

"All your waiting area furniture."

She gasped. "That's awesome!"

He nodded. "I should be able to get it all set up for you today. We'll just need to clean this whole front area first. No sense in putting down all the seating only to have to move it to clean."

"Agreed. I do have a couple of people coming in for interviews, though."

"Hmm." He looked around. "How soon?"

Trina checked the time. "First one's in an hour."

"Okay. If we can get your mom—where is your mom, by the way?" He looked around. "I thought she was coming with you today."

"She went down to the photography studio to see you. I'm sure she'll be back here any second."

"Good. If the three of us can get to work cleaning this area, I can probably have a few seats set up before your interview. Maybe even the table, depending on how quickly the pieces build."

The door opened and Roxie came in. She smiled at Ethan. "There you are."

"Morning." He winked at her. "Sorry I wasn't where you thought I'd be."

"That's all right," Roxie said. "I know where you are now."

"I'm going to be working in here until this front area is set up."

Trina interjected. "All of the waiting area furniture came in early, Ma."

"That's great," Roxie said. Then she shook her head. "But it can't go down until this floor is cleaned. And I mean vacuumed then mopped. It's looking pretty grimy."

Ethan nodded. "I just said the same thing."

"Good," Roxie said. "Because I'm going to need your help. Trina can't be getting all sweaty when she has interviews to do."

"I need to do something," Trina said.

Roxie glanced toward the back of the salon where a few of the workmen were. "There's still towels to be washed and folded. You can work on that."

"Okay." Trina smiled. Her mom had gone from feeling lost to doling out jobs. That had to be a good sign. "I'm on it. But if you need me for anything up here, just yell."

"We will," her mom assured her.

Trina went back through the shop toward the breakroom. The place was really looking good. There couldn't be much left to do before they could open. She'd have to ask Ethan about that. She set her laptop, drink, and purse on the little table in the breakroom, then went over to the washer and dryer.

Her mom popped in. "There's still a load of towels in the dryer that need to be folded and that box there on the floor has the last batch that needs to be washed. Ethan's got a steam mop at his office that he's going to let us borrow for today, but I think we should buy one. It's the best way to clean a floor like this."

Trina nodded. "I can order one today." She took her phone out of her purse. "Just tell me what kind."

"Let's see if we like his, then we can decide on a brand."

"Good idea." Trina stuck her phone back in her purse, then opened the dryer, took the towels out, and set them on the table. She and her mom each picked one up and started folding.

"I can't wait to see the furniture set up," her mom said.

"Me, too. It'll really look like a salon then. And when the reception desk is in."

"What about the computer and register and all of that stuff?"

"It's ordered. Should be here any day. Then I'll set it up. The company said they can either send a tech or walk me through it on the phone. I'm going to try the walk-through first. I'm hoping it's not that hard."

"Does it cost money to have them send a tech?"

Trina shook her head. "No, it's part of the service you get for buying through them. I just thought...I don't know. That maybe I could do it myself."

"If you think you can, then why not. But at the same time, if they offer a tech for free..." Roxie shrugged.

"Yeah," Trina said. "I keep going back and forth on that. Maybe you're right. Maybe I should just let them come in and get it done." She picked up her phone and found the company's number, then dialed.

"Are you calling them?"

Trina nodded. "You're right. Having the tech come is the easiest solution. I don't know why I'd want to attempt it when I could have it done for me." She laughed. "See how much I need you? You're helping me already!"

Roxie just smiled and kept folding while Trina talked to customer service.

The smile wasn't lost on Trina, however. She knew her mom was starting to see that Trina really did need her. And not just because she was Trina's mom. In reality, Roxie was so much more. She was Trina's sounding board, her protector, and her best friend.

Together, they made an incredible team.

Add Willie to the mix and they were pretty much unstoppable.

Trina set a date with customer service, thanked them, and hung up. She laughed and shook her head.

"What?" her mom asked.

"Nothing," Trina said. "Just so happy you're here."

Chapter Six

*K*at walked into the offices of Future Florida with a big smile on her face and a box in her hands. She wasn't just happy to be coming to work, she was happy to be coming to work *here*. She greeted the copper-haired older woman seated behind the reception desk. "Morning, Arlene."

"Morning, Kat. How are you today?"

"Ready to get to work, that's how I am. I even remembered to bring a lunch. How are you?"

"I'm great, thanks," Arlene said. She was wearing a pale blue blouse that had little bunnies printed on it. Kat couldn't help but smile.

Arlene gestured toward the back. "Coffee's made, by the way."

"I am very pleased to hear that. I'll be headed in that direction shortly." Kat went through the door and down the corridor a few steps to her office. Out in reception, the phone rang. She could just hear Arlene answering it.

Kat unlocked her office door and turned on the lights. Her office still had that new paint smell but she guessed that would dissipate now that the office was occupied. She'd brought a few things from home to give it a little more of a personal touch. The surfboard wall clock she'd got as a kit from the craft store and painted herself. Her framed college diploma. A charging stand for her phone that also held it upright. Her favorite coffee mug that she'd brought back from the Landry house.

The deep green and blue ceramic mug was handmade, very sturdy, and decorated with a seal from the Florida State Renaissance Faire. It had a thick handle that Kat really liked, and it probably held sixteen ounces, maybe more, meaning she didn't have to refill it nearly as often as a regular cup.

The only downside was that she'd gone to that fair with Ray, but she'd bought the mug herself, so it wasn't like it had been a gift from him. Anything he'd given her had already gone into the donation pile. She was beyond done with Ray. She didn't need anything around to remind her of those wasted years.

She glanced at the wave ring on her finger, at how the little diamonds sparkled in the light, and smiled. She was all about Alex now.

She put her box on the desk, stuck her purse in a drawer, then took her mug and her lunch down to the employee breakroom. The lunch went into the fridge and the mug got filled with coffee. She added some half-and-half and a few teaspoons of sugar before going back to her office.

She hadn't gotten nearly as much done yesterday as she'd hoped, but she'd had paperwork to fill out and she'd had to acquaint herself with the software Future Florida used. That had required watching a brief training video, but she was glad she had. The software was complex and watching the video had helped her learn about some interesting features she'd definitely be using.

Today, she could get right to work. She knew what she was doing and what she wanted to accomplish. She settled into her chair and fired up her laptop. She took a quick look around her office. It still needed some artwork and at least one plant in here, but there was time for that.

Maybe she'd see if Alex wanted to hit up some yard sales this weekend with her. She might find something for the walls that way.

She logged into the software and, using what she'd learned yesterday, created a new task so she could run a report on the last five years of contributions and donations. She wanted to look for patterns to analyze. Those would tell her a lot and help her make suggestions to the board about future decisions.

She had nearly finished setting the parameters for the report when Arlene knocked on her open door.

Kat looked up. "Hey."

"How's it going?"

"Good. I'm really digging in today." She made one more selection for the report and then hit Enter to start the report running.

Arlene stepped inside the office. She had a stack of folders about three inches thick in the crook of one arm. Using both hands, she held the folders out to Kat. "Sorry to bother you, but these are for you."

"No bother." Kat took them. "What are they?"

"Last week's requests. So far. Tom and Molly would like you to look through them and assess them for risk and reward."

Tom Phillips and Molly Hargrove were both on the board of Future Florida and the top-level executives who worked out of this location. Kat nodded as she set the stack down on her desk. "Sure. Those are all from last week?"

"We get a lot of them."

This kind of assessment was a big part of what she'd been hired to do. She just hadn't realized it would pertain to those currently seeking the help of the charity. She glanced from the folders on her desk to Arlene. "Please tell me that I'm not going to be the sole decisionmaker on who gets our help and who doesn't. That feels like a *lot* of responsibility."

Arlene smiled. "No. That gets done as a group. There will be a meeting to go through the requests and make determinations as to who we can best help. You'll do that with Tom, Molly, and Eloise. Sometimes, if he's in town, Waylen sits in."

"Waylen Crosby, the CEO? He actually has time to sit in on meetings like that?"

Arlene nodded. "When he can make the time, he does. He lives in Pensacola but he's usually here at least once every six weeks or so. Nicest man. Looks a little intimidating, but once you get past that you realize he's just a big softie with a heart of gold. You'll meet him soon."

"Good to know. Are Tom and Molly in today?"

"They should be at some point. I don't know when they got in last night from their out-of-town trip, just that they were supposed to. Eloise is here today, too."

"I should go say hi to her. Introduce myself." Kat got up. "Thanks for bringing me the folders. I'll dig into them just as soon as I go meet Eloise."

"You're welcome. Let me know if you need anything."

"I will." She went in the opposite direction down the hall as Arlene went back to reception. Kat stopped at the office door of Eloise French, the organization's director of marketing and social media. Kat knocked.

"Come in."

Kat opened the door. "Hi. I'm Kat Thompson. The new lead data scientist."

Eloise got up from her desk and stuck her hand out. She was a tall woman with silver hair cut short and artfully tousled on top. She wore a fitted cobalt blue dress with enormous matte black hoop earrings. Her nails were painted taxicab yellow. Her eyes sparkled behind thick black half-frame reading glasses. "It's a pleasure to meet you, Kat. We've been needing someone with your skillset for quite a while. I'm so glad you've joined the team."

"Thanks." Kat looked around. There was some very cool modern art on the walls, as well as a

striking chrome sculpture atop one of the filing cabinets. A long, narrow dish of succulents sat on the
windowsill. A collage of photos covered part of one
wall, featuring Eloise and a variety of celebrities.
"Have you really met all of those people?"

Eloise nodded. "I have. You'll meet your share of
them, too. It's part of the job. They come to help with
our fundraisers, mostly, but some of them get more
personally involved. Sometimes they want to help in
bigger ways."

"That's nice."

Eloise smiled. "There are a few who have been
incredibly generous. And a few who have only done
it for the publicity and goodwill, but their cash still
spends, so..." She shrugged and made a face.

"Right," Kat said. "I get it. I think. Have celebrities actually reached out to us? Or is it a case where
we've contacted them to be a part of something?"

"It works both ways," Eloise said. "I do my best to
get them involved when I can, but they all have crazy
schedules, so you can imagine how that goes."

"I can. It must be incredibly hard to coordinate
with some of them." Wheels started turning in Kat's
brain. "What if you had a celebrity who wanted to
help in a specific way? Or with a specific type of
need?"

"I'd find a way to make it work." Eloise's eyes narrowed. "Are you thinking of someone specifically?"

"I am. But I need to talk to them first."

Eloise's perfectly sculpted brows rose. "Do you know a celebrity?"

"I guess...sort of." Kat laughed and shook her head. "She's not a huge celebrity, except maybe in certain circles. I shouldn't say anything more until I talk to her. It was just an idea that came to me."

"Well, let me know what I can do to help if anything develops."

"I will. I'm really glad to meet you and really glad to be here. I finally feel like I'm doing something useful with my skills, you know?"

Eloise nodded. "I do know. If I can help with anything as you get settled in, you know where my office is. Don't be a stranger."

"Thanks." The offer meant a lot to Kat. Eloise seemed to be a pretty cool individual. "See you around."

Smiling, Eloise sat back down as Kat moved toward the door. "You will indeed."

Kat went straight to her office, the idea that had come to her percolating in her brain with big energy. She wasn't sure if her aunt would even be interested, but there was no way of knowing unless Kat presented the idea. She needed to think it through a bit, but she'd definitely see what Aunt Jules thought about it tonight when she got home.

As Kat let that idea simmer, she picked up the first request folder, opened it, and started to read.

Chapter Seven

laire finished wiping down one of the long, stainless-steel worktables, then stood back to inspect her work. Looked good to her. Nearby, the dishwasher hummed away, busy cleaning another batch of baking implements that she could then put away.

After that, another batch would be going in. There was a lot of cleaning to do to get things sanitized and ready for the real work of baking.

She'd already washed the mugs and plates they'd be using to serve people.

Danny pushed through the kitchen door from the retail side of the bakery. "Display counter is all set up if you want to come take a look." He glanced around, hands on his hips "You've been busy in here."

"Trying to get everything clean so I can start

production soon. Ingredients start arriving tomorrow, right?"

He nodded. "They do. What are you going to make first?"

"Starting with the basics. Cookies. I'll need popcorn eventually, too."

"I'll text Ivelisse and let her know about that. Regular and kettle, right?

"Yep. But I'm starting with chocolate chip cookies first. A classic for a reason. I'll bake a few to get used to the ovens, but I'm mainly going to make several batches of dough, portion it out, then freeze them so they're ready to bake. That will help us keep up with demand. Which I'm hoping we'll need to do."

His eyes narrowed in thought. "So you're going to freeze the dough, but what do you mean about portioning it out?"

"With one of the cookie scoops. That way, when we need cookies, all you'll have to do is grab a baking sheet, add the scoops of frozen cookie dough spaced out appropriately and pop the whole thing in the oven. No need to defrost. The dough will bake just fine from frozen."

His eyes stayed narrowed, but he tipped his head back slightly. "Why can't we offer that as an item for sale?"

"Frozen dough?"

He nodded, his eyes widening with excitement. "Think about it. Take and bake Mrs. Butter's cookies. For the fresh-out-of-the-oven bakery experience at home. I could easily add a small, glass-front freezer next to the sour orange pie cold case."

"I never thought about doing that."

"Could you write up baking instructions? We'd have to include them."

"Of course. That would be easy." She smiled at his creativity. "That's a really smart idea, Danny. No wonder you've been so successful in business. We'll need some kind of airtight container, so the cookies don't get freezer burn, but I'd still want to put them in a sealed plastic bag inside of that. Although, they should still probably be baked within six months of purchase to taste their best."

"Add that to the instructions. We'll need to figure out pricing, too."

"How many do you want to sell in a package?"

He hesitated. "Our cookies are going to be fairly large, aren't they?"

She nodded. "That was my plan. But we've got different sizes of scoops. Maybe they should be a little smaller than what we're going to sell in store. Not that smaller is inferior, but if they want the true

Mrs. Butter's experience, they should have to shop here. Making the cookies at home should be... second best." She wrinkled her nose. "That doesn't sound good, does it?"

"No, I know what you mean. The cookies should taste as good as what customers can get in-store, but it's never going to be the same experience, so there's no reason to attempt to recreate that. A slightly smaller cookie makes sense. How about we sell them as a baker's dozen?"

"Thirteen to a container. I like that. I can work up a price based on that."

"It should be less expensive than buying the equivalent number of cookies in the store, but obviously not so much less that we don't make money."

"Yep. And I agree. It really is a good idea."

"You gave it to me." He stepped back toward the door. "Come on out and have a look at the new display case."

"Right!" She followed him to the retail side. A lot of work had been done yesterday, but even more had been done this morning while she'd been working in the kitchen. The place was shaping up beautifully. The display counter was massive. The lights were on, illuminating the wire racks, waiting to be filled with trays of goodies. "It looks fantastic. That is a *lot* of space to fill."

"We'll have plenty of product to go in there based on the menu we worked out yesterday."

She nodded. "True. It just looks like a lot because it's empty." She turned to see the rest of what had been done. The tables and chairs had been unwrapped and put into position, two sets on either side of the door. "Napkins," she said, thinking out loud.

"Napkins?" Danny asked.

She pointed at the tables. "Maybe we should have some napkin dispensers on the tables. Or..."

"Or what?"

She pointed to the far wall. To the empty spot next to the glass-front refrigerator that would house the sour orange pies. "What about doing a coffee fixings station there? We are going to sell coffee. People need to be able to put cream and sugar in. Where are they going to do that?"

"Good point."

"Then we could just keep the napkins and straws and utensils and coffee stuff up there. If we do that, we don't have to hand out forks with every slice of cake or pie we sell. People can help themselves."

He nodded. "Smart. And something we should

have thought about already." He smiled. "I didn't mean 'we.' I meant 'me.' You've been plenty busy with recipes. This was my job." He sighed.

"Don't feel bad. You've never opened a bakery before."

"No, I haven't, that's for sure." He pulled his phone out of his pocket. "I'm going to call some of the restaurant supply places, see if they have anything like that prebuilt. Otherwise, maybe I can get Ethan to build us something."

"Sounds good. Whichever one you decide on works for me. I'm going back to the kitchen."

"Wait. There's one more thing I want you to see." He put his phone away. "I'll call in a second. First, look at these." He went over to one of the tables that had a medium-sized box sitting on it. He used his pocketknife to slit the tape sealing the lid, then reached in.

He pulled out a folded rectangle of black fabric. He shook it out and revealed it to be a long apron, emblazoned with the Mrs. Butter's Bakery logo in white, yellow, and pink. Underneath that was a long pocket. "What do you think?"

She smiled and nodded. "Looks great. I love it." She held her hand out. "Here, let me try it on."

He gave it to her.

She put the strap over her head, then tied the apron's strings behind her back. She held her arms out. "What do you think?"

"Looks great. That's going to be our store uniform."

"No T-shirts?"

He thought for a moment. "We could get T-shirts."

"If we can't afford them right away, that's all right. But I was thinking we'd have T-shirts, as well. Just so everyone working here looks the part. Also, it's something else we can sell." She took the apron off. "These, too. You never know what people might want to buy."

He grinned. "You're right. And obviously, I'm not the only one with good ideas. I'll take care of it."

"Thanks." It made Claire feel good to contribute more than just recipes, but in a couple of days, she'd be doing nothing but baking. She was looking forward to it. That's when her major contribution would kick in.

She couldn't wait. If the sweet aromas wafting out of that kitchen didn't attract customers, then the bright colors and tantalizing items on display would. When they came in to see what the bakery was all about, she didn't want them to leave until they'd left some money behind.

She smiled as she headed for the kitchen. She was excited. Not just to get open but for people to taste her creations.

And for those people to become regular customers. She wanted Mrs. Butter's Bakery to be a household name. A place people could depend on for delicious everyday treats and specialties for their celebrations. A neighborhood gathering spot. Somewhere locals and tourists would feel welcome. But also a viable business that made money and would someday provide her with the means to retire.

To Claire, it seemed like they were well on their way.

Chapter Eight

*I*t wasn't often Willie was alone in the beach house, but she was leaving soon anyway to go furniture shopping with Miguel, so it wasn't a big deal. She fixed herself a cup of coffee, then had a quick breakfast of cereal. Special K with Strawberries was all she could find in the cupboard.

She sprinkled a big spoon of sugar over it to make it edible. She sat in her chair to eat. Breakfast only had to last her until lunch, which she and Miguel would no doubt eat out. She was going to see if she could get him to go to Clipper's.

Willie wanted to see this Liz for herself.

She finished up her cereal and drained the last of her coffee. She put her dishes in the sink, since the dishwasher was full of clean ones. She'd take care of unloading it when she got back. From there, she went to her room to get dressed.

She opened a dresser drawer to get out a new pair of undies for the day. That's when she saw the baggies she'd tucked in there for safekeeping. One had a Q-tip in it, the other a few strands of hair. The DNA samples she'd taken from Nico, Paulina's baby, supposedly fathered by Bryan.

Willie frowned. In all the wedding excitement and then going off to the honeymoon suite at the Hamilton Arms, she'd completely forgotten about them.

Her plan had been to ask Miguel if he knew anyone who could run a comparison on the DNA to see if Nico really was related to Trina. A sample of Bryan's DNA was out of the question, since he'd been cremated.

But Trina's was easy to come by. Even easier now that Willie was alone in the house. She went back to the kitchen and took another baggie out of the cupboard, then she went into Trina's bathroom and found her hairbrush.

Trina was meticulous about keeping her brushes clean, but all Willie needed was one strand of hair. From watching plenty of *CSI* and *Law & Order*, she knew the strand had to have the root on it. She really had no idea how to determine that, so it was probably best if she gathered more than one hair.

There was only one left in Trina's brush, however. She took that then looked around on the floor. Trina had long hair. There was no way she hadn't shed a few extras.

Cursing her less-than-youthful eyesight, she got down on her knees on the bathroom floor to have a better look. She found all the hair she needed in the trashcan where Trina had apparently deposited everything she'd pulled from her brush.

"That'll do," Willie said. She stuffed a few hairs into the baggie and sealed it up, then took it back to her room and used a Sharpie to write Trina's name on the plastic. Now she just had to talk to Miguel.

She changed out of her robe into elastic-waist capris that looked like light blue denim but were much softer and a thinner fabric. To that she added a T-shirt with a bedazzled flamingo on the front and her orthopedic sandals. Her hair could have used Trina's help. She opted for a hot pink rhinestone sun visor and called herself dressed.

She clipped on her fanny pack and texted Miguel that she was on her way over. Before she made it into the elevator, he texted back that he'd called a car for them.

She'd already decided to have the DNA conversation over lunch. Talking about it in the car, which would be driven by someone they didn't know, didn't seem like a good idea to her. Then again, why would that person care? Maybe they wouldn't.

Still, Willie wasn't taking any chances that that person might somehow know Paulina. For privacy reasons, she was sticking to lunch.

First stop of the day was Pritchard's, a furniture store that catered to the Florida lifestyle. That meant lots of rattan for indoors and out, and the whole line of Tommy Bahama furnishings. Willie wanted lighter and brighter, though, to match the light, bright interior their new house was going to have.

And while she liked the tropical look, she'd really fallen for what the Dunes West decorating department called Modern Coastal.

She and Miguel stood in front of a large white sectional upholstered in nubby fabric. It wasn't bad looking. Clean lines, which was nice.

Even so, Willie sighed. "I can't stop thinking about that beautiful couch at Grace Stewart's house. That white one with the blue shells. It's not the couch so much as the fabric. It was so pretty."

"Maybe they have other fabrics for something like this," Miguel said. "We have a big living room to fill. We're going to need something this size."

She went over and sat on it, scooching back so

that she could rest against the back of the couch. Doing that meant her feet no longer touched the floor. "I look like the world's oldest toddler, don't I?"

He laughed. "Maybe that one's too big." He held out his hand. "Let's look through the rest of the store and see what we can find."

Willie saw a lot of things she liked, but she was hesitant to commit to anything until they'd looked at what the other stores had to offer. That was until they took the elevator to the second floor, where the bedroom sets were.

That's where she found the Glamor Girl collection and fell in love.

"Oh, Miguel. I have to have this." She ran her hand over the top of a creamy white dresser accented with an inch-thick band of glittering rhinestones. Every piece in the collection had the same accent of rhinestones. The fabric headboard was padded and quilted, with a big, single crystal set into the indented corners of each quilted square. "It looks like something out of an old Hollywood movie."

He didn't say anything right away and when she looked over at him, his expression was one of uncertainty. "For the master bedroom?"

She laughed. "No, sweetheart. For one of the

guest rooms. This furniture alone will get Trina to visit."

He smiled and seemed to exhale in relief. "Very good. For the guest room. I like that a lot."

"I promise I won't pick out anything this over-the-top for our room. We'll keep it simpler in there. Something nice and beachy, but easy to live with, too."

He nodded. "That sounds good to me." He sat on the display bed. "If you want this set for the guest room, let's order it."

"You don't think we should wait? See what the other places have?"

"You think they'll have this?"

"I have no idea. But I do really like this. And Trina will love it."

A salesman magically appeared. Nathan. The same young man who'd greeted them and intro-duced himself when they'd first walked into the store. "How are you folks doing? Can I answer any questions for you?"

Willie knew the sales people worked off commis-sion. She didn't begrudge them that. It couldn't be an easy way to make a living. "I like this set for the guest room in our new house, but they've only just broken ground on it."

Rob from Dunes West had texted while they were in the car to give them that update, which was *very* exciting.

"So you wouldn't be able to take delivery for a while, is that what you're concerned about?"

She nodded. "Exactly. But I'm also worried that if I don't order it now, it won't be available."

"That could happen," Nathan said. "Collections come and go. This one is brand new, so chances are good it would be available, but we can do a hold purchase, too. That would allow you to order the pieces you want but also set a delivery date up to a year in advance."

She looked at Miguel. He nodded. She looked back at Nathan. "Let's write it up."

By the time they got to Clipper's, Willie was so hungry she didn't care if they saw Liz or not. All she wanted to see was food. The cereal she'd eaten had done very little to keep her full. She'd expected too much from that weenie little bowl of diet flakes.

They were seated at a table for two near the window and given menus, which she opened right away. Everything looked good.

She glanced over the top of her menu at Miguel. He was looking around the restaurant, not at his menu.

"We don't know what she looks like, other than pretty and blond," Willie said.

He nodded. "I know. She might not even be working."

"Just like her parents might not have even said anything to her yet." It was a possibility they had to consider. Not that they were there to confront Liz or anything. Willie just wanted to see the young woman for herself. Maybe get a feel for what she was like.

Her stomach rumbled, reminding her that other needs were more pressing. She went back to the menu and quickly decided on the cold shrimp pasta salad trio. It was served on a bed of greens with coleslaw or potato salad and fruit salad. That sounded good to her. Filling, but sort of light at the same time.

She closed her menu just as their server arrived with two glasses of water. She was tan, blond, and pretty.

And her nametag read Liz.

Willie tried not to stare. Instead, she cleared her throat to get Miguel's attention, since his focus was now on the menu. "Sweetheart, our server is here. What do you want to drink?"

She looked up at Liz. "That is what you were going to ask us, wasn't it?"

Liz smiled. "I was. What can I get you?"

"I'll have a lemonade," Willie said.

"We have regular lemonade or strawberry."

"Strawberry," Willie answered. She was tempted to ask for a shot of vodka in it, but she figured she'd better keep her wits about her with Liz as their server.

Miguel nodded. "That sounds very refreshing. I'll have one, too."

"I'll be right back with those." Liz left.

Miguel leaned in and whispered, "That's her."

"I know," Willie said. "We just have to be nice to her and see if we can engage her in conversation. Maybe we can learn a little more about her. You never know."

"We must be careful not to talk about Trina so that she hears us."

"Good plan." She set her menu down. "Speaking of your step-granddaughter, there is another matter I wanted to ask you about. Do you know anyone who can run a DNA test on a strand of hair?"

His eyes narrowed. "Willie, what are you up to now?"

Chapter Nine

Margo didn't mind looking at condos with Conrad and Dinah. It was always interesting to see the decorating choices other people had made, and as she was about to embark on redoing an entire house, any ideas were welcome.

But the real star of the show was Dinah. Margo had a feeling she was about to be so entertained she was going to wish she had popcorn.

Jerry Whitmer, Conrad's realtor friend, was a gregarious older man who'd turned up at the first address in khaki pants and a turquoise polo shirt emblazoned with his name and the name of the real estate company. He was a broker and, as such, had his own firm. Judging by his Italian loafers and Rolex watch, he did all right.

She hoped they weren't putting him out too

much. She hated to think they were wasting the man's time. Maybe Conrad would make it up to him later. Take him out for dinner or something. She'd ask him about it.

Jerry unlocked the condo door. "Now, this isn't exactly what you asked for, it's a three-two, not a two-one."

"A what?" Dinah said, her face screwed up like she didn't understand.

Maybe she didn't, Margo thought. The poor woman wasn't the brightest bulb in the chandelier. Or at least she liked to play at being a dim bulb. Margo said, "Three-bedroom, two-bathroom. As opposed to a two-bedroom, one-bath."

"Ding-ding," Jerry said. "We have a winner." He smiled at Margo, who smiled right back. He glanced at Dinah again. "I'm showing you this because it just came on the market and it's a great buy. Now, it's going to need some work, which is why it's a great buy, but keep an open mind."

Margo snorted softly. An open mind and Dinah were not two things that went together.

They went inside and he flipped the lights on so they could see better. The condo was very dated. It reminded Margo of the house she was buying in Conrad's neighborhood. She'd already made peace with the idea of how much work had to be done there, so this place didn't seem that daunting at all.

After a small foyer, the space opened up into a large living room-dining room-kitchen combination with lots of space and probably plenty of natural light, if the blinds were open.

"It's got nice bones," Margo said.

"You bet it does," Jerry agreed. "Great-sized rooms, terrific breezes, and this view is stunning." He went over to the vertical blinds covering the sliders and used the loop of chain connected to the top bar to maneuver them to one end. Light flooded the space, just as Margo had imagined it would.

Conrad let out a low whistle as he walked over. "Wow. You're right about that view, Jerry. Look at all that water."

They were on the sixth floor and Margo had to agree the view was spectacular. Miles and miles of blue sky and water in both directions. She came to stand at Conrad's side. "Wouldn't be bad to look at while having your morning coffee, would it?"

"Not at all." Conrad smiled, his gaze still aimed at the horizon.

"What if a hurricane comes?" Dinah asked.

Of course she'd ask that, Margo thought. She managed not to roll her eyes but just barely. The woman was going to come up with every possible excuse under the sun why this place—why *any* place —wouldn't work for her.

Jerry answered right away. "Despite its age, Silver Palms was built to hurricane specs, which include impact-resistant windows and hurricane shutters. It's a very secure building."

Dinah shook her head. "I don't think I could handle putting up hurricane shutters. How would you even do that on the sixth floor?"

"There are no shutters to put up," Jerry said. "All the windows are impact-resistant, except for the balcony. Then you just pull the accordion shutters together manually and latch them from the inside. Super easy. Probably takes less than two minutes, unless you have a few things out there to bring in. No big deal."

"I don't know," Dinah said.

"What's not to know?" Margo asked. Dinah wasn't getting off the hook that easily. If the woman was going to make excuses, Margo wanted valid reasons for those excuses. She wasn't about to let Dinah threaten to move here and put Margo's future with Conrad in jeopardy and think she was going to get away with it so easily.

Not while Margo still had breath in her body.

Dinah shrugged. "It just seems like a lot to think about."

"What does?"

Dinah's lips pursed. "Hurricanes."

Again, Margo wanted to roll her eyes. She didn't. But she wanted to. "Did you just realize Florida gets them? Surely you had to know that when you decided to move here."

Conrad turned to look at his sister. "They're not a big deal. They happen pretty infrequently and if one does come up, I'll come over and close your shutters if that's too much for you to do."

"Oh, Connie. You're so sweet to offer, but I wouldn't want to inconvenience you."

Right, Margo thought. She wandered down the hall, mostly so she could finally roll her eyes. The woman was insufferable. Margo took a look around. The bedrooms were fairly roomy and bland enough, but the bathrooms were deeply entrenched in the '90s. They'd have to be fixed up a bit. Unless Dinah didn't mind that look.

Margo went back out. Everyone was now in the kitchen. And Dinah, it seemed, had found a new tact. "This has to be over my budget. How much is this place?"

Jerry cleared his throat softly. "It's about seventy

thousand over your budget, but the sellers are eager. I'm sure they—"

"Absolutely not," Dinah said. "That's not even worth negotiating. It's too much. I don't want to see anything over my budget." She crossed her arms for emphasis.

Jerry deflated slightly but held on to his ever-green smile. "It's worth a hundred more than they're asking."

Conrad looked at his sister with a challenge in his eyes. "I'm glad you don't want the place. I'm thinking about buying it myself."

Margo had no idea what he was playing at, but before she could say anything, he sidled up to her.

"What do you think? We could buy this place, do a quick rehab, and flip it. Wouldn't take more than some paint, new floors, maybe an appliance package. Cabinets refinished. That sort of thing."

Margo wasn't so sure about that. "You haven't seen the bathrooms yet."

"Outdated?"

She nodded.

"Connie. Seriously." Dinah walked toward him. "That's too much work for you."

He frowned at her. "No, it's not. I'm more than capable."

"You're not the young Marine you used to be."

Margo had had enough. And while Conrad might be interested in a project, one was enough for her. "Maybe we should move on to the next location?"

Dinah nodded. "I think that's a good idea, too."

The next location wasn't far and ten minutes later, they were walking into another condo. This one much newer, but also smaller. A two-bedroom, one-bathroom, which Dinah had said in the car was more than sufficient for her.

Jerry unlocked the door of the ground-floor unit and let them go in. "Now, this unit is actually three thousand *under* your budget."

Dinah nodded as she looked around. "That's good."

But Margo already knew she'd find faults.

A few minutes later, Dinah did. "It's awfully small, isn't it?"

"Nine hundred and four square feet," Jerry answered.

"It's a two-bedroom condo with one bathroom, Dinah," Conrad said. "How big did you think it was going to be?"

"It makes me feel claustrophobic," Dinah

announced. "And I don't like being on the first floor. That seems like a security problem."

Margo hadn't bothered to look around. She didn't need to see the place. "Is that because you think criminals don't know how to use an elevator?" She held her hands up. "Look, I know first floor units can be a greater target for thieves, but this is a very safe area. Isn't it, Jerry?"

"It is. And first-floor units tend to be very popular," Jerry said. "They have great resale value. A lot of people specifically request them so they don't have to deal with stairs or an elevator. You're only a ten-minute walk from the beach here, as well. This is a great property."

Conrad nodded. "It really is."

Jerry smiled.

So did Margo, because she knew no matter how many places they looked at, Dinah was never going to find anything she liked well enough to buy.

Because Dinah had no intention of actually moving here. And that was all Margo needed to know.

Chapter Ten

*R*oxie swept the front half of the salon, then immediately went to work with Ethan's steam mop the moment he returned with it. She was amazed by how much dirt and grime the washable pads picked up. Fortunately, he'd brought a bunch of them.

While she did that, Ethan and Trina, who'd finished folding the towels, worked on putting the new furniture together. That didn't seem to be too complicated. Mostly the chairs needed their legs attached. The low coffee table that was going in the middle and the racks that would hold all the retail merchandise seemed a bit trickier, based on all the pieces. The racks especially.

Head down, Roxie finished one complete pass of the floor, which put her on the side where the reception desk would eventually go.

"Done?" Ethan asked.

She shook her head. "No, I want to go over it one more time. It was really filthy." She swapped out the dirty pad for a fresh one. Her T-shirt was clinging to her sweaty back. Cleaning wasn't that hard, but it certainly got her heart rate up. "How are we doing on time?"

Trina answered her. "About fifteen minutes before my first interview arrives."

"Good enough. I'll start at the back wall where I finished and work my way out. That way you guys can move stuff into place as soon as the floor dries. Which is pretty fast with this thing." She started mopping again.

She'd just reached the halfway point when Ethan and Trina carried the first two chairs over. They were sleek and modern with thick cushions of black vinyl supported by chrome frames. Very sharp. She nodded her approval as she finished mopping the rest of the floor. "Nice. You did good, Trina."

Trina smiled. "Thanks, Ma."

Roxie was proud of her. She'd picked the furniture out herself with a clear vision of how she wanted the salon to look, and it was definitely coming together. With the crystal chandelier over the seating area, the chrome really gleamed.

All done with the mopping, she turned the steam mop off and helped carry the last of the chairs over. They were set up with three against the front window, then two and two flanking that row.

Ethan adjusted the placement of one of the chairs, so it was lined up straighter. "I'll get the table put together, then I need to get back to the photography studio, since that's become a priority. Is that all right? Or do you need the racks sooner? Might be a couple days before I can get to them."

"That's fine," Trina said. She looked at her phone, then out to the parking lot. "I think my interview is here anyway."

"All right," Ethan said. "You know where I am if you need me."

"Thanks for the mop," Roxie said.

"You're welcome. Might as well hang on to it for now. The rest of this place will need to be done. So will the photography studio eventually."

"Okay." She gave him a smile and a little wave. "If I go out to get us lunch, I'll stop by and get your order first."

He grinned. "Thanks." With a wink, he was gone.

A minute after he left, an older woman came in. Trina greeted her and got the interview underway, inviting her to sit on the new chairs.

Roxie went back to the breakroom where there were more towels to be washed. She finished folding the few that were still on the table, then pulled out the ones that were in the dryer and transferred the next load over from the washer. She got those going then returned to folding. After those were done, she'd wash all the mop pads she'd used.

She was just about done folding when her phone rang. It wasn't a number she recognized. "Hello?"

"Is this the Beachview Shopping Center?" a woman asked.

"It is. How can I help you?" Willie had told Roxie that she'd put a new message on her voicemail telling anyone who was calling about the shopping center to call Roxie's number instead. Made sense these days, since Willie was a little busy with her new house stuff.

"I was wondering if you still have any stores available to rent?"

Roxie smiled. This was good. "We have one left. What kind of business are you looking to set up?"

"A dog grooming salon. Top Dog. We have one shop already and are looking to expand to a second location."

Something fluttered in Roxie's chest. She'd been thinking about getting Trina a dog, now this.

This was a sign. It had to be. "That sounds great. Would you like to come see the store? I can meet you. I'm already here working in one of the other shops."

"Yeah, I really would. I'm Hannah, by the way. Hannah Song."

"Hi, Hannah. I'm Roxanne Thompson. When would you like to come by?"

"I'm coming from the other shop, so maybe twenty minutes? Does that work?"

"It does. Just bear in mind that the storefront needs to be cleaned out and remodeled, but we're glad to help with that."

"No problem. I'll see you soon."

"Great. Bye!" Roxie hung up.

Roxie quickly finished folding the last of the towels, then tucked them away on the shelf where they belonged. With that done, she slipped out of the salon. Trina was still interviewing the woman who'd come in.

Roxie went straight down to the photography studio and inside. Ethan had a saw set up and was cutting two-by-fours to frame out the office space he was building for Thomas Plummer, the photographer.

He finished the cut he was making, turned the

saw off, and pushed his safety goggles up onto his head. "Hey."

"Hey. I just got a call from a woman named Hannah who's coming by in about fifteen minutes to see the other store."

"Good news."

"It is. She wants to turn it into a dog groomers. Already has one location. Top Dog."

"I've seen it. It's all the way at the other end of town. I can see why they'd want one up here."

"Will that take a lot of work?"

"More than this place. Besides the extensive clean-out it needs, there will be construction to do. They'll need some extra plumbing for the sinks and plenty of electrical hookups. Some walls to separate the storefront from the working space, that sort of thing. I can walk through with you and answer her questions, if you want."

"That's exactly what I need. But I need one other thing, too."

"Sure. What is it?"

Roxie smiled. "I need someone to go with me to a local rescue or shelter and pick out a dog for Trina."

His brows lifted. "You're getting Trina a dog?"

She nodded. "Something not too big. She's wanted one all her life and not getting one was one of the big disappointments of her childhood, something I blame her father for. With the right dog, there's no reason she can't bring him or her into the salon with her. It's not like it'll have to be stuck at home all day alone. It's her shop, she can do what she wants."

"True."

"Plus, I'll be around. I can take it out for walks and whatever else it needs. We can get it a dog bed for the breakroom so it can hang out in there."

He laughed. "You've worked all this out, haven't you?"

"Mostly. What do you say? Will you come with me? I haven't even researched local shelters, but there's got to be one."

"There is. Family Friends. You might want to give them a call, see what kind of dogs they have right now."

"I'm going to do it right now. Thanks."

"Of course. And if you want, we can go down there later and see the dogs in person."

Roxie smiled. "I'd love that."

"Let me know when the new potential tenant gets here."

"I will. I'm just going to go outside and make my call so you can get back to sawing."

He laughed. "Thanks."

She went outside, looked Family Friends up on her phone, found the number and dialed.

"Family Friends Rescue." A man had answered. "How can we help you find a friend today?"

"Hi, there. I'm looking for a small to medium-sized dog with a nice temperament who's good with people." Roxie quickly added, "A dog that my daughter can bring to work with her at the hair salon she owns."

"That's pretty specific, but that's good that you know what you want. Are you trying to find a certain breed? Because that can be harder. Most of our dogs are mixed."

"Mixed is fine. I mean, we're all sort of mutts anyway, aren't we?"

He laughed. "Good point. If she's going to take the dog to work with her, something a little more hypoallergenic might be nice, like from the terrier family. As it happens, we have a small white terrier who's looking for a good home. He's been with us for about two weeks and his temperament is just perfect."

"How did he end up with you?"

"Unfortunately, his owner passed away unexpectedly. He's only about a year old, though. Still has a lot of puppy left in him. We think he has a good bit of West Highland White Terrier in him. He's very cute."

Roxie didn't want to get too excited, but so far, the dog sounded great. "What's his name?"

"His name is Walter and we recommend keeping that name, because he definitely knows it."

Her heart melted at the thought of a little dog with an old man's name. "I want to come see him. Do I need an appointment?"

"I'll be here until six. If you want, I can text you a picture of him. I'm Dave, by the way."

"I'd love that, Dave. Thank you." She gave him her name and recited her number. "I have some other things I need to take care of, but I'll be in touch."

"Looking forward to it, Roxie. Talk to you soon."

They hung up and, a few seconds later, her phone beeped with Dave's text. She tapped on it and Walter's face appeared.

Roxie sucked in a breath. Walter was just about the cutest thing she'd ever seen. She sent Dave a quick text back. *I already know I want him. I'll be by as soon as I can.*

Trina was going to love him.

Chapter Eleven

*A*fter the walk on the beach with Jesse and Shiloh, Jules had headed back to the beach house. Toby had seemed worn out by all the excitement of hanging out with his girlfriend and chasing seagulls, so no doubt he'd be sleeping the rest of the day. Jules was glad they'd both gotten the exercise, although *she* didn't have the luxury of sleeping all day.

She'd be working on finalizing the lyrics and writing the music for her two new songs, *Girls Night Out* and *Bad Boys Are My Bad Habit*. She didn't expect to get both songs done today, but getting one close to done and a good start on the second would be fine.

For the next few weeks, she was going to be incredibly busy. Besides finishing those songs, she had an entire album to record, which meant many more days of practice in the studio with her new band.

But before any of that happened, she needed coffee. And a shower. And breakfast. In that order.

She cleaned Toby's feet off, then set him free. She went into the bathroom and turned on the water in the shower before texting Cash, who was probably still sleeping.

Going to shower then make breakfast. Should I text you when it's ready?

She set the phone down on the bathroom counter, stripped off her sweaty clothes, and got into the shower. The water felt great. While she washed her hair and her body, she tried out a few melodies that might work for the new songs.

Both songs felt like they needed to be upbeat and danceable, which would help balance out some of the slower, more emotional songs on the album. She was pleased with how it was all coming together.

Her phone vibrated, moving a half-inch across the counter. Done, she cranked the water off and wrapped her hair and her body up in towels. Probably Cash. And he probably wanted to know what she was making for breakfast.

Then her phone vibrated again. And again. *And* again.

She grabbed it before it vibrated off the counter. If this was Lars... But it wasn't. Notification after notification had popped up, alerting her that she'd been tagged in some social media posts.

She clicked on the first one and found a TikTok video of a young woman dancing to *Dixie's Got Her Boots On*. There were all kinds of hashtags attached to the post: *#hotnewjam #summeranthem #newmusic #JuliaBloom #notyourdaddyscountrymusic*

She stood there, wrapped in a towel, mouth open in disbelief, and watched it through to the end. Then she clicked on another notification. And another. They were all alike. People on social media sharing her song. Some dancing to it. Some already lip-syncing to it.

But all of them loving it.

She was about to click on another one when her phone lit up with an incoming call from her agent. She answered right away. "Hi, Billy."

"Have you seen what's happening? Have you been online this morning?"

"You mean the social media stuff? My phone just started blowing up with notifications."

"It hasn't even gone live on any of the streaming sites yet, but with this kind of buzz, I'm guessing they'll push it through a little faster. You did it, Jules. You've got a verified hit on your hands."

She shook her head. "That's kind of you to say, but it's just a few people on social media. I don't think that means it's a hit. Not yet. It's not even for sale yet. I mean, it's great, don't get me wrong, I'm thrilled. But I'm also cautiously optimistic."

He snorted. "It's a hit, Jules. Trust me. This fervor is only going to build. Brace yourself—you're about to be more popular than you could have dreamed of. You'll see."

"I guess I will."

"Enjoy your day."

"You, too, Billy."

He hung up and she was left with her home screen again. A new stream of incoming notifications rolled by. There seemed to be no end to them.

She carried her phone with her into the bedroom and got dressed. Easy, comfortable clothes. Yoga pants and a tank top, the kinds of things she liked to work in. Still no text from Cash, but she headed to the kitchen anyway to see about something to eat.

She was digging around in the fridge when the sliders got pushed open.

"Mom, are you seeing this?"

She turned at the sound of Cash's voice.

He barreled into the house, his phone in his hand, screen turned toward her. "Macaulay Murphy just did a video of herself dancing to your new song. *Mom.* Macaulay freaking Murphy. You're gonna be famous! More famous. This is crazy. Good crazy. Holy cow, Mom. You've gone viral!"

She set the carton of eggs on the island. "I have no idea who Macaulay Murphy is, but I have gotten a lot of notifications about social media posts that I've been tagged in." She smiled, feeling a bit dazed. "I agree it's crazy."

"Macaulay Murphy is not only a massive influencer with, like, five million followers, but she's also Chad Murphy's daughter." Cash looked at her like that would explain everything.

Jules shook her head. "And Chad Murphy is..."

Cash laughed. "Mom, seriously. He's the editor of *Rebel Yell* magazine."

"Oh. You mean Ted Murphy. That is kind of a big deal." She'd thought the name sounded vaguely familiar and now she knew why. *Rebel Yell* was *the* magazine when it came to music. Mostly rock-and-roll, but they covered every genre.

A little shiver went through Jules. "What do you

think it means? Will she tell her dad? Will she play it for him?"

"There's a good chance he's already heard it. Macaulay prides herself on finding new music and 'influencing,'" he made air quotes around the word, "her dad."

Jules took a breath. "I might need to sit down."

"This is really good. Really good."

"I get that. I just wasn't expecting this." She stared out at the living room without really seeing it. "I need coffee."

"Go sit, I'll make it."

Her eyes narrowed. "You know how to make coffee?"

"I'm not twelve anymore. Yes, I know how to make coffee. In fact, I can make breakfast. That way you can sit on the couch and look through all your social media. You should start responding to those posts, too. Thank them for the mention, tell them you're glad they liked the song. You know, stuff like that."

"I'm not a hundred. I know how to respond to social media posts." She laughed. "Thanks. Whatever you want to make for breakfast is fine, because I'm hungry."

"Hungry enough for pancakes?"

Jules didn't generally go in for a lot of carbs. But this was sort of a special day. And she had gotten that walk in with Jesse. She nodded. "Okay, I'll eat pancakes."

"Cool." With a smile, he got to work on the coffee first.

While Cash occupied himself in the kitchen, Jules settled onto the couch. She went through the notification alerts and carefully wrote a comment on each post. But to Macaulay, who appeared to be one of the first to post about *Dixie*, Jules not only commented, but sent a private message of thanks.

I am so touched that you liked my new song enough to feature it on your channel. I can't say thank you enough for your kind, generous support of new music. Keep shining bright! Lots of love, Julia Bloom.

Probably over the top, but this was an over-the-top moment. Jules hit Send, then went back to scrolling through all the posts that had popped up when she'd done a search on her name as a hashtag.

By the time Cash brought her a cup of coffee, she'd commented on at least twenty different Instagram posts and probably twice as many on TikTok. She glanced at the cup he'd just set down on the coffee table. It looked ready to drink. "Did you put sweetener and creamer in there already?"

"Yes. Was that okay?"

"That's perfect. Wow, is this how stars live?" She gave him a big grin. "I could get used to this."

He snorted as he headed back to the kitchen. "I'm glad fame hasn't gone to your head yet."

Her phone pinged and she looked down to see a message from Macaulay Murphy waiting. Jules hadn't expected a response. But then, she hadn't expected any of this. She tapped on the message.

I haven't liked a song this much in 4ever. It's literally the best thing I've heard in ages. So danceable! I've already told my dad that if he doesn't interview you for Rebel Yell, I'm never speaking to him again. JK! Love this song so much. If you tour, I want front row seats. Not kidding. Hook me up? She signed off with a heart and a peace sign.

Jules got up and went to the door. She opened the slider and looked into the kitchen where Cash was standing over the griddle, pouring batter into ivory puddles. "Macaulay wants front-row seats when I tour. And she said she told her father to interview me for the magazine. Do you think she means it?"

"About the tickets or the interview?"

"Either one."

He pondered that for a second. "Probably both.

She wouldn't want to get a reputation for being full of hot air, you know." Then he frowned. "Did she say that to you in response to your comment?"

"No. I commented, but then I also sent her a private message to say thank you more personally."

He nodded. "Smart. You should send her a *Dixie's Got Her Boots On* T-shirt. Like the kind you sell in your store on your website."

Jules let out a little sound of frustration. "I don't have a store on my website. And I don't have any T-shirts."

He grinned. "Then you've got a lot of work to do."

"Sounds to me like something my business manager ought to be doing."

He made a face. "You don't have a business manager."

She grinned at him. "About that..."

Chapter Twelve

$\mathcal{T}$rina's last interview was done. She was torn between two of the women she'd spoken to. Both of them had a lot of experience and both of them were only interested in working part-time. Part-time was all Trina was hiring for, someone to fill in on the days when the regular crew was off and possibly to work a few later evening shifts.

Maybe her mom could help her decide. She looked around for her mom. Roxie had been in and out of the salon most of the day. She seemed to be out at the moment. She'd been out a lot, actually.

Trina got up, admired the new chairs once more, then went toward the back to make sure her mom wasn't just in the breakroom. Not there. She must be with Ethan, who was probably down at the photography studio.

She thought about texting, but she wanted to stretch her legs after sitting for so long. Plus, she hadn't seen the progress on the studio yet. She stuck her phone in her back pocket and walked out of the salon. The photography studio was next to the bakery, leaving one empty store between it and the salon.

Hopefully, that would be filled soon, too. Trina wanted her grandmother to have the income from all the rents. Trina peeked into the empty store as she thought about rent. Mimi had never said how much she wanted a month for the salon.

Trina had a feeling the answer would be nothing, but that just couldn't be. She wanted to pay her grandmother back for everything she'd done for her. That would take some time, obviously, but the least she could do was pay rent.

Something to talk to Mimi about this evening.

She continued on to the photography studio. Ethan had put paper up over the windows to a height of about six feet to block the view inside while he worked. She tried the door and found it open. Ethan and her mom were standing with their backs to her, chatting.

"Hey, there," Trina called out. "I wasn't sure

where you were, Ma. I need to talk to you about something."

Before her mom could answer, a little white ball of fluff came running toward Trina.

Her mouth fell open as she realized it was a dog. The precious little creature stopped by her feet and looked up at her, letting out one short, happy bark.

Trina blinked. "Hello, there. Aren't you the cutest thing?" He really was. Probably the cutest dog she'd ever seen. Her whole being ached with want at the sight of him. She crouched down to pet him. He was so soft.

She glanced up at her mom. "Is he lost? Where did he come from?"

Her mom and Ethan had weird smiles on their faces. Like they were both super happy and slightly worried.

"He's not lost," her mom said. "His name is Walter." Her mom paused. "Walter Thompson."

Trina frowned. "He has the same last name as us?"

Her mom nodded. "Unless you don't want him."

Trina's mouth came open again. "I don't understand. Is he *our* dog?" Her heart beat faster. Was this really happening?

"He's *your* dog," her mom said. "If you want him.

I went down to the rescue and got him for you today. You deserve a dog, Trina. I know how much you've wanted one."

Emotion narrowed Trina's throat. "All my life."

Walter licked her hand.

Trina scooped him up in her arms and buried her face in his fur as the tears flowed. "I can't believe he's mine. I love him already."

"I knew you would." Her mom's arms came around Trina in a quick hug. Roxie sniffed. "He's the handsomest boy ever, don't you think?"

Trina nodded and adjusted Walter's position in her arms. She couldn't believe he was hers. "He's amazing. He's absolutely perfect."

Walter licked her face, making her laugh.

Ethan came over. "I think he likes you, too."

Roxie nodded. "He's about a year old. His name stays, because he knows it. He was at the rescue because his owner passed away and none of the remaining family wanted him."

"How could no one want this angel?" Trina said. She looked at him. "Don't worry. I want you. And I'm going to give you the best life." She kissed his face. "I think Walter's a pretty good name for him, too."

Her mom was all smiles. "Because Walter is a terrier, Dave, the guy at the rescue, said Walter's pretty hypoallergenic, which means you can bring him to work with you and no one should have allergy issues."

Trina took a breath. "I can bring him to work with me?" The very idea of that, of being able to keep him with her all the time, filled her with joy. And she was already happier than she imagined she could be.

"Why not?" Ethan said. "It's your shop. You make the rules."

Trina grinned. "Walter, you and me are never going to be apart. I can't wait to introduce him to Miles."

Roxie nodded. "I'm sure Miles will love him, too. Does that mean you're definitely going to keep him?"

Trina hugged Walter a little tighter. "He's a hundred percent my dog now."

"Good," her mom said. She pulled out her phone. "I told Dave I'd send him a picture of you and Walter once you got acquainted. Say cheese." She took a quick snap and sent it.

Trina looked at Walter. "It's official. You're adopted."

"I have some more good news, too," her mom said.

Trina wasn't sure how much more good news she

could take. There wasn't anything she could imagine that would be better than having her very own dog. She kissed Walter again, just because she could. "What's that?"

Her mom hooked her thumb toward the empty store. "The place next door is about to be occupied by a dog grooming salon, if you can believe that." She chuckled. "When the woman called to ask about the space, hearing that she was looking to open a dog grooming place seemed like a sign that I should get you a dog. I'd already been thinking about it. Anyway, the woman, Hannah, came by earlier to look at the space and she loved it. Top Dog Grooming Salon. This will be their second location. They'll be moving in as soon as Ethan and his crew can make the necessary changes."

Ethan brushed some bits of sawdust off his T-shirt. "The photography studio is my main priority, along with whatever remains to get the bakery and your salon open, of course, but once that's done, I'll be focused on the groomers. Your grandmother should be happy. She's got a full house."

Trina glanced at her mom. "Did you tell Mimi?"

"Not yet." Roxie looked at Walter. "I've been a little busy."

"I guess so. How did you do all of this today?" Trina asked.

Her mom nudged Ethan. "I had help. He walked through the empty storefront with me and Hannah, although calling it empty is a laugh. The previous tenants left a lot of garbage behind. Anyway, Ethan answered all of her questions, and then he went down to Family Friends with me to get Walter."

"And now," Ethan said. "I need to get back to work. I'm happy for you, Trina. He looks like a great dog, and I know you're going to treat him like a prince."

Trina nodded. "Prince Walter."

He let out a little yip.

"Are you trying to tell me you're royalty?" Trina asked him. She laughed as she hugged him. How could she be this in love with a creature she'd only just met? She had no idea, but she was crazy about him.

"Come on," her mom said. "Let's let Ethan get back to work and we can go show Walter where he's going to be working as the beauty shop's mascot."

"Okay," Trina said. She waved at Ethan, Walter still in her arms. "Thank you."

He was putting his safety goggles back on. "You're welcome."

Trina and her mom headed for the salon.

"We'll need to go by Happy Pets before we go home," her mom said. "Walter needs everything. A leash and collar, a bed, some bowls—"

"Toys," Trina added. "Treats, a brush...I should probably get some poop bags and a holder for them for when I take him for walks. Jules has those for Toby." She kissed his face again. "I'm going to spoil this dog rotten. Thanks, Ma. I love him so much."

"You deserve him, Trina. You do so much for everyone else. It was well past time you had a dog." Her brows bent as they went into the salon.. "You said something when you first came in about needing to talk to me. What about?"

"Oh, just some help deciding who to hire. Two of the women I talked to today were really good. I can't decide between them."

"It's for the part-time position, right?"

"Right." Trina set Walter down, interested to see what he'd do. She couldn't stop looking at him. He was literally perfect.

Roxie shrugged. "So hire them both and spread the hours out. You can always give more to whoever wants them."

"I guess I could. I really would like to hire them both. So that's my solution then. Thanks, Ma."

"You're welcome. Now, let's take Walter on a shopping spree."

Trina watched him sniff everything in his path, loving the way his nose wrinkled and his ears twitched. Everything he did was magic. "There's nothing I want to do more."

Chapter Thirteen

*K*at let out a heavy sigh as she put the last folder down. She hadn't anticipated what those folders would hold, but if she'd thought about it more, she would have.

She'd known they were all requests for help from Future Florida, which meant they were all stories from people who were in great need in some way or another. She just hadn't anticipated how much they'd affect her.

Some were looking for help with medical situations. Those were particularly hard to read about. Some wanted to start a business but didn't have the funds and couldn't get financing. Some were seeking help for family members or friends and had written on their behalf.

There were groups in search of donations, too.

Schools. Beach cleanup organizations. Animal shelters. Food pantries. Blood drives. Veterans charities.

The list of those in need was endless. And to think all of these had come in in just the last week. It was staggering. And Kat felt the weight of the requests as if they sat squarely on her shoulders.

It was a lot to take in. She needed a break. She checked the time. Well past lunch. Another hour and she'd be headed home. She got up, feeling like she'd been mentally rung out, and made her way back to the breakroom to eat. Mostly she needed to decompress and felt like the change of scenery would be a good thing.

Eloise was already there, sitting at the end of the dining table, a container of Publix's sushi and a bottle of sparkling imported water in front of her. "You missed lunch, too?"

Kat nodded. "Yeah. I hope you don't mind the company."

"Not at all." Eloise peered at Kat a little harder. "You okay? You seem...upset. Or at least bothered."

Kat got her lunch out of the fridge, realized she hadn't thought about a drink, and filled a cup from the cabinet with tap water. She brought all of that to the table and took a seat one chair away from Eloise.

"I don't know what I am other than reeling from the support requests I just read through."

"Ah," Eloise said knowingly. "Baptism by fire, I see." She nodded as she used a pair of chopsticks to pick up a piece of sushi. "Those are hard. It's a lot to take in but it's a very important part of what we do."

"I can see that. I just...I never thought about it." She took her sandwich, a baggie of pretzels, and a baggie of grapes out of her lunch sack. "Never thought about how someone would have to be the person who read through all of those and helped decide who gets the help and who doesn't."

Eloise smiled. "I'll let you in on a little secret."

Kat unwrapped her sandwich. "What's that?"

"We do our best to help all the legitimate requests. Even if we can't fulfill their exact wish, we try to help in some way. Sometimes that means sending them a small amount of money. Sometimes that means referring them to another charity. Sometimes it means trying to get someone else on board who can provide the help they need. A doctor, a lawyer, an angel investor, someone like that. A lot of times we can get the professional people to do pro bono work."

Kat felt some of her tension ease away. "That's really good to know. I'm so glad you told me."

"Feel better?"

"A little. Better than I did when I walked in here."

Eloise ate her bite of sushi, then used her chopsticks to point at the treadmills that were set up on the opposite side of the room. "That's also why we have the exercise equipment. You should really take advantage of it. Even if it's only for ten or fifteen minutes, the adrenaline boost will really help balance your mood. I keep a set of exercise clothes here just for that very purpose. You might have noticed there's a shower stall in the women's bathroom, too."

"I did see that." Kat took a bite of her sandwich and chewed while she looked at the machines. "That's a great idea. I'm going to bring a change of clothes in, too."

"Trust me," Eloise said. "This is a great place to work, but it's also a *hard* place to work. Not physically, but emotionally. We have to take care of ourselves and take care of each other. Tom and Molly know that. More importantly, Waylen knows that."

She ate another piece of sushi before going on. "A lot of people might see a room like this and think we've misspent money that could have been better used to take care of someone in need, but a lot of people have no idea the toll working at a charity like this can take."

Kat hadn't honestly thought about it. "I certainly didn't."

"You just wanted to do something that felt like you were making a difference, right? A job that mattered instead of one that just paid the bills?"

Kat nodded immediately before sipping her water. "That's exactly right. You, too?"

Eloise gave her a slow nod in return. "Eight years ago. I was working in PR, getting business for companies that already had a lot of business and were just using their profits to line their pockets." She smiled. "I had what most people would call a breakdown, but it was really a crisis of self."

"Meaning?"

"I didn't like who I'd become. And the job I was doing wasn't helping at all. It seemed so superficial and, honestly, pointless. For a while, I considered selling everything, buying an RV, and traveling the country with my cat."

Kat laughed. "That doesn't sound like such a bad plan."

"It's not, really. But now it'll be for my retirement. Isaac spends most of his time laying in the sun that comes through the sliding doors in my house. I'm not sure how he'd feel about living in an RV."

"Isaac is your cat?" After making that guess, Kat took a bite of her sandwich.

Eloise nodded, a look of pure happiness in her eyes. "Sir Isaac Mewton. He's twenty pounds of ridiculousness and I love him dearly."

"I love that name. That's great. Are you married, too?" Kat sat back. "Sorry, that's none of my business."

"No, it's okay. I'm divorced. Happily. No kids, but that's okay, too. I have nieces and nephews and I get to spoil them, so it's all good."

Kat liked Eloise a lot. She seemed to be a few years older than Aunt Jules, but with a similar sort of coolness. Actually, Eloise might be a tiny bit cooler in a different way. She was just so put together and hip.

Aunt Jules was put together and hip, too, but in a more down-to-earth way. Eloise looked like she could have easily just arrived from Manhattan.

"How about you?" Eloise asked. "Are you married?"

Kat shook her head. "I almost was but I came up for air before it actually happened." She smiled and glanced at the wave ring on her finger. "I'm with someone new now. Someone amazing. He's kind of the reason I'm here."

"Oh? How's that? Did Future Florida help him in some way?"

"No, but he's a fireman and he volunteers to work with kids at a surf camp sometimes. He just really inspired me to do something bigger with my life. Alex." She smiled again. "He's teaching me to surf, too. He's really just changed my whole perspective on life."

"That's great. He sounds amazing. You're brave to surf." She shook her head. "I don't think I could do that."

"I didn't think I could, either, but Alex helped me get into the right kind of mindset and after trying it, I was instantly hooked. As soon as I get my first paycheck, I'm buying my own board."

"A surfer girl. I love it. It's a lot of work. And a great workout. Not that you're in bad shape."

"No, you're right. After that first time surfing, I was so sore. But it's a good kind of hurt, because you know you did something worth doing."

"It'll be a great way to balance out working here, too."

Kat nodded. "Yeah, it will be. I hadn't thought

about that." She popped a pretzel into her mouth. "Now I'm even more determined to get good at it."

Eloise ate her last piece of sushi and started to clean up. "I'd better get back to work. I meant what I said about how we have to take care of each other. You need anything, you know where my office is."

"Thanks."

Eloise got up and put her garbage in the proper receptacles, some in recycling, some in regular trash. She washed her hands at the sink, then headed out giving Kat a smile and a wave. "Thanks for the chat. See you later."

"Later," Kat said, waving back.

She was glad she'd come in. Talking to Eloise had helped a lot. Kat understood now that this job was going to require some self-care in ways she hadn't imagined. That was all right, though. She should be taking care of herself anyway.

Now she just had a solid reason to. Buying that surfboard couldn't happen soon enough.

Chapter Fourteen

Claire wiped sweat off her forehead as she leaned against one of the stainless-steel worktables and let out a soft sigh. She'd gotten a *lot* done. There was pretty much nothing left to do in the kitchen as far as the cleaning went. She was ready to start baking as soon as the ingredients arrived.

Danny was at one of the sinks, washing his hands. He glanced over at her as he rinsed them. "Long day, huh?"

She nodded. "It was. That's all right, though. Got a lot done in here. I'm ready to start baking now, which I am really looking forward to."

He smiled. "There's cleaning to be done out front and a few minor things, but we're really close. I'm going to see about ordering containers and plastic bags for the frozen cookie dough tonight. I'm sure I can get them from our supplier who provides us with our big plastic popcorn buckets."

"Seems like something they should be able to do."

"Yes." He dried his hands on some paper towel as he came over to her. "You want to stop by someplace on the way home and pick up some dinner? I don't know about you, but I'm in no mood to cook."

"Neither am I but I should check in and make sure no one else has plans. Cash has been talking about cooking dinner for everyone, I just don't know what night he intends to do that." She pulled out her phone and sent a group text asking about dinner. "I'm sure someone will answer me soon."

He nodded. "I think all I want to do is take a shower and crash."

"I'm pretty close to that myself." She smiled at him. "Although, you know what I'd like to do again before we open?"

"What's that?"

"Go out on your catamaran again."

His brows lifted. "Yeah?"

She nodded. "And not just because I want to see dolphins. I do, and they definitely inspired me, but it was a lot of fun, too. I really enjoyed it. I was thinking maybe you could even show me how to operate it. If you're willing. Not like there's much for me to crash into out on the open water."

He laughed. "I'd be happy to show you. I'd like to go out on it again, too. Being on the water with you reminded me of just how much I'd missed it. We could probably do it tomorrow afternoon. What do you say?"

"I say—" Her phone beeped, signaling that she'd gotten a message. She glanced at the screen. "Yes to the boat tomorrow and yes to Cash making dinner tonight. He says for me to bring you. You up for that?"

"So long as I can go home and shower first. That's really nice of him." Danny made a face. "Can he actually cook?"

"I'm not sure, to tell you the truth. For as much as he eats, he ought to be decent in the kitchen, because I don't know how else he was feeding himself when he was in California. I wonder what he's making. Let me see if I can find out." She typed another message to the group. *What's for dinner?*

Cash responded shortly and she read his answer out loud. "He says barbequed chicken with his homemade sauce, grilled veggie kabobs, and rice. Dessert is up to someone else."

"That sounds good. I'd be happy to stop by

Publix and pick something up." He leaned closer to Claire. "I know it won't compare to anything you could make, but no one should be expecting you to bake something after the day you just put in."

"Amen," Claire said. "Tell you what—if you get something from the bakery, I'll pick up one of their big fruit bowls. That's always a nice option after dinner, too."

"Deal." He pushed away from the worktable. "Let's get out of here."

"Right behind you." As they turned off the lights and locked up, she realized she was about to go out in public looking very much like she'd just put in a hard day's labor, which she had. Wasn't like her to go out that way, but it couldn't be helped.

Hopefully, she wouldn't see anyone she knew. Probably not, seeing as how few people she'd met in the area.

Publix was busy, too, with lots of people stopping by after work to grab something for dinner. She and Danny split up a short way inside, with him headed to the bakery and her going into produce.

The two were right across from each other, so as soon as she'd selected a fruit bowl, she found him at the bakery counter. "What are you getting?"

He pointed at the glass display case. "An assortment. Two of those little fruit tarts, two of the turtle brownies, six petit fours, and four chocolate-covered strawberries. You think that'll suffice?"

She nodded. "With this fruit, it's plenty. Even without the fruit, it's plenty."

They took their items to the express lane, paid, and got back in his truck. Without seeing anyone. Thankfully.

Danny dropped Claire in front of her house, then parked in his driveway. They gave each other a wave before heading inside to their respective homes.

Claire found Cash in the kitchen, prepping for the meal he was about to make, when she stepped off the elevator. "Hey, Aunt Claire. How was your day?"

"Good. Long." She couldn't wait to wash off the sweat and grime of the day.

"Is Danny coming?"

"He is. He'll be over after he showers, which is what I'm about to do." She held up the Publix bag. "I got a fruit bowl and he's bringing some other goodies from the bakery."

"Cool." He grinned suddenly. "By the way, your sister is on her way to becoming a major celebrity."

"What? What happened?"

He shook his head. "I'll let her tell you, but my mom had a *good* day."

"I'll be sure to ask." Claire put the fruit in the fridge, then went to her bedroom. After her shower, she was about to put on pajama pants and an old T-shirt when she remembered Danny was coming over. She changed, going with capri leggings and a cuter T-shirt, instead.

Cash was no longer in the kitchen. She figured he'd gone downstairs to get the chicken on the grill. She filled a big glass with ice water and took a sip.

Jules came in through the back porch sliders, an empty cup in her hand. "Hey, I didn't know you were home. Good timing. I think we're eating in like twenty minutes."

"Danny's coming over, too."

"Great." Jules took the cup into the kitchen and put it in the dishwasher.

"Cash said you're about to become a major celebrity and that I should ask you about it."

Jules laughed and nodded. "My new song kind of blew up today. Lots of social media mentions by some pretty big influencers. Things look...good." She pulled a quick face. "I just don't want to over-expect. This could be a flash in the pan. I mean, the song's not even available to buy yet, because it's still going through the approval process that happens after uploading."

Claire frowned. "Then how could anyone on social media talk about it?"

"Billy. He sent it out to a lot of people, hoping something like this would happen."

"Seems like it worked."

"It did. I just...I don't know. I feel like I shouldn't get too excited about it yet."

"Why?"

Jules put her hands on the kitchen counter, leaning on them. "I don't know. I guess I'm afraid it's not real. That I might not actually be on the cusp of the success I've always dreamed about. It's a strange feeling."

"Like you don't deserve it? Like you haven't worked hard enough for it?" Claire laughed. "Sweet Jules. You *do* deserve it. And you have worked harder than anyone I know. Stop doubting and enjoy it." She went over and hugged her sister, who hugged her back.

"Thanks," Jules whispered. "It really doesn't feel real, though."

Claire pulled back. "It will at some point. I'm so happy for you." For a long time, Jules had been overshadowed by Lars and his success. There was a point where she'd even discussed walking away from music entirely to be a full-time mom.

Jules was too talented to deny her gifts, though. And while she'd had a good deal of success, enough to live off of and make a small name for herself, Claire knew it was nothing like what some of her contemporaries had achieved.

"Thanks," Jules said. "I needed that. How was the bakery today?"

"Good. Got a lot done. I'll be baking before you know it. Mostly cookies, which I'll freeze. Danny wants to sell packages of frozen cookie dough that people can take home and bake themselves. They'll be varieties of the cookies that we sell in the store, obviously."

"That is a great idea," Jules said. "I love that. So smart. I can't wait until you're open. I want to be one of the first customers."

Claire laughed. "I'll make you whatever you want. You don't have to buy something."

"I want to. Haven't you bought all of my albums?"

"Yes, but—"

"No buts," Jules said. Her phone chimed with a new message, but she ignored it. "Besides, I have a whole studio full of musicians that will happily eat whatever I bring them, I have no doubt. Hey, that reminds me—have you talked to Danny about doing a deal with Jesse so he can offer the sour orange pie at the club?"

"I've mentioned it, but we've been so busy that we never really worked anything out. I promise I'll talk to him tonight. Speaking of Danny, he should be here by now. I hope something hasn't come up."

Jules looked at her phone. "Cash texted me. Danny's with him downstairs. I'm supposed to be bringing him a drink."

"Danny?"

"Cash." Jules grabbed a soda from the fridge.

"Let me just put some shoes on and I'll go down with you," Claire said.

"Okay."

"Does Toby need to go out, too?"

"No, I took him out about an hour ago. He's good."

"Be right back." Claire ran to the bedroom and got her flipflops, then she and Jules went down in the elevator.

The tantalizing aroma of barbecuing chicken wafted over to them as soon as they stepped off. Danny was standing next to Cash at the grill, a ginger beer in hand. The two of them were laughing about something.

He smiled when he saw Claire. "Hey, there. Nice to feel human again, huh?"

She laughed. "Yes. That shower was exactly what I needed."

"Me, too. Ginger beer?" He gestured to the big cooler near his feet.

She lifted her glass of water. "I'm good for now. Are your desserts in there, too?"

He nodded. "Yep."

"Speaking of desserts, we need to figure out some kind of deal for Jesse."

"The sour orange pie, right?"

"Right."

"Okay," Danny said. "We need to cost out the recipe and see where our pricing is at, then we can give him a number. We'll make it happen. It'll be good for us. Good for him, too, being able to offer something no one else has."

"Unless they buy a pie from us."

Danny smiled. "Which is exactly what we want them to do."

Chapter Fifteen

*W*illie lay on the couch. Not her usual spot, but she was too tired to sit upright. They'd looked through three massive furniture stores today. She had no idea when furniture stores had gotten so big, but the three they had been in today were some of the largest buildings she'd ever been inside. Football fields could have fit inside them.

They weren't just one floor, either. Most of them were at least two. One of them had had a third floor, which was where all the clearance was. They hadn't bothered going up there. Willie had nothing against a good deal, but by that point she and Miguel had been exhausted.

She was still exhausted. She hadn't done that much walking in a long time. She imagined that was a sign that she ought to get in better shape. When they went to Puerto Rico, they'd be doing a lot of walking, too.

The good news was she and Miguel had accomplished a lot. Besides buying furniture for Trina's guest room, they'd found a beautiful set for the master bedroom. A big king-size bed, two nightstands, and a dresser with a mirror for Miguel. Willie planned to have drawers in her closet and keep everything in there.

She wanted a nice chair for the master bedroom, too. She'd found a few she'd liked, but she just wasn't sure. She'd taken pictures of them and was going to see what Roxie and Trina thought when they got home.

Which sounded like now, since the elevator doors were opening.

"Mimi!" Trina called out. "Guess what?"

Trina usually sounded excited about something, but this was a whole new level of excitement. "What?" Willie called back.

Trina rushed in, arms full of white fur. "I got a dog. Ma got him for me. His name is Walter. Isn't he amazing?"

Willie sat up. "Are you fooling me? That's a stuffed animal." But then the dog moved. "For Pete's sake, it's real."

Trina laughed and put Walter on the floor. He came running up to Willie, looking about as happy as a dog could look.

Willie gasped. "He's beautiful, Trina." Willie looked at Roxie, whose eyes shone with happy tears.

Willie felt a little emotional herself. Trina had wanted a dog all her life, but that rat weasel Bryan had never thought it was a good idea. Now she'd finally gotten her pup. "Where'd you find him, Roxie?" A dog like this had to be expensive. Not that Willie was going to say anything, no matter what Roxie had spent. Looking at Trina, it was clear to see the dog had been worth every penny.

"I got him from a rescue in town," Roxie said. She had shopping bags from Happy Pets in each hand. "He came from a place called Family Friends. Isn't he just perfect?"

Willie nodded. "He really is. I can't believe you got a dog like him from a rescue."

"Neither can I," Roxie said.

"I'm already crazy about him." Trina gestured toward the elevator. "I need to run back to the car and get the rest of his stuff. We took him to Happy Pets for a little shopping spree to get him all set up. Keep an eye on my baby while I'm gone, will ya?"

"We will," Roxie said.

As Trina headed downstairs, Roxie started unpacking the shopping bags. Most of what she was taking out seemed to be dog toys, but there was also a bag of food and a pair of stainless-steel bowls.

Willie grinned. "Spoiling the little guy, huh?"

"Like you wouldn't believe."

"Has he met the weiner dog upstairs?"

"Not yet, but Claire and Jules were outside grilling when we got home, so they got to meet Walter. Trina and Jules talked about introducing them to see if they'd want to play together."

"Very good." Willie patted the couch and Walter hopped up, turned around twice, and laid down next to her, putting his head on her leg and looking up at her. She shook her head. "He's a heartbreaker, this one. Just look at him. Have you ever seen anything so cute? I swear, if he could talk, I'd give him anything he asked for."

Roxie laughed. "Pretty sure we already bought him anything he might ask for at Happy Pets."

"I'm glad." Willie petted the little dog's head. He was very soft. "You did a good thing, Roxie. A really good thing."

"Thanks, Ma. I was a little nervous that Trina might rather pick out a dog herself, but after I talked to the man at the rescue and saw Walter's picture, I just couldn't say no. I figured if Trina didn't want him, I'd keep him for myself."

"I could see that. Maybe you should get a dog, too."

"I think we're good for now."

Trina returned, carrying a dog bed, another shopping bag, and a large empty plastic container. "Did you miss me, Walter?"

He sat up and his tail wagged, thumping against the back of the couch.

Willie got up, energized by the new addition. "I'll scooch over to my chair so you can sit with him." She did just that, settling in and putting her feet up. Walter tipped his head at her as if he was wondering why she'd left.

"I'm going to put a blanket on the couch for him," Trina said. "So he knows where his spot is. Plus, it'll help keep his hair contained. We got one at the pet store. Got him a brush, too. They're in this bag."

She put the bed and the plastic container on the breakfast bar, then pulled the blanket out of the bag but left the brush in it. The blanket was about the size of a baby blanket. White fleece with a pink and blue paw print pattern. She pulled the tag off, then spread it out on the couch. She patted her hand on it. "Come on, Walter. Over here. This is your spot. Your blanket."

He moved over and laid down, after doing two more turns.

"He's a smart cookie," Willie said. "What made you pick Walter for his name?"

"I didn't," Trina said. "He came with that name, and he knows it, so he's keeping it." She told Willie his story.

"Sad he lost his owner, but he's in high cotton now." He really was a good-looking dog. All that white fur and those big dark eyes.

Roxie opened the bag of dog food and transferred the kibble into the big plastic container, making sure the lid was on tight when she was done. "We've got more news, Ma. The last unit at the shopping center is rented."

"Is it? That's fantastic," Willie said. "That happen today, too?"

"It did," Roxie answered.

"And guess who rented it?" Trina asked. She didn't wait for Willie to answer. "A dog grooming place! Top Dog. Don't you just love it?" She bent down to kiss Walter's head. "And I already know who their number one client is going to be."

Willie snorted. "Maybe we can get a discount.

What are you going to do with him when you're at work, my girl?"

"Take him with me, Mimi." Trina took the tag off a bright blue stuffed bone and put it next to Walter on the blanket. "His breed is hypoallergenic, so customer allergies shouldn't be an issue. Besides, he won't be in the way. He's little. And I'll make sure he has a bed in the breakroom to chill out on."

Willie nodded. "You're the boss, my girl. You make the rules. Seems to me like some people might really get a kick out of seeing a dog at the beauty shop."

"Hopefully." Trina shrugged. "I know there's always a chance some people won't like it, but what's done is done. Walter is the official new mascot of A Cut Above. Anyone who has an issue with that can get their hair done somewhere else."

"Then again," Roxie said. "It might bring some people in." She looked at Willie. "Are you hungry, Ma? Trina and I were thinking about ordering pizza and salads."

"Fine with me. Miguel is on his way over, too. I'm sure he'd like something to eat. And while you're up, I could use a drink, if you wouldn't mind. One of those diet cherry sodas, if we have any."

"I think there's one left. You want ice?"

"Yes, thanks."

"Coming up. I'll order an extra salad for Miguel."

"I appreciate that."

Trina finally sat down next to Walter. She put her arm around him. "How was your day, Mimi? Did you guys find a lot of good stuff?"

"We found a few things." Willie grinned. "Wait until you see the furniture I picked out for your guest room. You're going to love it."

"I'm sure I will," Trina said. "I just need to know if I'm going to be able to bring Walter with me when I come. That's kind of important."

Roxie brought Willie's drink over and set it on the table next to her chair.

"Of course!" Willie winked at the little dog. "My great-granddog is always welcome at my house."

Trina laughed. "Thanks, Mimi."

"Granddog." Smiling, Roxie shook her head. "I'll order the pizza and salads, then I'm sitting down."

"Maybe I should take Walter out again before we eat," Trina said. "Do you need to go out, baby?"

Walter's ears twitched, but that seemed to be the extent of his interest.

Trina shrugged. "I guess not. I still need to put his collar and his new tag on him. We got those at the pet store, too."

"And a matching leash," Roxie added as she prepared to call in their supper order.

"Did you tell your boyfriend he's got competition?" Willie asked Trina, laughing at her own words.

Trina nodded. "I sent Miles a picture and told him the whole story. He's excited to meet Walter. We're going to take him to the beach with us next time we go."

"Make sure you've got shade," Willie said. "White dogs and cats are susceptible to sunburn. I read about it in a magazine."

"I promise, we will," Trina said. She gave her grandmother an amused look. "You like him, don't you?"

"Who? Miles? I think he's a very nice boy," Willie teased.

Trina laughed. "No, Mimi. I mean Walter."

Willie chuckled. It was plain the dog was going to be a big part of Trina's life and that he already occupied a special place in her heart. Good for her. She deserved to be happy and loved and to have one of her childhood dreams come true. "I like Walter tons, my girl. I think he's a very nice boy, too."

Chapter Sixteen

Margo didn't like to think the day had been wasted, but the truth was, all of the window shopping they'd done with Dinah had been just that: Window shopping. Wasted time. The woman had no intention of moving to Diamond Beach.

Margo felt sure of that now. All the talk about moving here had been a big ploy to disrupt Margo and Conrad's plans for being together and writing. Which Dinah had done, successfully. They'd gotten approximately half a page written today. Not great.

Of course, they had no one to blame but themselves. It had been her and Conrad's idea to look at properties, thinking they would call Dinah's bluff.

In that sense, their plan had succeeded. But Dinah had yet to vacate Conrad's home. That part was a fail. Margo desperately wanted Dinah gone so they could get back into the groove of writing. And of her spending the day with Conrad.

She missed him more than she could say. Missed the bantering and working on the book together, the keen discussions they had during their breaks. The closeness. The occasional kiss. In a remarkably short period of time, she'd grown used to being with him.

All of that had come to a screeching halt with the arrival of Dinah. Margo was *more* than ready for the woman to go home.

She sat at dinner, pondering how she might make that happen, lost in her own thoughts, all the while aware she was being terrible company.

"You okay, Grandma?"

Margo looked up at her granddaughter and smiled. "Sorry, Kat. Just something on my mind."

"Everything all right?"

Margo wasn't much of a liar. "Not really. Dinah is still here. She's been talking about moving to Diamond Beach, but Conrad and I went with her to look at some condos for sale today and all she did was come up with excuse after excuse for why all of them were wrong."

Kat made a face. "You really want her out of your hair, don't you?"

"Very much so."

"You think she's really going to move here?"

"No. Not after today. Someone who was being honest about moving to a new place would show more enthusiasm about looking at available homes in the area. All we did was waste a day we could have spent writing." Margo sighed. "It's frustrating me to no end."

Kat nodded. "So why don't you just ignore her and get back to your life?"

"I'd love to do that. I think Conrad would, too, at this point. I'm just not sure how. She's staying with him."

"He could come here," Kat suggested.

"It's not the same. He has a dedicated office. And an empty house. When Dinah's not there, obviously. We'd have to work here at the dining room table. We'd be in the way of Jules and Cash. Or you and your mom."

"Or we'd be in your way. Although I'm at work from nine to five these days, so it wouldn't bother me. Everyone else is sort of in and out sometimes, so I see what you're saying. What about going to a coffee shop?"

Margo shook her head, touched by Kat's concern and suggestions. "We have to be able to talk freely so that we can discuss what happens next in the book. We talk a lot. It's a big part of how we write."

"That makes sense." Kat ate a bite of chicken. "It's too bad there's not a college library around. You know, we had these study rooms where two to four people could fit in and have their own private space. They were great for when the dorms were too noisy or you just needed a place to get away and get work done."

"That would be good." Margo narrowed her eyes as she tried to remember the layout of the public library in Diamond Beach. "I know the library here has a big meeting room. That's where the book club meets. Not sure about them having any smaller rooms."

"I bet Conrad would know."

Margo nodded. "I bet he would, too." She'd left her phone by her chair in the living room. She didn't particularly like phones at the dinner table. She glanced at it.

Kat laughed. "Go on. Go text him and see what he knows."

With a little half-smile, Margo got up and went to retrieve her phone. She sat in her chair to send him the message. *Do you know if the public library has study rooms?*

She gave him a few seconds and was rewarded for waiting.

They do. Why?

Can we reserve one and work there tomorrow?

A smiley face came back immediately. *That's a brilliant idea. The rooms are first come, first served, so we'd just have to be there when they open at nine.*

Works for me, Margo typed. *Breakfast first?*

Digger's?

Where else. 8am?

See you there. He finished his message with a heart.

She smiled and sent him a heart back before returning to the table. She took her seat, putting her hand on her granddaughter's arm. "You're a genius, Kat. Thank you. The library does have study rooms and Conrad and I are going to write in one tomorrow. I owe you."

"You don't owe me anything." Kat wiggled her brows. "But I do want to be one of your first readers."

"I promise I will make that happen."

"I'm all about that." Kat helped herself to another piece of cornbread. "Were you able to reserve the room so you'd have it all day?"

"Conrad said the rooms are first come, first

served, so we're going to be there when the library opens at nine."

Kat nodded. "You know that means you could lose the room if you go out for lunch. That's how it worked in college."

Margo frowned. "I hadn't thought about that."

"My suggestion, and I'm telling you this because it's what we used to do in college, is to sneak lunch in. The library probably has a no food or drinks policy, but if you take a big purse, you can probably fit a couple of sandwiches and bottles of water in there. Maybe even some fruit or chips or something."

Margo nodded. "I do have a tote bag that could pass as a purse. That's a splendid idea. We're meeting at Digger's for breakfast first, but I'll just bring the tote in with me so the food doesn't sit in the car. Once again, an excellent idea."

Kat grinned and looked pleased with herself. "Feel free to mention me in the acknowledgements."

Margo laughed. "I might just have to do that. We'll see how the study room works out, but I feel like it's going to be exactly what we need."

Anyplace where they could work and be away from Dinah's constant interruptions would be a godsend. And if the study room turned out to be as conducive to writing as Margo thought it would be, Kat wasn't just getting a mention in the acknowledgments, she was getting a present, too.

Margo wasn't sure what. Maybe a good pair of earrings. Maybe a good pen, engraved with her name. That would be a nice gift, considering Kat's new job. Which Margo realized she hadn't asked her granddaughter about.

She'd been far too caught up in all the nonsense with Dinah. That rotten woman. She wasn't even here, and she was taking Margo away from her family. Well, that was enough of *that*.

She patted Kat's arm. "How is your new job? I want to hear all about it. Every detail."

"Yeah?"

"Yes," Margo said. She'd already heard a few things, but not enough. She didn't want to miss out on sharing Kat's life just because of her own issues. "Very exciting that you have your own office. Have you decorated it yet or isn't that allowed?"

"No, it's allowed. I've brought a few things in. Still need some art for the walls and at least one plant, but I'm getting there. I love the job. It's tough, but very rewarding." Kat looked at Jules. "That reminds me, Aunt Jules. I have a proposition for you..."

Margo ate the last few bites of her dinner,

smiling and nodding while Kat told Jules all about Future Florida, a coworker named Eloise, and Kat's idea for how Jules could get herself some great press for her new album while doing a good deed.

Margo was proud of her granddaughter. Proud of how far she'd come in such a short period of time.

Margo was also much happier to be listening to Kat than thinking about Dinah.

Chapter Seventeen

The house was quiet, and Roxie figured that, as usual these days, she'd gotten up before Trina and Willie. That surprised her today, however, since she thought Walter might have woken Trina up so he could go out.

Maybe he'd slept a little harder than normal considering it was his first night in his forever home. It was a happy thought.

She quickly got a pot of coffee going, then went out the sliding doors and down the spiral stairs to get her workout in.

Trina was standing at the side of the house in shorts and a T-shirt, hair unbrushed, yawning as Walter sniffed around the grass.

Roxie smiled. "I thought you were in bed."

"Nope. Walter had to pee. Gotta take care of my

baby," Trina answered with a sleepy smile. "Mimi and Miguel are definitely still sleeping, though."

"How'd he do last night?"

"He slept great." Trina beamed down at Walter. "Oh, Ma. I love him so much. I can't get enough of him. Even when he's peeing he's the cutest thing I've ever seen. He slept right next to me, too, all cuddled up. He's just a perfect little baby."

Walter finished up his business and sat by Trina's feet, looking up at her expectantly.

"He is pretty perfect," Roxie agreed. "I started the coffee. I'm off to get my workout done and then I'll be back."

"Okay. I should walk him, too, but I'm just not that awake yet."

"You want me to take him?"

Trina gave her mom an apologetic smile. "No. I mean, it's super nice of you to offer, but it would interrupt your workout, I know that. Also, I don't think I could stand not doing it myself. Sorry."

Roxie laughed. "I totally get it." She waved as she headed for the beach. "Back in a bit."

She was all right with Trina not wanting to let Walter go without her. Roxie was running more and more during these morning walks, and she wasn't sure the little dog could keep up. Although it would be fun taking him for a walk in the evening with Trina.

Maybe they'd do that tonight.

She walked for a few minutes to warm up, then launched into a slow, easy jog. She'd do a sprint or two later, but for some reason, she felt like she wanted to run. Just to see what she could do, maybe.

Yesterday had been an amazingly good day. Getting the last unit rented and finding Walter? There was no way she'd top that. But she didn't need to. Her head was clear and her heart was happy. Her desire to be needed no longer hung over her like a dark cloud and for good reason.

She'd figured out that she was already needed. By her family. And by Ethan. Helping Trina out at the salon would be enough. Something had clicked in Roxie yesterday and she'd suddenly understood a few things.

The job Trina was offering her really wasn't out of pity. Trina had told her that, but she'd also made it plain she wanted Roxie there. Needed her there. Not only that, but she knew now that the job could be as big or as small as Roxie wanted it to be. The job could become whatever she made it.

If she wanted to be super busy and work a lot, there would be plenty to do. If she wanted to take things slower and work less, that was also a possibility.

What she realized now, and something she hadn't realized previously, was that the job was Roxie's personal opportunity to help her daughter succeed.

Why she hadn't seen it that way before, she had no idea. Maybe she'd been too stuck in her own head. Maybe she'd been sideswiped by all the stuff with Paulina and that had clouded her judgment.

But she got it now.

And that realization had set a new determination in her. A real drive to lift Trina and the business up. To do as much of the heavy lifting as she could so that Trina could concentrate on the fun part of the salon. Doing hair and making people look and feel great.

Trina excelled at that. Roxie would figure out how to do the inventories and how to keep things stocked. She'd take on all of that, plus focus on client happiness and building the business as much as she could.

Oddly enough, she was energized by the idea of all that work. By the thought of figuring out how to do new things. It invigorated her.

She stopped running and went back to walking,

hands on her hips, her chest rising and falling with her fast breathing.

She knew Trina had hired an assistant for the salon who would handle things like keeping the place clean, doing laundry, getting drinks for clients, making sure the stylists had what they needed, and any other little jobs that required doing. That was all good. But Roxie had already determined she'd be the one to keep an eye on the assistant.

Trina didn't need to worry about that. Roxie would make sure the woman was doing her job. Not in a micro-managing kind of way. She wasn't going to become anyone's worst nightmare. But she was going to make sure things were getting done.

She'd also help look after Walter. That was only fair. He was in Trina's life because of Roxie, so it was partially her responsibility to assist in taking care of him. It would be a nice break anyway. And he really was the sweetest thing.

She smiled just thinking about him and how happy he made Trina.

With a new burst of energy, she took off in a sprint, running hard and fast and digging her feet into the sand. When her lungs didn't feel like they could take any more, she slowed down again.

She was going to concentrate on her and Ethan a

little more, too. With Willie married, her mom just didn't need her quite as much. So why not focus on her relationship with Ethan? He was a fantastic man. She liked his parents, too.

And now that they were going to the same church, there was even more time for them to spend together. Which reminded her that she still needed to call the church to ask about outreach programs she might volunteer with.

No matter how busy she was with the salon or Ethan, she wanted to make time to do something that qualified as giving back. Being involved that way felt important.

She turned around to head back to the house, throwing in one more sprint for good measure. She did a round of walking lunges on her way back, too, then headed upstairs to see if Trina had managed to stay awake.

She left her sandy sneakers by the door and went in. Trina was sitting on the couch drinking coffee. Walter was eating breakfast out of one of his new stainless-steel bowls.

Roxie inhaled the aroma of the coffee. She was definitely getting some of that.

"Good workout?" Trina asked.

"Yes. Still need to do some pushups and

crunches in my room before I shower, but yeah, pretty good. What's on the agenda today?"

"No interviews but I do need to call those two women I interviewed yesterday and ask them a few more questions. Depending on how many hours they want, I'm going to try to hire them both and make it work. Then I'll probably head to the salon and do some cleaning. Maybe even attempt to put those retail racks together, since Ethan's so busy."

"I'll help you with that. If we both work on them, it shouldn't take so long." Roxie went into the kitchen.

"Cool. I was hoping I'd have time this afternoon to start visiting local businesses and hand out cards and flyers to anyone interested. I was going to wait until we had an opening date, but I don't want to wait. I want everyone to know about us, so we'll have clients."

Roxie nodded. "Good plan. I'll drive myself over today. After we're done at the salon, I'm going to see about helping Ethan. I know he's in a bit of a crunch, since Thomas needs to be in his space soon."

"That's nice of you." Trina drained her coffee cup.

Roxie shrugged as she got a mug down from the

cabinet. "It's helping him, but it's also helping your grandmother. It's helping all of us, really."

Walter finished eating and went over to the sliders. He whimpered softly and looked at Trina.

She put her cup down and got off the couch. "And now, Walter and I are headed for our first walk on the beach. Hang on, baby. I have to get your leash."

Roxie filled the mug with coffee. "Have fun. It's beautiful out there."

"Thanks."

Roxie took her mug into the bedroom and set it on her dresser. She did pushups, crunches, some leg lifts, then finished up with some squats. She really needed some hand weights.

She took her cup into the bathroom with her and cranked on the shower. She drank most of the coffee while waiting for the water to warm up.

She took her time in the shower, because the water felt so good. When she was out and dressed, she brought her cup back out to the living room. A lot of happy conversation greeted her. Willie and Miguel were up, having coffee and chatting with Trina while watching Walter play with a ball.

"Morning, Ma. Morning, Miguel."

"Good morning," Miguel said.

"Morning, Roxie." Willie saluted her with the cup in her hand. "Thanks for making coffee."

"You're welcome." She went to refill her mug. "What have you two got planned for the day?"

"Nothing too strenuous after yesterday," Willie answered. "But we are going grocery shopping."

Roxie looked at her mother. "You are? That seems pretty strenuous."

"The two of us can handle it. Besides, we're low on everything. And with Miguel staying here some nights, it's only fair we contribute."

Roxie smiled. "That's not necessary."

"Very kind of you to say," Miguel answered. "But I want to. Plus, I was thinking I might make dinner tonight for all of you. Nothing too fancy. Pork chops and Spanish rice. Would that be all right?"

"Sure," Roxie said. "That sounds great."

He smiled. "Then we will be off to the store to get everything we need."

Willie nodded. "If there's anything you need me to pick up, just let me know."

Roxie sipped her coffee. It was amazing how much more her mother seemed capable of accomplishing with Miguel at her side.

But then, a good man had a way of doing that.

Chapter Nineteen

"You know everything that needs to be done?" Jules asked her son as she drove them to the Dolphin Club for their day of rehearsal.

"Yep," Cash answered. "Well, maybe not everything, but I know how to get started. I just need to get everyone's email address from Jesse. Then I'm going to send them a link to fill out the tax forms. Once that's done, I'll get payroll set up."

She smiled. Asking Cash to be her business manager had definitely been the right move. He was more capable than she'd imagined, having learned about some of what was required in school, but also from his life as a working musician, even if he hadn't worked as much in that capacity as he'd wanted to. "Excellent."

"Hey, I know I didn't say much about it last night,

but I think it's cool that you're going to donate a portion of the proceeds from *Dixie* to that charity Kat is working for."

Jules nodded. "I'm really happy to do it. Especially since Kat said they can make sure it goes toward battered and abused women. I've done a few benefit concerts, but nothing like this. It feels good."

"It'll be great press, too."

"Which isn't why I'm doing it."

"I know," he said with a smile. Then he changed the subject. "It's just you, me, Sierra and Bobby today in the studio."

"That's right." Rita and Frankie both had prior commitments. "But tomorrow we'll have a full crew. I don't think we'll need much time to get *Folsom Prison Blues* knocked out. Everyone knows it."

"Sierra didn't. Not really. But she's been practicing it on her own."

"That's good." Jules really liked Sierra. And not just for her musical talents. She was a lovely, sweet young woman. She and Cash seemed to be getting along great. Jules hated to change the subject to something a lot less lovely, but it had to be done. "Hear from your dad at all lately?"

Cash shook his head, his expression immediately

getting darker. "No, thankfully. I think Fen's been dealing with him."

"That's nice of him. I hope your dad is getting back on track."

"Me, too." Cash sighed. "I should text Fen. See what's up." He took his phone out and started typing.

Jules pulled into the parking lot of the Dolphin Club. "Tell him I said hi."

"Will do."

She found a spot while he finished up his text, then they grabbed their gear and went in. She already knew Jesse wouldn't be there yet but that was all right with her. He'd given her a key.

As she was unlocking the door, Sierra and Bobby showed up.

Cash greeted them as Jules got the door open. "Morning. Ready for some Johnny Cash?"

"Always ready for the Man in Black," Bobby said.

Jules pushed the door open and held it while the rest of them filtered in, then she let it close so she could lock it. "I'm excited to work on this one. It's a real honor to be covering such a classic."

"Agreed," Bobby said.

Softly, Sierra said, "I hope I get it right."

"Don't worry," Jules said. "We'll work on it until

we all get it right. And we have all day to do that. We're not going to even attempt to record until tomorrow afternoon when Frankie and Rita are with us."

Sierra nodded, but still looked concerned. "Thanks."

Jules put her arm around the young woman. "It's okay to be nervous. I know you want to do the best you possibly can on this."

"I do," Sierra said.

Together, they walked back toward the studio. "Well, I'm going to tell you something, and I want you to really listen to what I'm saying, all right?"

"All right."

Cash glanced over his shoulder like he wasn't exactly sure what was going on.

Jules ignored him and continued speaking to Sierra. "You wouldn't be here if you weren't talented and if I didn't already know you have what it takes. I know you're new to all of this, but you've got the chops."

Cash, who'd slowed to walk beside them, nodded. "She's right, Sierra. And my mom is internet famous, so you know she knows what she's talking about."

Sierra laughed. "Thank you, Jules. That means a

lot. And huge congrats on blowing up social media yesterday. That was the coolest thing I've ever been a part of. Although I think that contributed to my self-doubt today. It kind of made me realize how many people are going to be hearing this music. That really got me thinking."

"Don't get too much in your head," Jules said. "I want you focused on the here and now. Not what comes after all of this. It's the only way to get through it. You can't be on stage thinking about the after-party. You need your head in the performance."

Bobby cleared his throat softly. "She's right. Let the music be everything to you in the moment. Because it has to be. Anything else means you're not giving it a hundred percent. And the people listening will pick up on that."

"Wise words," Jules said. "Thank you, Bobby." The man had years of experience in a lot of different aspects of the music business. She'd also recently found out from Jesse that Bobby was a member of the Grand Ole Opry, just like she was.

She smiled thinking about that. The man definitely hid his light under a bushel. She'd looked him up online after Jesse had shared the Grand Ole Opry bit. He had done some amazing things, but she got it. He was semi-retired and probably felt too out of the game to make a fuss about the life he'd lived but she was impressed.

He smiled back. "I didn't mean to butt in like that, but—"

"Uh-uh," Jules said, shaking her head. "You have nothing to apologize for. You probably know more about music and the music industry than the three of us put together. Butt in all you like."

Cash got a funny look on his face, like he didn't know what she meant.

Jules went on, tipping her head at Bobby. "That man right there, children, has been on stage with Ray Charles, B.B. King, and Bonnie Raitt, just to name a few."

"Dang," Cash whispered. "Bobby, is that true?"

Bobby laughed. "That was a long time ago, but yes. Worked behind the scenes on Raitt's last album, too."

"No wonder you knew how to master Mom's single." Cash shook his head and looked at Jules. "Jesse was better connected than we realized."

She grinned. "Apparently."

She unlocked the studio and turned on the lights. They filed in and got themselves set up. It was strange to be here without Jesse. She missed his presence. He always had a smile on his face and words of support. She realized she'd come to rely on him in that way. In a lot of ways, really.

She also just missed *him*. She felt like she'd forgotten something at home. It was an odd feeling. But Bobby was right. She had to get her head in the game or her own performance would suffer. Didn't matter that this was just a rehearsal. She needed to be as good as she could be or everything she'd said to Sierra held no water.

Within a few minutes they were tuned up and settled in, ready to go. Jules counted them down and they got to work.

Bobby seemed livelier on the fiddle than she remembered. Maybe having his accomplishments noted had given him a boost. Whatever the reason, he was on fire and did an incredible job with the song.

Jules sang lead with Cash, Sierra, and Bobby harmonizing beautifully on the background vocals. For as good as it sounded, Jules wasn't happy.

When they finished the run-through, she said, "Sounds too much like the original. We're missing something. We need to honor the original but give it a fresh feeling at the same time."

Cash and Sierra nodded, but Bobby spoke up. "It's the tempo. We should pick it up. Just a little.

Give it some more pep up front. When we get Rita and Frankie in there, that slide guitar and banjo are only going to contribute to the sound you're going for."

"True. I think I'm missing them a bit," Jules said.

Bobby looked at Cash. "Can you do a little finger picking on the intro, too?"

"Sure," Cash said. "I can give it a whirl."

Bobby turned to Sierra next. "Have you got percussion on that keyboard?"

"I do," she answered. "We need a little beat, don't we?"

"I think so." Bobby grinned. "If Jules does, too."

"Heck, yes." Jules laughed. She wasn't about to say no to help. "Let's give it a try. You have any suggestions for me, Bobby?"

He hesitated, like he wasn't sure he should answer.

"Come on," she said. "I want your input."

With a gentle smile, he nodded. "Lean into it a little. You sound like you're holding back. Maybe you're not warmed up yet, or maybe you're worried about doing injustice to such a famous song, but you sound a little tentative. Sorry."

"You're completely right. I have been thinking about what all those people online are going to say about me taking on Johnny Cash. But I need to push that aside and do what I know I can do."

"That's right," Bobby said. "Because you're going to kill it."

Jules lifted her chin. "Are we ready then?"

"Hang on," Cash said. "I need to play with this a minute."

"Same," Sierra said as she put headphones on and plugged them into the keyboard. "I have to work things out on my end, too."

"Take your time," Jules said.

About twenty minutes later, Cash and Sierra were ready.

"Okay," Jules said. "New and improved *Folsom Prison Blues*, here we come." She counted them down and they began.

It felt different this time. Lighter, where before it had plodded. Breezier, when it previously hadn't moved much at all. Jules closed her eyes and poured her heart into the vocals, opening up her voice to do the song justice.

When it ended, they were greeted with clapping. Jesse stood at the door from the control room, grinning. "That was outstanding. Holy cover song. I thought you guys were only rehearsing today. You sound ready to record."

Jules smiled. "Not quite. We still need Frankie and Rita. But Bobby got us tuned up on that one. Nice to see you."

"You, too," Jesse said.

"Let's take five," she told them. She put her guitar on its stand and went to greet him with a kiss.

"I have some good news," he said.

"Lay it on me."

He laughed. "I found a manager for the club."

She sucked in a breath. "You did? Someone who can really take over for you?"

He nodded. "By the time you're ready to tour, I'll be ready to go with you."

Chapter Nineteen

*A*ttempting to put the retail racks together was no fun. Way more complicated than Trina had imagined. No wonder Ethan had put all the parts back into the boxes and postponed the assembly.

She hadn't made any progress, other than getting all the pieces out of the box. She sat on the floor and stared at the parts laid out in groups so that all the same kinds were together. She read the first few steps of the instructions again and shook her head. Her brain didn't seem to be grasping them.

The floor around her looked like something had exploded. She sighed. She and her mom were never going to figure this out. At least not in the amount of time Trina had thought it would take. She'd really hoped to do some canvassing today to spread the word about the salon.

Her mom, who was eager to help, was out walking Walter, who'd gone to the door and given Trina the look that said he needed to do some business. He was a smart pup, that was for sure.

The door opened and Trina looked up, expecting to see her mom and Walter. Instead, it was Miles. She grinned, her construction project forgotten. "Hi. I didn't know you were coming by today." She got to her feet and hugged him, adding a kiss for good measure. It was always good to see his handsome face.

"I wanted to surprise you. And meet Walter. And see the salon." Miles looked around. "Where is the little guy?"

That's when Trina saw the small brown paper bag in his hand. "He's outside with my mom. He had to pee." Movement caught her eye. She pointed through the window. "There they are now."

Miles turned as Roxie and Walter were coming up the sidewalk. He opened the door for them.

"Hi, Miles. How are you?" Roxie asked.

"Good, thanks. How are you?"

"Just fine." She and Walter came inside, and Miles let the door swing shut. Roxie took Walter's leash off and nodded at Trina. "Definitely a good idea to take him out. He did *everything*."

"Good boy, Walter." Trina smiled at the adorable creature. "Walter, this is mama's boyfriend, Miles."

Miles crouched down. "Hey, little man." He dug into the bag he'd brought and took out a small nubby tan cookie. He looked at Trina. "Organic locally made peanut butter dog cookies. Is it okay to give him one?"

"Absolutely." Trina was touched. The fact that Miles had gotten something so special for Walter wasn't lost on her. But that was the kind of guy Miles was. Always going out of his way to do the extra thing.

Miles held up the cookie. "Do you know how to sit, Walter? Sit."

Trina shook her head. "I don't think—"

Walter sat and looked eagerly at the cookie.

Trina gasped. "He knows a trick! Ma, did you see that?"

"I did," Roxie said. "Very impressive."

Miles gave him the cookie. "I bet you could teach him all kinds of stuff."

"Maybe," Trina said. She had no idea how to do that, but YouTube could probably show her.

He straightened and handed her the bag with the rest of the cookies in it. "Here you go. I'm glad he likes them."

"Thank you. That was really nice of you."

He smiled, then tipped his head toward the disaster that was retail rack number one. "What are you building?"

Roxie snorted. "Nothing yet."

Trina sighed. "She's right. It's supposed to be a tall rack with four shelves to display the retail products on, but it's a lot more complicated than I thought it was going to be. The worst part is, I bought two of them."

Miles shrugged. "You want some help?"

"Um, *yes*." Trina bit her bottom lip as she nodded. "That would be great."

"All right." He rubbed his hands together. "Let's get this thing built then. Maybe we'll even have time to do the other one."

As much as she wanted his help, she didn't want it to come at the expense of his job. "Don't you have to get to work?"

"Not for a while yet." He winked at her. "I always have time for you, T."

She smiled. "Thanks."

Miles picked up the instructions and read them over. He nodded a few times. Then he looked at Trina. "You have the Allen wrenches that came with it?"

She pointed. "I think they're in that little plastic bag. I didn't open it yet. I hadn't really gotten past making sure all the parts were in the box."

"Were they?"

She nodded.

"Then we're good to go." He got down on the floor and, with the instructions in hand, found the pieces he needed to start with.

In a few short minutes, it was clear to Trina that Miles had things pretty well under control. Her mom seemed to realize that, too.

"Miles, you look like you've done this before," Roxie said.

He shook his head. "No, but I used to build a lot of models as a kid. This is really just a bigger version of that."

"Well, if you two don't need me, I think I'll go check in with Ethan and see if he could use some help." Roxie looked at Trina. "If you don't mind?"

"No, go ahead. I'm sure he'll appreciate that." She also knew her mom loved spending time with Ethan, regardless of the circumstances. Trina understood completely.

"Okay. See you later then. Bye, Miles." Roxie waved to Walter. "Bye, Walter."

As her mom left, Trina found a spot on the floor near Miles. "What can I do?"

"Hold this." He handed her the piece of the rack he'd already assembled.

She took it from him. "I really appreciate you helping me with this." Then she laughed. "Except you aren't really helping me so much as you are putting the whole thing together by yourself."

He snorted and looked up at her without stopping what he was doing. "I know you appreciate it. And I don't mind doing it at all. At least this way I can feel like I contributed something to your shop."

She smiled. He was just the best. "That's super sweet of you."

Walter came over and sat next to Miles.

"Oh, boy," Trina said. "I think you and your cookies made a friend."

Miles ruffled the dog's fur. "He's a cool little dude. That was pretty awesome that your mom got him for you."

"She's done a lot of amazing things for me over the years, but Walter tops the list. He's going to come to work with me and everything, aren't you, boy?"

Walter smiled at her in that little way of his, mouth open, tongue out. Adorable.

Miles nodded. "That's cool."

"I'm going to set up a bed for him in the break-room along with a water bowl and food dish. And with my mom working here, she's already promised to take him out whenever he needs to go, that sort of thing. It's going to be great."

Miles nodded as he attached the piece he'd just built to what she was holding. "You have a good family."

"I do, don't I?" She was blessed that way and she knew it. But hearing Miles say it made her happy, too.

They worked for a few more minutes without talking about anything but the directions for what came next.

As Miles was attaching a new piece, he asked, "Have you heard anything from Liz recently?"

"No," Trina answered. "You?"

He shook his head, tightening the screw while he responded. "No. But I did get a call from her dad, which was odd."

"What was that about?"

"He said he understood Liz had been rude to my new girlfriend and he wanted to apologize. He also said if it happened again, to let him know."

"Okay, that's weird."

"I thought so, too."

"When you were dating her, did you have a good relationship with her parents?"

"Yeah, it was all right. They're nice people. At least, they were always nice enough to me. Maybe not as nice as your mom and grandmother, but you know, decent."

"Still weird."

"Yep." He finished the section he was working on and looked at her. "All the same, anything happens, you let me know."

She nodded. "I will." She couldn't help but wonder how Liz's dad had found out about her behavior. Trina had her suspicions—her grandmother couldn't mind her own business if she tried—but she wasn't going to do anything about it. If Liz was out of their hair, she didn't really care how that had come to pass.

Just that it had.

Chapter Twenty

*N*ow that she'd gone through them all, Kat organized the request folders into three groups. Those she thought they should help through the charity. Those who they should help in some way. And then a No pile for those she knew weren't right and those she wasn't sure were legit.

Those were the worst ones. People who seemed obviously disingenuous about their situation. That was such reprehensible behavior that it turned her stomach. And it made her want to confirm her suspicions the best she could.

Maybe it wasn't her job to dig into people, but she'd been hired to assess and determine risk and reward. To her, that seemed like a logical reason to find out more about the people requesting help.

One of the requests had just sounded off to her. She couldn't exactly put a finger on why. Maybe it was the wording of the letter. The feeling it had given her. A kind of sixth sense she supposed all risk analysts got over the years.

She'd done a deep dive online to find out more about the person making the request, only to discover that his story of cancer striking him down didn't match up to the active life he was showing off on social media.

It seemed to Kat that someone with a debilitating brain tumor, which was what the man claimed to have in the letter he'd sent, probably wouldn't be going out boating and waterskiing. Not when he was supposedly unable to work or, on some days, feed himself.

Then there was the post showing a picture of a new boat with the caption, "I have a feeling this baby's going to be mine soon!"

Was he actually referring to scamming Future Florida? Sure seemed like it to Kat.

The nerve of such a post left a bitter taste in her mouth, especially when there were so many legitimate requests.

One of the others in the No pile was a letter from a woman requesting a million dollars to start a bird sanctuary. That wasn't really what Future Florida did.

Kat checked the time. She had her first meeting with Tom and Molly in fifteen minutes. She was a little nervous about it, since she'd never done it before, but she'd present her opinions and hope for the best.

She also planned on talking to them about the report she'd run on the charity's past five years. She'd found some interesting things that she hoped could help them make better decisions in the future.

She took her big cup to the breakroom to get a refill on her coffee. While she was there, she slipped into the bathroom, just to get a look at herself and make sure she was still presentable. She was. She slicked on a fresh coat of berry gloss then checked out the tan pants and brightly patterned pink and navy blouse she had on. She'd brought a white cardigan, too, but didn't have it on at the moment.

She hoped the outfit wasn't too casual. She hadn't thought so when she'd left the house, but now she wasn't so sure.

Too late if it was.

She took the coffee back to her office, put on her cardigan, then gathered up her folders, her notes, and her coffee and took them into the conference room.

Molly was already in there, but hadn't sat down yet. "Hi, Kat. How are you doing?"

"Great, thank you."

"Settling in all right?"

"I am."

"Sorry Tom and I haven't been around much, but you just never know when a possible donor might want to meet." Molly smiled. "That's not something we can ignore."

"No way," Kat said. "And you shouldn't. How did your meeting go?"

"Very well. Mr. and Mrs. Higgins are leaving us a substantial part of their estate in their wills."

"That's great. I mean, it's probably a long ways off, but still excellent news."

"I agree."

"About what?" Tom asked as he came in.

"I was telling Kat about the Higginses."

He nodded. "Good people."

Eloise walked in behind him, mug of coffee in hand and a notebook tucked under her arm. "Hi, everyone."

"Hi, Eloise," Kat said. She really liked the older woman. She was smart, insightful and so nice. And how could you not like someone with a cat named Sir Isaac Mewton?

"Hi, Kat."

Arlene came in with a steno pad and pen in one hand, a coffee cup in the other. She gave everyone a big smile.

They all took their seats.

Tom started things off. "Welcome, everyone. Kat, let me officially welcome you, since this is your first status meeting."

"Thanks," Kat said.

"How are things going?" he asked. "Finding your way?"

"I am. Things are going well." So far, anyway. She'd yet to give them her report.

He nodded and went back to addressing everyone. "As you may have heard, the trip Molly and I made to visit our most recent donors was a success. Mr. and Mrs. Peter Higgins have promised a portion of their estate to Future Florida in their wills. We believe that sum will be no less than a million dollars, but could be as much as five, depending on a variety of factors. Of course, due to the Higginses' ages, we don't anticipate that funding coming in for some time."

Arlene took notes.

"Furthermore," Tom went on, "We have another donor meeting next week in Gainesville and a few days after that, we'll be flying to Key Largo to speak to yet another possible donor."

"Excellent," Eloise said.

Tom looked at Molly. "Anything I forgot?"

"Fourth of July?" she answered.

"Right," Tom nodded. "We're partnering with Beach Keepers, a volunteer organization that helps maintain the local beaches by cleaning them, planting dune grass, that sort of thing, for a Fourth of July fundraiser. More details to come as we get closer."

Eloise gestured with her pen. "Molly, can we get together on that? The sooner I can start trickling it to social media, the better."

"Definitely," Molly said. "I'll email you my notes, too."

"Perfect."

Tom looked at Kat. "All right, Kat, you're up. What have you got for us?"

She took a breath. "I've sorted through the requests and have divided them into three piles. Yeses, Maybes, and I Think Nots."

Eloise laughed. "Nice."

Tom smiled appreciatively. "Thank you for taking that on. I realize it's a tough job. Tell us about them."

Case by case, Kat briefly went through the various requests. Somehow, Tom and Molly agreed with her on every one. That was a huge relief.

"Outstanding work," Molly said.

"Thank you." Kat took a sip of her coffee. "I have more. I ran an analysis on the last five years of business here at Future Florida."

Tom's brows lifted. "A report card of sorts."

"You could say that," Kat said.

"How'd we do?" Molly asked.

"Not bad," Kat answered. "But I found some places where we could be doing better." She passed out copies of the report, then went over the big details about how they were missing out on fundraising campaigns during the most lucrative months.

She further noted where they were doing things well, so it didn't seem like she'd only found fault, but talked about how there was room for improvement there, too, just by paying attention to cyclical indicators. She explained how there were certain times of the year when people were more likely to give, and certain times of the month when that was true as well.

"By doing the bulk of our fundraising, whether through phone calls or emails or even social media posts, during those time periods, we should be able to increase our donations by as much as fifteen percent."

She looked up from her notes and saw Tom and Molly staring at her. Arlene and Eloise were writing.

Kat couldn't get a read on Tom or Molly. She wasn't sure what they thought.

Tom shook his head. "That's...amazing."

Molly nodded and looked at him. "I told you she'd be good at this."

"You were right." He smiled at Kat. "Not that I didn't think you'd be good at this, but we've never had anyone with your particular skillset at the company before. I wasn't sure what you'd really bring to the table, to be honest. You've shown me very succinctly just how valuable this kind of input is."

Kat exhaled. "I'm so glad. And I'm happy to answer any questions."

Tom looked at the copy of the report she'd given him. "This is very clear. Beautifully and gently done. I knew in my gut we weren't maximizing what we could be doing. Now I see exactly how we can fix that. It's perfect."

She smiled. "There is one other thing."

"Go on," Molly said.

"My aunt is a singer-songwriter, and she's got a new song out that's getting some notice. She'd like to donate a portion of the profits to Future Florida to be earmarked for helping battered and abused women."

"That's great," Tom said. "Who is your aunt?"

"Julia Bloom?" Kat wasn't sure they'd have heard of Aunt Jules. She knew country wasn't everyone's thing.

Eloise flattened her hands on the table, obvious delight on her face. "Please tell me you're talking about *Dixie's Got Her Boots On*."

Kat laughed. "Yeah, that's the song. You know it?"

"It's all over social media. There's even a new TikTok dance challenge that goes with it." Eloise blinked a few times. "Julia Bloom is your aunt?"

"She is," Kat confirmed.

Molly looked immediately interested. "I wonder if we could talk to her about performing at our Fourth of July event."

Kat shrugged. "I can ask once we have a few more details. I know she'll be going on tour at some point, but I don't know when that is."

"Fantastic," Eloise said. She glanced at Tom and Molly. "I don't think you two have ever made a better hiring decision than this young woman."

Chapter Twenty-one

Claire touched one of the dolphin-shaped sugar cookies laid out on the racks to see if it was cool enough to ice. It was. She'd already made and colored a few batches of icing and had it ready to go in piping bags.

There was something a little bittersweet about making these cookies. They were probably the last batch she'd ever make here at the beach house. Soon, all of her baking would be done at Mrs. Butter's. Sure, the day might come when she'd bake in this kitchen again, but she couldn't really imagine the circumstances under which that would happen.

If she needed baked goods for some reason, why wouldn't she just bring something home with her from the bakery? Seemed like the most reasonable thing to do.

She picked up the bag of blue-gray icing and

started outlining the first cookie. The cookies were lemon-flavored with real lemon juice and a little bit of super-fine zest. Claire's thinking had been that dolphins were happy, fun, summery creatures, and lemon was a happy, fun, summery flavor.

She'd used lemon juice in the icing as well, to enhance the flavors in the cookies. Decorating cookies wasn't complicated work. It allowed her to think while she did it.

Once the outline was done, she moved on to the next one. She wasn't going to decorate them all. These were just a test batch of six to show Danny. Cash would probably demolish the rest and he wouldn't care if they looked fancy or not.

She'd still ice them, but mostly to use up whatever was left from decorating these samples. She was making the bodies blue-gray and the little sliver of belly that showed white. She'd do the bellies last, when the rest was dry, which would allow her to add some edible glitter and have it just stick to the white icing.

The eyes would be black and expressive, with tiny white accents. They were going to be slightly cartoonish to make them extra cute. And, she hoped, very popular with kids.

By the time she finished outlining the last one,

the first one was dry enough for her to go back and start flooding. That just meant filling in the outline with the same color to cover the entire area inside the outline with icing.

She worked like a one-woman assembly line, doing each section then moving on to the next cookie. She lost track of time a bit, but she had it to lose track of. Danny was at the bakery until at least after lunch, finishing up some things on the retail side and taking delivery of some of the ingredients that were due in today.

She smiled, thinking about her kitchen being that much closer to launch status. Not that it was just *her* kitchen. But she'd begun to think of it that way. Exciting stuff. The kind of excitement that filled her with breathless anticipation.

She could not wait to get in there and start baking. To fill that display case with all sorts of delicious treats, and to fill that cold case with sour orange pies.

With the main section of the dolphins done, it was time to let the icing really firm up. She took a break to eat some lunch, a couple of leftover pieces of Cash's barbequed chicken and a scoop of fruit salad. She ate outside on the screened porch, looking out at the beach.

The water sparkled a warm, welcoming blue under the sun. The plan was for her and Danny to go out on the catamaran this afternoon when he got back. If he wasn't too tired. She didn't want to make him work more than he already had just to entertain her.

But a little sunset sail sounded so nice.

She cleaned up her lunch stuff and went back inside, where she put her fork in the dishwasher and her paper plate in the trash. She refilled her glass of ice water, washed and dried her hands, then delicately touched the surface of the icing on one cookie to see how dry it was. Good enough. She could start with the next color.

The white bellies went on quicker, since it was a much smaller area. Once the first belly was done, she sprinkled it with white edible glitter, then held the cookie by its edges and tapped off the excess. She straightened to see her creation better.

Pleased with the result, she smiled. They looked good and she hadn't even put the eyes on yet.

She went back to work, again in assembly line mode, and soon had the bellies done. She let them dry for a few minutes, using the time to clean up and casually ice the remaining batch that would be Cash's. They weren't pretty but he wouldn't care.

With those cookies taken care of, she returned to the test batch. She piped the eyes in black, added the little white accents, and was done. Or was she? The eyes looked great. The sparkly bellies looked good, too. There was a lot of blue-gray. Maybe...

She picked up the bag of white icing and added a thin accent line along the dolphin's back, then just a hint of a smile. She stepped back for a better look and nodded. That was exactly what the cookie had needed. A little personality.

She fixed the rest of them and left them all to fully dry. Toby wandered in from the bedroom where he'd been sleeping as she was washing the last icing tip. "Hi, Toby. What's up? Did the smell of cookies wake you up?"

He whined softly and she realized that had nothing to do with cookies. He needed to go out. "Okay, Tobes. Hang on." She went into the bedroom to get her flipflops on, then grabbed his leash from the laundry room and connected it to his collar. She pushed the elevator button.

As soon as it arrived, they got on.

When they got off, Toby made a beeline for the patch of grass that apparently looked the best to him, which happened to be a strip that ran between the Double Diamond and Danny's house.

Danny's car was in the driveway, and he was getting out. "Hey, there. Do I have good timing or what?"

She laughed. "Yes, great timing. Although I'm not sure Toby wants an audience. How did everything go today?"

"Great." He closed the car door and came over. "Once the cold goods come in tomorrow morning, you can pretty much start baking."

She grinned. "That is so exciting." She glanced down to see if Toby was done and groaned.

"What's wrong?" Danny asked.

She grimaced. "I didn't bring a poop bag."

Danny laughed. "Hang on." He ran back to his truck and returned with a plastic bag. "Here."

"Thanks. Sorry."

"No big deal. You ready to head out on the cat?"

She finished bagging Toby's business and tied it off. "You feel up to it?"

"You bet."

"Then I am, too. But first, I want you to come over and check out the new lemon sugar cookie I made."

He nodded. "Let me change and I'll be right over."

"Okay. See you in a few." She tugged on Toby's

leash. He was sniffing one of Danny's palm trees. "Come on, Toby. You want a cookie?"

That got him moving. Back upstairs, she set him free of the leash, gave him the promised treat, then washed up.

She quickly changed into her tankini and put on a pair of loose, drawstring shorts. She pulled her hair back into a tiny ponytail to keep it out of her face, then grabbed her sunglasses. She still didn't have a waterproof phone case, so her phone would have to stay behind.

The elevator's hum announced Danny before he arrived. He stepped off the elevator in swim trunks, a T-shirt, flipflops and a Mrs. Butter's Popcorn ballcap. His gaze went straight to the cookies on the island. "I love them already."

She chuckled. "You haven't even tasted them yet."

He came over and picked one up. "That might not matter. People are going to buy them just because of how great they look. Nice job."

"Thanks. But you should still taste it."

He took a bite, nodding and making happy noises. "Yep. This is a winner. Lemon is such a great choice for warm weather."

"That's what I was thinking. The tartness is somehow cooling and refreshing."

He ate another bite. "I'm sold. We should package these in their own cello bags, tied with a nice bit of ribbon, and sell them by the register like an impulse buy."

"You think?" She'd been imagining them on their own tray in the display case.

He nodded. "Is this the only decorated sugar cookie we're going to sell?"

She shrugged. "I don't know. We could do a whole sea life thing. A shell, a seahorse, a starfish. That sort of thing."

"If that's the case, we should do a tray of them. If this is the only one, then let's make it even more special by bagging it separately. This is exactly the kind of item that will appeal to people as they're checking out."

"We do have the coated popcorn bars that we're selling that way already."

"And this will compliment that nicely."

"Works for me."

He took her hand. "Let's get out on that water."

She gave him a nod. "The cookies have been fun, but I'm ready to see some real dolphins."

Chapter Twenty-two

Willie and Miguel got the grocery shopping done, but they'd made a very important stop first, to see an old friend of Miguel's. A man named Gabe Rodriguez.

Gabe had been a police detective, but he was now retired and worked part-time as a private investigator. And he had connections. DNA processing connections.

He'd taken the samples Willie had collected and promised to use his clout with the local lab to get a report in two days. It had cost her three hundred and fifty dollars, but she was okay with that.

Finding out once and for all if Trina and Nico were really related was worth a heck of a lot more than that.

Now, as she and Miguel unloaded all the groceries they'd bought—and brought up on the elevator—she couldn't stop thinking about what the outcome of that report would be. Part of her wanted it to prove that Nico was related, for Trina's sake. She loved having a brother.

But part of Willie was hoping the test results would show Paulina was lying about the whole thing so they could be done with her. That would just be easier. And it would mean that there was no way Paulina could come after Roxie for more money.

Willie couldn't help but want to protect her family.

"You're awfully quiet, my love. Everything all right?"

Willie looked over from putting a package of granola bars in the pantry. "Sorry. Just thinking."

"About the test?"

She nodded. "I can't help it. Two days isn't a long time to wait, but at the same time, it feels like forever."

He put cups of yogurt into the fridge. "It will go by fast. Are you prepared to accept whatever the results say?"

"I am. But I have mixed feelings about it."

"How so?" He set the pork chops aside, because she knew he was going to marinate them.

"Because Trina really loves having a little brother."

Miguel's eyes narrowed. "Do you think Roxie got her that dog to keep her too busy to see Nico?"

Willie opened her mouth to answer. Then closed it again. She hadn't thought about that. "I honestly don't know. If she did, Roxie's a lot more cunning than I realized." Then Willie shook her head. "No. I think Roxie got her that dog because Trina has always wanted one and she thought the timing was right."

He nodded and went back to putting things away. "And if the results say Nico is not related to Trina?"

Willie breathed out softly. "I have to tell Roxie. And Claire. I can't keep that kind of information to myself. That woman took six hundred thousand dollars of Bryan's life insurance. Three hundred of that was for Nico. If that's not his kid? Roxie *and* Claire both deserve to know. Don't you agree?"

"I do. But there will be some hard feelings."

"I know. Paulina's not going to like that I called her bluff."

"Roxie and Claire will be upset, too. Upset that they were lied to. That money was taken away from their children."

Willie hadn't thought about that. "I can't not tell them."

"No, you can't. But you must be prepared to deal with the fallout."

"You think they'll be mad at me?"

He shook his head, eyes partially closed as if that was unthinkable. "No. What you're doing might be... sneaky? But it comes from a good place. You wanting to protect your family. No one can fault you for that."

She sighed. "Maybe I shouldn't have done it."

"If the test shows that Nico is Trina's brother, then you never have to say a word."

"True." She didn't want to talk about it anymore. The whole thing was making her feel uneasy. "What can I do to help you?"

"Nothing." His sweet smile made her feel better right away. "I'm going to make the marinade, put the chops in it, then I'm going to make us some pina coladas and we are going down to the pool. You do have a blender, don't you?"

"We do. Just a second." She got it out of the cabinet and put it on the counter. "There you go."

"Perfect. We might not be at the Hamilton Arms anymore, but that doesn't mean we can't still live like we're on our honeymoon."

She laughed. "I like that idea a lot. If you don't

need me for anything else, I'll go put my suit on. I need to clean out a drawer for you, too."

"I'll be in shortly to change."

She went back to her room. Their room, now. Miguel had brought a duffel bag with him when he'd come over earlier. A few things to keep here for when he spent the night. She needed to pack a bag to take to his place, too, for the same reason.

Tomorrow night, she'd be over at his house. She wondered how that would make her feel. Being one house away from her daughter and granddaughter. And her great-granddog. Walter was a nice addition to the family. Maybe she and Miguel should get a dog.

She worked on cleaning out the second drawer of her dresser. It was mostly just folded pairs of capri pants. She could find somewhere else to put those.

Getting a dog, as appealing as it sounded, would mean having to walk it and take care of it. She and Miguel weren't getting any younger. Maybe it wasn't such a good idea. An animal was good company, though. Although she'd have Miguel for company. She sighed at herself and her ideas.

They didn't need a dog. They had each other. And Trina would be visiting, so Willie would still get to see Walter.

She took two pairs of the capris and set them aside to go to Miguel's. From the third drawer, she picked two T-shirts that went with those capris and set them aside as well. She added underthings, a nightgown, and a light jacket that went with both pairs of pants.

That made some room. She consolidated the T-shirts in the third drawer to make room for the capris and just like that, the second drawer was empty.

She worked on her closet next, finding an old dress that she thought she'd gotten rid of a long time ago. She laid that over her chair to donate. Maybe at that thrift shop Roxie liked so much. She found a pair of orthopedic sneakers that could go to Miguel's. She tucked two pairs of shortie socks into the pile, too.

She found a big tote bag in the closet, probably meant for a beach bag, but it would work to carry her things to his house. She placed everything in it, nice and neat. What was she forgetting?

A swimsuit. She needed to put one on, but she also needed to pack one. Miguel had a pool at his place just like they did here.

She heard the blender going and smiled as she

got two suits out. Regardless of the outcome of that DNA test, things were going to be fine.

She had Miguel in her life now. And he was just the right person to take care of her. She quickly changed, putting on a short, fringed caftan made of gauzy material. Hmm. She'd need a coverup at Miguel's, too.

She found another one with a trim of beads and sequins. She folded it up and added it to the bag. Then added a pair of sandals to wear down to the pool.

Miguel came in. "Drinks are ready."

"I've got a drawer for you." Willie opened it to show him, giving it a little flourish of her hand like the models on *The Price Is Right*. "All yours, honey."

"Very good. Now I can unpack." He took his duffel bag off the floor where he'd left it and put it on the bed. He got his trunks out, then put the rest of the contents into the drawer. "There. Now we're really like a married couple."

She went over and gave him a big kiss. "I'm glad."

"About what?"

"That I married you."

His eyes twinkled with amusement. "I thought *I* married *you*."

She laughed. "However it happened, I'm very happy it did."

"So am I." He unbuttoned his shirt. "There is no one I'd rather lay by the pool and do nothing with."

"Pina coladas are made?"

"They are. And the pork chops are in the refrigerator, marinating. Tonight's dinner will be simple, but delicious."

"You spoil me."

He winked at her as he changed. "I promised you I would."

"I'm also very glad you keep your promises."

Chapter Twenty-three

The study rooms at the library were small. Barely room for a table, two chairs, and a small trashcan in the one Margo and Conrad currently occupied. She loved it. Being close to Conrad was never a problem.

There was something about being in the study room with him that gave everything a whole new feeling. She couldn't quite name what that feeling was, but working in the library space with him suddenly made the writing feel real in a different way. Which wasn't to imply that it had felt fake before.

There was something much more earnest and intentional about working this way. Almost like they were students cramming for an exam.

She let out a soft laugh at the thought.

He looked up from her laptop where he'd been

typing away on the next chapter. "What's funny?"

"I was just thinking about how working in here feels different. Kind of like we're students."

He looked around the little room. "Is this what being a student feels like?"

"You say that like you weren't one."

"Not a college student. I went straight from high school into the Marines."

"Did you?" That surprised her. "I had no idea. You're so well-read and knowledgeable about so many subjects, I just assumed you had."

He shrugged one shoulder. "I read a lot. Always have. It's the best way I know to educate yourself."

"I would agree with that." She smiled at him. "You really are a remarkable man, Conrad."

He laughed. "If you're trying to get me to make out with you, it's working."

"Conrad!" She laughed, feeling warmth flood her cheeks.

"Isn't that what students do when they're supposed to be studying?" He sat back and cracked his knuckles, clearly amused by himself. "This really was a good idea. We're getting a lot done. And bringing lunch was genius. Your granddaughter deserves a treat for suggesting this."

"I was going to get her a plant for her new office."

"I have some beautiful aloe veras I just potted up. Babies from one of my big ones. You could give her one of those. They're great little air cleaners, and useful for some minor first aid, too."

"You wouldn't mind?"

"Not at all. Be happy to after she led us here."

"Thank you." She glanced at the laptop. "What's next?"

"This scene where the former Marine hero starts to suspect our killer."

Margo nodded. "Okay. Should we really have him suspect her this early in the book?"

Conrad sighed. "No, probably not."

"Then we need a red herring, don't we?"

He stared at the screen. "We do. But I'm not sure we've really set anyone up who could fulfill that role."

Margo thought about that, then leaned forward in excitement. "Yes, we did. The hospital orderly."

"Reggie?" Conrad blinked. "He's not perfect as a decoy, but we can fix that. A few tweaks where he's mentioned earlier. Maybe even give him a slightly bigger on-page presence." He nodded. "Yes, he will work nicely. Good thinking."

Conrad's hands went back on the keyboard.

"You know what else I'm thinking?"

He stopped typing to look at her. "What's that?"

"How we should do something more than this."

His brow furrowed. "What do you mean?"

"I mean we should...go out after we're done here and get a drink somewhere. Or go for a walk in that park near your house. Or maybe have a small cone at Beach Freeze." She shrugged. "Something like that. Just the two of us. We've worked pretty hard today."

Not that doing something with him required justification, but she wasn't ready for her day with him to end after having just been about work. It was quality time, for sure, but she wanted a different type of quality time, too. Boyfriend-girlfriend quality time.

He nodded, seeming to understand. "I like all of those suggestions."

"I know Dinah's waiting for you at home and probably expects you, but I feel...needy today. I'm sorry, but I do." She sighed, frowning at her own admission. "Not sure if her visit is getting to me or what. But at least I can be honest about it."

"I know it's bothering you. It's bothering me,

too." He took her hand. "I am happy to do any of those things you want."

"You are?" She laced her fingers through his. She never got tired of how big and strong his hands were.

"Sure," he said. "Dinah's a grown woman who chose to overstay her welcome. Well, not exactly. She's my sister and she's welcome anytime, but she's not been the most pleasant houseguest. Nor has she been that nice to you. And she has stayed longer than she said she would."

"I get it. You love her even if you don't always like her."

The look of truth on his face spoke volumes. "That pretty much sums it up. So what do you want to do?"

"Maybe the ice cream *and* the walk in the park? Or is that too much?"

He laughed. "Sounds perfect. Let me make a few notes on this new idea with Reggie and we can pack up and get out of here."

"Wonderful."

Traffic was a little heavy, so it took them twenty-odd minutes to get to Beach Freeze, each in their own cars, since they'd met at Digger's for breakfast before going to the library. The line at the little ice cream shack wasn't long, though. Most people were probably headed home to make dinner or would be soon.

Margo ordered a small pistachio cone, which was the soft serve flavor of the week. Conrad ordered a medium coffee ice cream, also in a cone, but his was hand-dipped, not soft serve. They sat at one of the picnic tables under the metal roof-covered area.

They sat side by side, looking out at the road and the cars going by.

"This was a good idea," he said. "I haven't been here in a while. Used to come here a lot."

"We always brought the kids here." She took the top off the pale green swirl filling her cone. It was delicious.

"I need to set up a time to interview Claire for that article on the sour orange pies. I guess she's still pretty busy with getting the bakery going, huh?"

"I have no doubt she'll make time for whatever you need."

"Maybe I'll go over to the bakery and just talk to her there. I'd like to see the place anyway and the photographer has to go, so I might as well."

"I can text her right now, if you like," Margo offered.

He shook his head. "Eat your ice cream."

"Okay."

They sat in companionable silence for a while, watching the traffic and enjoying their cones. It was nice and exactly the sort of thing Margo had been missing.

She finished her cone first. "Did Dinah say anything this morning about her supposed desire to move here?"

"No. Doesn't mean she's given up on it, though. She's probably just reformulating her plan." He rolled his eyes. "If you think this is bad, wait until things get more serious between us."

She glanced at him. "*More* serious?"

He grinned. "Don't worry about what that means, just enjoy the ride."

She laughed and gave him her attempt at a salute. "Yes, sir."

He leaned into her slightly. "You don't think I'm going through all of this nonsense with my sister to not get more serious with you, do you?"

"I don't know what I thought."

"Not to mention, we're about to be neighbors." He took another bite of his ice cream. "I'm going to be around a long time, Margo. You'll see." He glanced at her. "I hope you're okay with that."

"I'm not only okay with it, I'm happy about it."

Her smile was coy, and she knew it. "I can't renovate that house by myself, you know."

He snorted and shook his head, eating the last of his ice cream. He wiped his mouth with the paper napkin that had been wrapped around the cone. "Now we need that walk to burn off that ice cream."

Getting to the park in Conrad's neighborhood only took six minutes. Any other time, they would have parked at his house and walked over but doing that today would mean alerting Dinah. Instead, they parked on the street.

They came together on the sidewalk, Conrad taking her hand right away. "You know, I don't come over here very much, but I should. It's a great park. The playground is nice, too. And this path goes all the way around."

"Maybe we can make walks part of our routine when I move over here."

"I'd like that," he said. They walked along the shady path. "What else will be part of our routine?"

"Besides our daily writing sessions?"

He nodded and she could tell he wanted her to spin out that future for him. Maybe so he could think about it. Maybe so he could make it a reality.

"We'll have dinner together most nights."

"Your house or mine?"

"Depends where we work that day."

"Makes sense. What else?"

"Some nights, after dinner, we might watch a movie. One of the really good ones from the days when Hollywood still had some class and dignity."

He smiled. "John Wayne and Maureen O'Sullivan."

"William Powell and Myrna Loy," she answered. Then she went on. "We'll go to that monthly dance at the Legion."

He smiled. "Definitely."

"On weekends, we might take a Saturday off now and then. Have lunch in town. Or maybe spend time by the pool doing absolutely nothing but enjoying some cocktails."

His brows lifted. "I could get used to that. Maybe your pool. It's bigger."

She nodded. "Anything you want to add?"

"Sure," he said. "We've still got book club at the library."

"Right." That was how they'd met, after all. "Anything else?"

"Romantic dinners out once in a while. Maybe an occasional weekend trip? There are a lot of nice places to visit within driving distance."

That wasn't something she'd considered but she

liked the idea of it. "It's good to know you've had some thoughts about our routine, too."

He smiled, still looking straight ahead, lips pursed like he was infinitely pleased with himself. "Oh, I have all sorts of plans for us."

Chapter Twenty-four

*R*oxie shouted a hello to everyone when she got home from helping Ethan, then got straight into the shower. She needed it, because she'd definitely helped. In fact, she'd done things she hadn't thought herself capable of. Like holding up part of a framed-out wall while Ethan nailed it into place.

She'd swept and picked up construction debris, too. Nothing overly strenuous, but dirty, sweaty work all the same.

She was glad to be under the hot water and getting clean. The scent of her peach body wash filled the shower with a delicious fruity aroma. Ethan was probably doing the same thing, since he was due here for dinner shortly. Although not with peach body wash. Probably.

She laughed at the thought. She didn't know

what soap or cologne or whatever he used but he always smelled nice. Masculine.

Her stomach growled. She'd seen Miguel, Willie, Trina, and Walter all in the living room and kitchen when she'd come home. Miguel would start cooking soon. Roxie was ready. After all she'd done today, she was hungry.

It had been a good day, though. Really good. She'd gone back to the salon to check in with Trina and found that Miles had assembled both shelving units. By the time Roxie had returned to see how things were going, Trina had cleaned them and was stocking them with some of the retail products that had arrived.

The salon looked more like a salon every day. It was nice to see. And it looked great. All of the choices Trina had made for fixtures and paint and wallpaper worked so well together. Bright and modern and very sharp. The salon would be up and running soon. There was no way clients wouldn't be impressed with how fun and hip it was.

And once Trina got her hands in their hair, they'd be sold on her skills. Success seemed practically inevitable.

Roxie got out of the shower, dressed in cute white denim cutoffs that showed the golden tan she was getting from her morning workouts. She added a simple blue tank top with a daisy on the front, then fixed her hair and makeup. Nothing over the top. Just enough so that she'd look nice for Ethan.

She flexed in the mirror. Hmm. Her arms could use more work. She definitely needed to pick up some weights. Pushups alone weren't cutting it.

Happy to be clean and refreshed from the shower, she went out to see if there was anything she could help with for dinner. "How's it going? Can I do anything?"

Miguel shook his head. "Thank you for offering, though."

"Sit," Willie said. "Relax."

Roxie remained at the breakfast counter. "I don't mind helping, really."

"Ma," Trina said. "Sit already." Walter was at her side on his blanket, his head on Trina's leg. He looked so content. And maybe a little worn out from his day at the salon.

Roxie gave him a little scratch on the back before sitting in her usual chair. "Did you show Mimi Walter's new trick?"

"I did," Trina said. "Miles thinks he can teach him how to shake paws, roll over, and play dead, too."

"That sounds like a lot of work," Willie said, a drink in her hand. "You're going to wear that poor dog out."

Roxie laughed. "I don't think dogs get tired of attention, Ma." She then realized there was a blender full of pale yellow slush that looked very much like a frozen beverage. She pointed at it. "Is that pina colada in there?"

"It is," Miguel said. "Would you like one?"

Roxie thought about it for less than a second. "Yes, I would."

Willie got up. "I'll get it. You want whipped cream?"

"No, thanks," Roxie said. There would be enough sugar in the drink without adding to it. "Straight up is fine with me."

"Coming up," Willie said. She poked Miguel in the arm. "You'd better start cooking, honey, or we're going to be too sloshed to eat."

He laughed. "I will. I'm going to get the water on for the rice right now." He already had a pot out and was filling it.

Willie poured Roxie's drink into a glass and brought it to her. "Here you go."

Roxie took it. "Thanks." She sipped from the hot pink straw Willie had added. The combination of pineapple and coconut never disappointed, but Miguel's version was so fresh that it made the drink something truly special. She hadn't seen him make this, but it tasted like it had fresh pineapple in it. "That is so good. Easily the best pina colada I've ever had."

Trina, who had one in front of her on the table, picked it up to take a sip. "Isn't it?"

Miguel smiled, his chest puffed up. "I know what I'm doing."

Roxie laughed. "No argument from me."

The three women sat like that, enjoying each other's company, a game show on the television, although the sound was turned down, chatting while Miguel worked in the kitchen. This was a life Roxie could get used to.

Sad that it was only going to be until Willie and Miguel's new house was built, but maybe they'd have some evenings like this over there. Roxie suddenly needed to know. "Ma, are you going to have us all over like this at your new house? With Miguel fixing drinks and amazing Puerto Rican food?"

"You bet," Willie said. "This is just practice."

"I like that," Roxie answered.

Miguel looked up from whatever he was doing.

"Hopefully, Danny will be there, too. And maybe Claire."

"That sounds so nice," Roxie said. "A real family night."

He nodded. "Exactly."

The doorbell rang. Roxie got up. "I'll get it. I'm sure it's Ethan."

It was. She kissed him in the foyer, where no one could see them, taking a little moment to themselves. "Hi."

"Hi yourself," he said, all smiles. He had a cooler in one hand. "I brought a little something."

"That was nice of you. Come on in." She took his hand and led him through the reading nook and into the living room. "You have to taste the pina coladas Miguel made. Best I've ever had."

"I'm in," Ethan said. He waved to everyone as he walked into the living room. "Thanks for the invite. Willie, I brought you another six-pack of that cherry soda you liked. And two pints of ice cream. Coconut mango and vanilla."

"Coconut mango?" Miguel smiled. "That sounds like something you'd find in Puerto Rico."

Ethan nodded. "It seemed appropriate."

"Very kind of you," Willie said. She took the ice cream out of the cooler, wiggled past Miguel in the kitchen, and tucked the cartons away in the freezer.

Ethan handed her the six-pack of soda over the breakfast bar, then left the cooler by the door. He tugged on Roxie's hand, a strange look on his face. "Can I talk to you outside for a second?"

"Sure." She gave him a look, silently asking him for more information, but he didn't offer any, just opened the sliding glass door for her.

She stepped out. He followed, closing the door behind them.

"What's going on?"

He smiled. "Nothing. Just wanted a second with you alone." He stuck his hand in his pocket and came out with a small black velvet box. "So I could give you this."

Her breath caught in her throat. She stared at the box.

"I told you I was going to get you a ring and I did." He opened the lid, revealing a swirl of sparkling white diamonds and gleaming yellow gold in the shape of two hearts intertwined. "I hope you like it. You didn't give me any hints about what you wanted, so…"

His smile faltered and she could tell he was nervous about his selection.

She took his face in her hands and kissed him. "It's beautiful. I'm a little unhappy at how expensive it looks, but it's stunning."

His smile returned. "You like it?"

She nodded, looking at the ring again. "It's perfect. I love it. Although I'm a little afraid to wear something that nice."

"It wasn't cheap but it didn't break the bank, either, so don't be afraid. Besides, if you don't wear it, what's the point?"

"True." She stuck her hand out, fingers splayed.

He took the ring from the box and slipped it on her finger. Right where she'd once worn her wedding ring. That was now tucked away in her jewelry box. Ethan's ring was the perfect replacement.

She looked from the ring to him. "How did you know my size?"

"Trina helped me out."

Roxie frowned. "How? I don't think she knows my ring size, either."

"She traced the inside of one of your rings on paper and I took that to the jewelry store with me. It's a six, in case you were wondering."

Roxie shook her head, amused by the craftiness of the two of them. She stared at the ring on her finger. "This means you can't date anyone else, right?"

"No, it just means *you* can't date anyone else." He laughed. "Yes, that's what it means. You good with that?"

She kissed him again. "I've been good with that for a while."

Chapter Twenty-five

*J*ules let out a deep sigh of contentment as she lounged on a chaise on the back deck of Jesse's house. She was grateful for the salt-tinged breeze blowing over her and the distant sound of the waves. She was grateful that Sierra and Cash had gone out after the day's rehearsal session, leaving Jules free to spend some time with Jesse. She was grateful that Kat had agreed to take Toby out for a walk when she got home from Future Florida. Jules was also grateful for how well rehearsal had gone.

Life was good. There was a *lot* to be grateful for. Just today alone she'd had thirteen requests for interviews. Some from magazines and newspapers, but a lot from bloggers, vloggers, podcasters, and other social media types.

All because *Dixie* had hit and hit *hard*. Pretty

much like everyone, except maybe her, had thought it would.

Was that a lesson in faith? She wasn't sure. It was a lesson in something. Trusting her gut more? Being more confident in her work, even when it was new and different? Whatever she was supposed to learn from this, she wanted to take it in and keep it close. To remember it.

Jesse came through the sliding glass doors, which he'd left open. He was carrying two glasses of white wine. He handed her one, then lifted his in a toast. "Here's to *Dixie* and whatever happens next."

She smiled, lifted her glass, and touched it to his. "I'll toast to that."

As she took a sip, he stretched out on the chaise beside hers. Shiloh was curled up on her bed, content to be near the humans. Jesse let out a sigh that mimicked the one Jules had just done herself. "This is nice."

"Really nice," she agreed.

"The food should be here in about half an hour."

"Perfect." He'd ordered Indian cuisine for them. She didn't eat it a lot, because it was rich and a bit of an indulgence when it came to carbs, but she definitely liked it. Although if there was ever a time for a little indulgence, it was this evening. Things were good. Tonight felt very celebratory.

"Talked to the video people for quite a while today."

She sat up a little. "You did? You didn't say anything to me about that."

"You were pretty busy rehearsing. I didn't want to take you away from what was going on."

"Yeah, probably a good call." She would have been upset if they'd lost the groove they'd gotten into. "So, come on. What did they say?"

"They're excited about it. They've never done a music video, but they clearly want to expand their services, so they're in." He grinned.

"That's great news." She stuck her leg out to nudge him with her toe. He was obviously enjoying dragging this out. "Details. I need details."

"They're willing to give us a discount on production costs in exchange for making sure they get visible billing wherever the video's posted and in the credits."

"As they should, so no problem there. That's awesome." She smiled, because it *was* good news, but also because Jesse had said "us." They were in this together. That was nothing new to Jules. He'd been more supportive than anyone in this journey, but it was still sweet to hear him say it.

"Even better than that," Jesse went on, using his wine glass to punctuate his words. "They love the rodeo idea. Love the song, too, which I sent them. Anyway, they know a location where they can get the footage they need for the script Cash and Sierra came up with."

"Really? Where?"

"Bellstead, Florida. They have a huge rodeo there every Fourth of July, but there's a lot of practicing that goes on at the arena year-round. Rick— he's the owner of First Reel, the video production company—thinks they can absolutely get the shots they need there. We'll have to figure out who the lead actors are going to be and all of that, but it seems pretty doable."

"That's amazing. I guess I knew Florida had rodeos, but not that it was such a big thing here."

"Thankfully, it is in certain parts." He sipped his wine and looked out at the water. "They want to get started right away."

Jules nodded. This was a big financial commitment, but with the way the song was going, it would be foolish not to do a video. A good one would only give the song stronger legs. "What do we need to do to get them going?"

"Sign a production contract and give them a deposit."

"How much?" She almost didn't want to know.

He took a breath, watching her as he answered. "Ten grand."

She drank a little more wine and swallowed before answering. "All right. I knew it would be a big number. How much do they think it'll be in total?"

"I told them not to go crazy. Explained that this is new territory for you. They have assured me they can give you a sixty-thousand-dollar production for about thirty to thirty-five-grand total. Of course, if you want to spend more, you can. That's up to you."

She let that sink it. That was a great deal. And as music video costs went, thirty-five grand wasn't awful. But it was all coming out of her pocket and while she was all right financially, she hadn't had new music out in a while. She'd been living off royalties for quite a few years. She was all right financially, because she'd been careful with her money. Even so, she needed to get her house in Landry up for sale.

"Are you second-guessing it?" he asked. "Having doubts?"

"No. It's not that." She smiled. "Just absorbing that figure and doing a bit of thinking."

"About that..." He ran a hand through his hair, then shifted position like he'd suddenly gotten uncomfortable. "I... already gave them the deposit."

She looked at him, shock running through her. "You did?"

He nodded. "Please don't be mad. There were a few things they wanted to get to work on right away, so I wired them the money. I know, I should have talked to you first. That was impulsive of me. But with the way the song was blowing up and how good you guys sounded in the studio today, I got carried away. If you don't want to do this—"

"No, I do." She set her glass down, reached out, and laid her hand on his arm. "That was very kind of you."

"But I need to discuss this stuff with you first. I know that." He shook his head. "I get ahead of myself, Jules. I realize that. I'm sorry. I probably shouldn't think of us as a team the way I do, either. I know we are. Sort of. But this is your business and—"

"Jesse?"

He looked at her sheepishly. "Yeah?"

"It's okay. We *are* a team. But, yes, this is also my

business. If I didn't have that money to pay you back with, I'd be upset. You shouldn't do things like that." She smiled to soften her words. "It's sweet that you did, though."

"I screwed up, didn't I."

She laughed and patted his arm before taking her hand back. "It's not that bad. It really was a kind gesture."

"Kind and overly enthusiastic." He stared at the water again. "I'll try to do better. I really will."

She knew that was true. He meant well. And it really wasn't a big deal. He wanted the best for her. She got that. "There's one more thing I need to say."

He frowned. "What's that?"

"Thank you. For believing in me the way you do. For making all of this possible. For being the most amazing support I've had in a long time. I'm not mad at you."

"You're not?"

She shook her head. "Not a lot of women have a boyfriend who can just throw ten grand down to make sure something important happens for them. That's pretty impressive. Even if it was impulsive."

His frown slowly righted itself as he looked at her. His expression softened. "I'm crazy about you, you know."

"I feel the same way."

He swallowed. "Then marry me."

Her mouth opened but no sound came out. She just looked at him. That was not what she'd expected him to say.

"I don't mean immediately," he explained. "But someday in the future. I understand that we're still getting to know each other. But I need you in my life, Jules. You're all I think about. When I wake up in the morning and you're not here, all I can focus on is when I'm going to see you again. I would do anything to make you happy."

He'd certainly proven that.

He took a breath. "I love you. I know that with as much certainty as I've ever known anything." He glanced down at the chaise. "I also know you might not want to get married again, because things didn't go so well the first two times. So if you say no, I understand."

"Okay." The word came out as breathy as a whisper.

He looked up at her, confusion filling his eyes. "Wait. Okay, it's a no? Or okay, it's a yes?"

She smiled. "Okay, it's a yes." She quickly held a finger up. "But it's not happening tomorrow. This is going to be a long engagement. We definitely need to get to know each other better."

Although she loved everything she knew about him already. But he was right. Her first two marriages hadn't been great. She was a little gun-shy.

Maybe her heart didn't know that, though, because every cell in her body felt like it was radiating happiness.

"I'm good with a long engagement." He inched closer to narrow the gap between them and kissed her.

She kissed him back, keeping her hand on his cheek when the kiss ended. "I love you, too. I can't help but love you. You've come to my rescue several times already. You might be the best man I've ever known."

And she'd be a fool to let him get away.

Chapter Twenty-six

*A*fter Miguel's delicious dinner and a scoop of coconut mango ice cream, Trina packed Walter and herself into her car and headed for the firehouse. Earlier, Miles had invited her to come by, and had told her Walter was welcome.

She absolutely wanted to come by. Any chance to spend time with him was a welcome one.

She also thought it would be a good opportunity to see how Walter did around a lot of people. Kind of important, considering that was going to be his everyday routine once the salon was open. If too many people freaked him out, bringing him to the salon wasn't going to be an option. She really hoped the station's alarm didn't go off. That was another thing that might spook him.

She parked beside the firehouse, happy that she and Walter were arriving after everyone on shift had eaten dinner. Walter wasn't a beggar, and she didn't want him to become one. She didn't want the guys sneaking him scraps of people food, either. Walter had such a cute face it was hard not to spoil him.

The organic dog cookies Miles had gotten him were a much better option for Walter's health. She'd still be spoiling him, just with good choices.

The big firehouse doors were open, the trucks ready to go at a moment's notice. She clipped Walter's leash to his collar, locked the car, then she walked him in. She found the guys all in the lounge, hanging out and watching a few of the crew play a video game on the big-screen TV.

Miles was on one of the couches near the back of the room, almost like he was waiting for her. Maybe he was. Alex was sitting with him. Alex's arm was still in the sling, meaning he couldn't work. In fact, Trina knew he hadn't been cleared for duty yet, but Miles had mentioned he'd been hanging out with them more since Kat had started her new job.

Miles saw Trina before she even walked through the lounge door. He put down the magazine he was flipping through and came to greet her in the hall.

"Hey, there." He gave her a quick peck on the cheek, then crouched down to scratch Walter on the head. "How are you, little man?" Miles stood back up. "The crew is going to go nuts for him."

"I hope they don't scare him. I have no idea how he's going to be around a lot of people. Especially because I get the sense he was used to a pretty quiet life with an older person. I guess we'll see, huh?"

"He'll be all right, won't you, boy?" Miles looked down at Walter, who was wagging his tail. "See? He already looks excited."

Trina nodded. "He does. All right. In we go."

Miles went ahead of them. "Hey, guys. Trina's here. And she's got someone new with her."

The crew turned to see. Trina gave them a wave, then quickly picked Walter up. "Hi, everyone. This is Walter. My new puppy."

Nothing but smiles and nods and kind words. Alex came over and gave the dog some attention. "Hey, buddy."

Walter licked his hand.

Alex laughed and looked at Trina. "He's a cool little dude."

"He really is."

Walter squirmed as a few of the guys called to him. Trina put him down and unclipped his leash, something she wasn't completely sure about.

Miles went behind her and closed the lounge door. "Just in case," he said.

"Yeah, thanks."

Walter seemed oblivious that any means of escape had just been removed. In fact, escape didn't seem to be anywhere on his horizon. He was too busy being petted by a lot of different hands. The guys were acting like they'd never seen a dog until Walter, showering him with affection and baby talk and scratches.

Walter was in dog heaven.

Trina laughed. "Not sure what I was so worried about. He's doing just fine."

"He's eating it up," Alex said.

Miles snorted. "You might not get him back."

"He's not going to want to leave." She crossed her arms as she watched her dog being treated like a celebrity.

"I knew the guys would love him," Miles said.

Alex glanced at her. "Congrats, Trina. He's great."

"Thanks. No Kat tonight?"

He shook his head. "She's still getting into the groove of things at work and has been kind of worn out at the end of the day. We're hanging out tomorrow night, though. Send Walter over to see me when he's done with his rounds."

"Will do," Trina said.

Smiling, Alex went back to his seat.

Trina looked at Miles. "How's Alex really doing?"

"Bored but that was expected. He's all right." Miles shrugged. "You want something to drink?"

"I'm okay. I don't need anything. Just came to hang out."

"I'm glad you did. Thanks."

"I think Walter's the happiest of all." Someone had found a tennis ball and was now playing fetch with Walter.

Miles laughed. "That dog is going to sleep good tonight."

"All right with me," Trina said.

"Are you letting him sleep on the bed with you?"

"I am." She made a face. "You probably don't think I should, huh?"

Miles shook his head. "He's your dog. Up to you where he sleeps. I couldn't say no to him, I know that."

She smiled and slipped her arm around his waist. Miles understood. "I'm trying not to spoil him too much, but it's hard. I just want to give him everything."

He put his arm around her shoulders. "You'll

probably feel that way about your kids someday, too."

Our kids, she wanted to correct him. But she didn't have a crystal ball. As much as she adored Miles, she didn't *really* know if they'd end up together. Wanting something didn't always make it happen. So instead, she just nodded. "I'm sure I will."

"You're going to be a great mom, Trina." He pulled her closer.

"Thanks. And thanks again for coming by today and putting those shelving units together. My mom and I would probably still be working on them."

"You know you can call me whenever you need help. I mean that."

She lifted one shoulder in a little shrug. "I know. I just hate to bother you. I know how hard you work and you need your downtime."

He released her just enough so that he could look at her. "But I need you more. I wish..." Then he just shook his head.

"What?"

Walter scampered past, chasing the tennis ball.

"Nothing," Miles said. He smiled. "I just need you. That's all."

She narrowed her eyes at him. "What were you going to say?"

He pressed his lips together in a firm line, then glanced over his shoulder. "Alex, keep an eye on Walter, okay?"

"You got it," Alex answered.

Miles led Trina out of the room, closing the door behind them. "I feel like my life is on hold sometimes. I see you and I know how good we are together, just like I know what our life could be like, but we can't be there yet because society says you can't just be with someone you've only known a short while. Well, that sucks. I know what I want and it's you. My feelings aren't going to disappear. In fact, they get stronger every day. I love you, Trina. I want us to be together."

She went all warm inside. "We...are together."

"I don't mean the way things are now. I mean permanently. I want to sleep next to you at night and come home to you when my shift is over and make you coffee in the morning and do all the little things to take care of you that I can't do now."

Her heart thumped wildly in her chest. "Are you saying you want to live together?"

"Yes. But I also want more than that. I want to marry you and get on with our future."

She smiled up at him. "We really haven't known each other that long."

"I know. That's the holdup. But are you saying that you don't feel the same way about me?"

She quickly shook her head. "No, not at all. Just that you're right about society frowning on that kind of fast decision-making."

"Didn't stop your grandmother."

"No, it didn't." Why was she arguing against this? She wanted it, too. But she had some fear despite her feelings. Fear that maybe they *were* moving too fast. "But she and Miguel are a lot older than us, and they wanted to spend as much time together as possible."

"Which is exactly how I feel. I know my job isn't as dangerous as if I was a firefighter, but I see how close people come to death every day. None of us are promised tomorrow. Waiting doesn't appeal to me." He sighed and looked up at the ceiling for a moment.

When he looked at her again, he was smiling. "I'm not trying to push you to do something you don't want to do, T. I'm really not. I guess I just wanted you to know where I'm at when it comes to us."

She smiled. "I love that you told me. I love you, too."

"Does that mean if I were to propose, you'd say yes? Wouldn't mean we'd have to get married right away. I know you have a lot going on with the salon and that needs to be your focus right now, but we could be engaged."

She nodded, her heart just about bursting with happiness. "We definitely could be. And then, when the time is right...we'll make everything official."

He grinned. "Any kind of wedding you want. Beach, church, underwater, I don't care."

She laughed. "Underwater? I think a beach wedding would be great."

She could see his point about not waiting. She really could. For all of his reasons, and one of her very own. Mimi wasn't getting any younger. The longer Trina waited, the less likely she was to have her grandmother at the ceremony.

That alone seemed like reason enough.

Chapter Twenty-seven

*K*at's mind wandered as she relaxed in front of the television, only half-watching the forensic show her grandmother had on. There were probably more interesting shows to watch, at least to Kat, but this was more about being with her grandmother than it was entertaining herself. Her mom had gone to her bedroom to work on bakery stuff, Aunt Jules was at Jesse's, and Cash was with Sierra.

Kat didn't want her grandmother to be alone, although her grandmother was a pretty independent woman. She might not have minded being alone. Kat still wanted to hang out with her, regardless. Her grandmother was a pretty cool individual.

She knew her grandmother was proud of her for making such a big change in her life. Kat was proud of herself, too.

She loved her new job. How fulfilling it was. How it meant something. She didn't love how surprisingly tired it left her. She'd been feeling brain-drained when she got home, but she imagined that was all part of getting used to being back at work and getting into the swing of her new routine. Eventually, that wouldn't be an issue.

She hoped that eventually came soon. Then again, working at Future Florida wasn't just sitting at a computer, punching in numbers and creating reports. It required more thought than any other job she'd ever had. More emotion, too.

That part would probably never go away. She was okay with that. The job was important, and she was finally doing something to help people in a meaningful way.

All of that was awesome.

Not getting to see Alex as much wasn't. She missed him. Him being unable to work because he was on sick leave, and therefore available to spend time with, only made it worse. No matter how she felt tomorrow night, she was going to see him.

Even if all they did was sit on the couch and watch a movie, that would be great.

Actually, she planned to make dinner and do a few chores for him while she was there. Maybe a little cleaning, vacuuming, straightening up. Whatever needed doing. No matter how tired she was.

"You all right, sweetheart?"

Her grandmother's question pulled Kat out of her thoughts. "I'm all right. You need something?"

"No." Her grandmother nodded at Kat's hand. "You've been twisting that ring around your finger for the last fifteen minutes. I was a little worried you were going to cut a groove in your skin."

The last sentence was said with a grin, telling Kat her grandmother was only kidding. Kat snorted. "I didn't even realize I was doing it."

"Is that the ring Alex gave you?"

"Yeah."

"You miss him, don't you?"

"I do." Kat sighed.

"You feel guilty, too, right? Because he's recovering from the shoulder injury and you're working, but you feel like you should be with him."

Kat slanted her eyes at her grandmother. "When did you develop psychic abilities?"

Margo smiled. "It's human nature to want to be with the person you love. And when something gets in the way of that, even something wonderful as a new, worthwhile endeavor, it's natural to feel like you're shortchanging that

person. You're not, you know. And I have no doubt
Alex understands that."

"I'm sure he does, too. Doesn't change the way I
feel, though."

"I know," Margo said.

"Do you feel that way about Conrad?"

There was a moment of hesitation before her
grandmother answered. "What I feel about Conrad
right now has been overshadowed by the meddling
behavior of his sister." She frowned. "I know it won't
last, but it is *tiresome*."

"So tell her," Kat said. "Be kind, but be honest.
Tell her how you feel about Conrad, about her inter-
fering in both your lives, and how nothing she does
is going to change how you feel about him. Couldn't
make things worse."

Margo smiled kindly. "I'm not so sure about
that."

"I can't imagine how frustrating it is to be dealing
with her. I'd have given her a piece of my mind ages
ago. Like at the wedding."

"Conrad stood up to her at the wedding and that
seems to be why she's still here."

"Yeah, but have you told her how *you* feel? I
mean really had a heart-to-heart with her?" Kat
shook her head. "Seems to me that she's got all kinds

of insecurities of her own going on. Otherwise, why would she care what her brother did? She thinks she's going to lose him."

"She won't. He'll be as available to her as he ever has been. He just won't be all hers anymore."

"And that has to be what's bothering her." Kat twisted to face her grandmother, resting one arm along the back of the sofa. "Although I can't imagine why. What does she need Conrad all to herself for?"

"She has no one else," Margo said. "That's the real problem. Dinah's pretty much alone now but losing Conrad to another woman has to feel like a whole new kind of isolation. The thing is, if she were *nice*, she could be adding to her circle of friends."

Kat nodded. "Because she'd be as welcome with you guys and even here with us as Conrad is."

"That's exactly right." Margo exhaled a long, exasperated sigh. "Unfortunately, I think that ship has sailed. I don't think she'll ever get over her hatred of me."

"Grandma, I don't think she *hates* you."

"Kat, trust me. The woman loathes me."

Kat grimaced. "That's no way to get through life. No wonder she's alone and miserable."

"I'm not so sure she's miserable. She seems to enjoy her own crankiness quite a lot."

Kat laughed, all the while wishing she could find some solution for her grandmother. "At least she's probably not serious about moving here."

"No, probably not. Although I've stopped caring about that."

"Really? Why?"

"Because if she really does move here, she'll see that Conrad and I are serious about each other. This isn't some fling or whatever she thinks it is." Her grandmother threw her hands up. "For crying out loud, I'm moving into the neighborhood. Conrad and I are going to be more a part of each other's lives than ever before."

"Does she know that? About you moving a few houses away?"

"I'm not sure," Margo answered. "I don't think so."

"You'd better not say anything then," Kat said. "There's no telling what she might do." She tried to smile, but that wasn't really so funny. "Grandma, what *are* you going to do about this woman?"

"I don't know, Kat. Pray she goes home soon, I guess. Other than that…" Margo shook her head, then let out a deep sigh. After a moment, she said, "I think I might turn in. Thanks for the chat."

"Anytime." Kat turned off the television, got up,

too, and headed for her bedroom. She felt for her grandmother, but she didn't have any ideas to offer. Something really had to be done about Dinah. Kat wondered if she should reach out to Conrad. See if he had any suggestions.

Would that make her grandmother mad? Maybe not mad, exactly, but...

Kat decided to sleep on it. Things sometimes looked clearer in the morning.

Chapter Twenty-eight

Claire had slept hard, maybe because of the work she'd done at the bakery, but more likely because of being out on the water with Danny. Something about the combination of fresh air, Gulf water, and warm sun did wonders for her sleep.

She got ready for the day with a sense of lightness and joy. She'd worked for a while last night, translating several of her recipes into the right amounts for bakery production. Scaling up like that wasn't always just about math.

Baking was a science more than most types of cooking and she needed to be sure her equations were right. Too much or too little of one ingredient could throw the whole thing off. But she'd researched how to scale recipes and felt confident she'd figured it out.

Today would be the first test.

She drove to the bakery fully prepared to take on the day and the challenges ahead. She was unsure about a few things, namely working with commercial-grade tools, equipment, and appliances, but she was sure she'd figure them out. If not, Danny would be there to help her. It would all be fine. Nothing was going to dampen her happiness.

Hard to believe she'd finally be baking in her new kitchen. After the perishables came in, anyway. She'd driven separately from Danny today, since he'd gone in earlier. He hadn't wanted to miss the delivery and was there now, waiting on it. Thinking about him, she stopped on the way in and got two large coffees.

When she arrived at the shopping center, she parked and went into the bakery. Two of Ethan's guys were knocking out some final items. One was installing a large ceiling fan in the center of the dining area. The other was securing the new Sour Orange Pie sign over the tall cold case.

She stood for a moment, admiring it. The sign fit above the glass-front refrigerator and matched the rest of the décor in the bakery, except for the addition of the orange color. It featured hand-painted artwork depicting a tantalizing slice of sour orange pie on a plate with a swirl of meringue on top and an orange blossom alongside like a fancy garnish. All of that was against a black background that made the colors pop.

Over the illustration were the words, "Try the Florida original: Sour Orange Pie," painted in white. Underneath the artwork, more words in white: "Take one home today!"

She smiled and nodded her approval. The sign had just the right amount of old-fashioned character to it. She loved it. Maybe the *Gulf Gazette* would feature a photo of that sign in their article.

She heard a little noise from the kitchen, so she went through, taking the coffees and her purse with her.

Danny was checking things off a list as a delivery guy hauled in a dolly stacked high with perishable ingredients. Some of those ingredients were two crates of Seville oranges. He smiled at her. "Morning."

"Morning." She lifted one of the cups. "Coffee?"

He sighed as though she'd just saved his life. "Yes, thank you."

She handed him the cup. "How's it going?"

"So far so good. Looks like everything's here, although he's still got two more loads to bring in." He sipped the coffee. "That's just what I needed."

"We need to start making coffee here. Seems silly to pay for it when we have the capability."

"I agree."

She took a drink of her own coffee. Maybe not as good as homebrewed, but not bad, either. "Hey, I *love* the pie sign. It's just perfect. It's got exactly the right sense of nostalgia about it. You did good."

"I'd love to take credit for that, but I can't. That was the design team at the sign shop." He smiled. "They really nailed it, though, didn't they?"

"They did. I'm going to work on a batch of those after I get some cookies in the oven. Provided the Lorna Doones arrived yesterday?" She thought she'd seen them, but things had been a little hectic.

"I'm sure they did."

"Great. For now, though, should I get in that walk-in and start organizing or wait until he's done bringing stuff in? I can always work in the dry storage." Then she'd know if the Lorna Doones were here or not. Without them, there'd be no crust for the sour orange pies.

"Up to you. Did you bring a sweater or something? It's cold in that walk-in."

She frowned. "No. I didn't even think about that."

"I've got a sweatshirt in the office. You can wear that if you want."

"Thanks. I'll borrow it and get to work." She went into the office, a small room off of the kitchen, and found the sweatshirt easily, as it was hanging over the back of the desk chair. She put her purse and her coffee down and pulled on the sweatshirt.

Traces of Danny's aftershave lingered, a subtle clean scent with a soft spicy note beneath that. Sort of like a good gingerbread cookie, but much more masculine. She smiled as she rolled the sleeves back. Then she tucked her purse into a drawer, grabbed her coffee and headed back out.

Danny was checking off things on the second dolly full of stuff, so she let him work and went straight to the walk-in. It was definitely chilly, making her glad for the sweatshirt. The walk-in was deeper than it was wide, with metal shelving from floor to ceiling all the way around. Lots of room, which was good, because they were going to need it.

They also had a dry storage area for shelf-stable ingredients, and a walk-in freezer, but that would be more about storing already-made items, like the pre-portioned cookie dough, cake blanks, tubs of prepared buttercream, those sorts of things.

She took a look at what had been brought in. She'd given a great deal of thought as to how she was going to organize it. The most-used ingredients would go on the right, prepared bakery items on the left.

First up on the right-hand side would be butter, since it was something that would be used a lot. Then eggs, heavy whipping cream, milk and so on. Fruit would go into bins on the back wall. Lemons, limes, mangos, the bitter oranges required to make the pies, and whatever else they needed.

She worked as quickly as she could while still being careful, especially with the eggs, which had arrived in large, square cardboard flats, each egg in its own divot.

By the time the deliveryman had brought everything in, and Claire had gotten it all put away where she wanted it, the sweatshirt was no longer doing enough to keep her warm. She came out of the walk-in shivering.

Danny wasn't in the kitchen. Probably out front. The A/C was on, so she slipped out the back door that led to a strip of parking and the shopping center's dumpster. She stood in the sun, letting it warm her until the feeling came back into her fingers.

Getting the cookie dough together would probably help warm her up, too. Or her coffee, though she'd left it on one of the worktables and chances were it wasn't very hot anymore. She could stick it in the microwave.

Finally warm, she went back inside and returned Danny's sweatshirt to the office chair. She took the Mrs. Butter's apron off the wall hook where it was hanging and put it on. Then she got her bakery recipes, written out on folded sheets of notebook paper in her purse, and went into the kitchen to make some cookies happen.

The first thing she did was make sure the large, industrial stand mixer was operational. She attached the paddle beaters and turned it on. It started right up. That had been easier than expected. Pleased, she turned it off and got out the scale she'd be using to portion the ingredients. That was the only way to be sure she was using the right amount. With large-quantity recipes like she was about to make, measuring cups just weren't accurate enough.

Next, she gathered the ingredients she'd need.

Danny showed up as she was getting eggs and butter out of the walk-in. "Hey, you want some help setting up that big mixer?"

She shook her head. "Nope. Already did that."

"You did?"

"Wasn't that hard."

He smiled and put his hands on his hips. "Do you need help with anything else?"

She looked around. The ovens needed to be turned on and brought up to temperature, but she wanted to do that. She wanted to do all of it, so that she knew she could. Danny wasn't always going to be here. "No, I've got it."

"Doesn't surprise me. Yell if you need me, although I guess you won't."

She laughed. "I'll call you when the first batch of cookies is out of the oven and ready to be tasted." Though she was going to freeze most of them for later, she wanted to test the ovens out.

"I can definitely do that." He started toward the retail side of things again, then stopped. "You look good in that apron, by the way. Very...in charge."

"I feel in charge," Claire said. And it was a *very* good feeling.

Chapter Twenty-nine

Margo had given Kat's words from the night before a lot of thought. What was stopping her from sitting down with Dinah and just having a heart-to-heart? Could it make things worse? Maybe.

But it might also make things better.

She'd texted Conrad that she was coming to his house this morning. He'd questioned her decision, reminding her that Dinah was indeed still there.

I know, she'd texted back. *I want to talk to her.*

Is that really a good idea?

Not sure. But I promise it's not with the intent of being combative or worsening the issue. I've had some time to think and I'd like to speak to her.

All right.

She couldn't really explain to Conrad the feeling she had that this was the right thing to do. And if it wasn't exactly the right thing, it was the necessary thing.

She tried to pick an outfit that made her look nonthreatening. White pants and a printed blouse. Then she thought better of the blouse. She wanted this to be a casual, calm chat. The blouse was too much. Too dressed up. She chose a T-shirt instead. It had a soothing watercolor scene on the front of sailboats. That felt casual.

She wore crisp white tennis shoes and kept her jewelry to a minimum. Her grandchildren had told her she was intimidating. She hoped this outfit would help soften her appearance. There was nothing she could do about her face.

She drove to Conrad's, rehearsing her words. She had no idea, obviously, as to what Dinah's responses would be, but Margo planned to at least say what she'd come to say. How Dinah reacted to that remained to be seen.

Margo would have to respond as best she could. But she'd realized a few things as she lay in bed thinking last night.

Dinah was only an issue to her and Conrad because they were letting her be an issue. If they didn't allow her to take that role, the problem of Dinah would cease to exist.

At least that's what it seemed like to Margo.

She pulled into his driveway and parked, but didn't get out immediately. She sat there a moment, gathering her courage, reminding herself to be kind and understanding, and saying a little prayer that things would go well.

Then she got her purse and walked to the front door.

Conrad answered. "Thought you'd changed your mind for a second there."

She smiled. "No. Just gathering my thoughts."

"Come on in." He moved out of the way to let her in. "Dinah's in the kitchen having coffee."

"I wouldn't mind a cup myself." She stepped inside.

"There's plenty." He stepped in front of her and kissed her. The kiss lingered longer than she expected, almost like he was deliberately defying his sister. "I'll get you a cup."

She smiled at him. "Thanks."

"Do you need me to do anything?"

She shook her head. "Just back me up. If you feel so inclined."

"I can do that."

They walked into the kitchen together. Conrad announced, "Dinah, Margo's here."

Dinah was at the kitchen table, looking at a copy of the *Gulf Gazette*. She barely glanced up. "I see that."

Margo sat across from Dinah. "Good morning."

With a sigh, Dinah put the paper down. She made it seem as though Margo speaking to her was a major inconvenience. "Good morning. I suppose you're here to write?"

"Yes, but I wanted to chat with you first." Conrad put a cup of coffee in front of Margo, fixed the way she liked it. She smiled at him. "Thank you."

Dinah stared at Margo. Her eyes narrowed slightly. "Chat with me about what?"

Margo sipped the coffee, which was delicious, then put the cup down. "About us. About you and me and Conrad." She had an odd sense of peace within her. Her voice remained calm as she spoke. "I know you don't like me. I don't quite know why, other than I think you believe your brother's involvement with me will somehow limit the time he'll have to spend with you. Is that right? Or do you not like me for a different reason?"

Dinah opened her mouth and looked at Conrad, who was standing by the coffee maker, leaning on the counter. His arms were crossed, and he seemed to be attempting an impartial expression. He shrugged. "It's a valid question. Why don't you like Margo?"

Dinah cleared her throat, finally returning her gaze to Margo. "I never said I didn't like you."

Margo let out a gentle laugh and kept her tone light and non-confrontational. "I know you didn't. But you've made it pretty obvious with your attitude toward me. And the way you keep trying to come between your brother and me. I'm just attempting to understand what you're afraid of. And I guess in that way understand you."

"You don't need to understand me," Dinah snapped.

"I feel like I do." Margo picked up her coffee cup. "And I want to. You seem hurt by something that hasn't yet happened. Maybe by what you think is going to happen if Conrad and I continue to see each other, which is our plan, by the way. We're crazy about each other. We make each other happy. You want your brother to be happy, don't you?"

Dinah sputtered. "What is this all about? Why are you here?"

Conrad pushed away from the counter and let his arms fall to his sides. "Dinah, she just told you what it's about. Stop avoiding the questions and answer them. Do you want me to be happy?"

Dinah's lips pressed against each other. Finally, she spoke. "Of course I do."

"Then what's your problem with Margo?"

Dinah took a few long breaths through her nose, her chest rising and falling. But she said nothing.

Margo glanced at Conrad. He looked more than a little irritated. He closed his eyes and exhaled. An attempt to calm himself down maybe? When he opened his eyes, his expression had changed into something much more resolved. And a bit sad. "Come on, Dinah. It's time for you to pack your things and go."

"What?"

"You heard me." He shook his head. "Nothing is going to change by your staying any longer. You're not going to drive Margo and me apart. You're just not. Any relationship you could do that to is one I wouldn't want to be a part of anyway."

"You're talking nonsense." Dinah's chin quivered. Quivered!

Margo gave the woman props for her acting abilities. There was no way she was genuinely about to cry.

Conrad smiled. "Dinah. I love this woman. Don't you see that? I don't know why my desire to be happy upsets you so much, but it clearly does. And if you can't be happy for me, and you can't be civil to Margo, then why are you here?"

Dinah sniffed. "I want to spend time with my brother."

"And we have. A lot of time."

Margo had to say something. "If that's really what you want to do, then move here like you said you were going to."

Dinah's lips pursed. "Yes, I'm sure you'd like that."

"If we were on civil terms, I'd be fine with it."

Dinah snorted, tears forgotten. "You're lying."

"No, I'm not. In fact, I was just talking with my granddaughter last night about how your circle of friends would increase if you lived here. And had a change of heart toward Conrad and me, obviously."

Dinah stared at Margo like she'd grown horns. "You and your granddaughter were talking about me."

Margo nodded. "We were. Because, honestly, I feel for you. You seem so unhappy. So...like me just a few short weeks ago." She looked at Conrad. "Before I realized how much life I had left to live, and how happiness really is a choice."

Conrad came over to stand next to Margo. Like

they were a team. "You could make that choice, too, Dinah."

She shook her head. "I've already decided I can't move. It's too much at my age."

But those words felt like a defense to Margo. She could see a crack in Dinah's shell, and she wanted to break it open entirely. "We could help you with the move." She glanced up at Conrad. "Couldn't we?"

He nodded. "You bet."

"It would be a fresh start," Margo said. "It's never too late in life to have one, you know." She was proof of that.

Dinah said nothing.

"Think about it," Margo went on. "You and Conrad would be able to see each other more often. The three of us could do things together."

"Book club," Conrad offered. "Trips to the farmers market. Movies. We went to a play just the other week. There are all sorts of things we could do."

Margo threw another option into the mix. "Big family dinners."

Dinah frowned. "Big family dinners?"

Margo nodded. "With my two daughters and their children. And the partners that come with them. All the people who were at the wedding."

Dinah swallowed. "I-I don't know. I have to think about it."

Conrad put his hand on his sister's shoulder. "Take all the time you need. There's a park just a couple blocks over if you feel like a change of scenery. It's really beautiful."

Dinah stood, picked up her coffee cup, and took it to the sink. "Maybe I will go over there. The fresh air might do me good." She had yet to look either of them in the eye. "I suppose you'll be here writing."

"We will," Conrad said.

With a short nod, Dinah left the room. A few moments later, the front door opened and closed. The house seemed oddly quiet after that.

Conrad took the seat Dinah had occupied, reaching for Margo's hand.

Margo exhaled. "You think that had any effect on her?"

"I have no idea," he said. "We'll have to wait and see."

Chapter Thirty

Waiting sucked, Willie thought as she lay in the bed and stared up at the ceiling in Miguel's room.

She wanted the answer to the big DNA question *now*. She wasn't going to get it, but she wanted it all the same. One more day and she'd have it. Then things would either change...or they wouldn't.

She still didn't know which outcome she preferred, but it wasn't something she'd have to think about too much today.

She and Miguel were headed to Dunes West to explore some more and get to know the community they were about to move into. But first, they were stopping by to see Rob at the sales office so they could pick out the exterior colors for their house. Apparently, they needed to do it soon, because the colors had to be approved by a committee.

Willie rolled her eyes at the thought. So fancy. A color approval committee. But that was what you had to deal with when you lived in an exclusive place like the Preserves. She laughed to herself.

Miguel rolled over. "What's funny?"

She hadn't meant to wake him. "Sorry. Go back to sleep."

He faced her, eyes sparkling with amusement. "Too late. I'm awake now. What were you laughing about?"

"How fancy it is to have to go through a color committee. They must be afraid we're going to want a hot pink house with lime green trim."

He chuckled. "Maybe we should make that one of our choices, just to see if they're paying attention."

She snorted. No wonder she loved him. "What colors do we want?"

"I don't know. But I like color, so nothing too bland."

"I'm in agreement with that."

"Maybe they'll have something for us to look at. Some options? Some ideas?"

"That would help. Or we could leave a little early and drive around the Preserve to see what other people have done."

"You, my love, are a genius. For that, I'm going to

get up and see if Danny left us any coffee." Miguel pulled the covers back and pushed himself upright. "If not, I shall make us some."

"And bring it back to bed?"

He glanced over his shoulder, smiling. "Is that what you want?"

"Coffee with you? Back in bed with me? When we're all alone?" She grinned. "Do you really need an answer to that?"

He laughed. "I will return shortly."

He left and she got up to use the bathroom and brush her teeth. Wouldn't do to have morning breath if they were going to fool around.

He returned about five minutes later with two cups of coffee. Danny and Miguel made very strong coffee. She was getting used to it, but Miguel usually added extra cream and sugar to hers to make it more to her liking.

As she took the cup from him, she could tell he'd done that for her just by the color of the coffee. "Thank you."

"Anything for you." He put his coffee on the nightstand and got back into bed. Once he was settled, he picked the cup back up and took a sip. "What time should we leave?"

"Well, I need to shower. And have some breakfast."

"We could eat breakfast over there. At the café. See what that's like." He glanced at her. "If you can wait. Otherwise, I'll make us something here."

"No, I like that idea. We should see what it's like, since we're going to be living there." She drank a few big sips of her coffee. All the extra creamer had cooled it down to a very drinkable temperature. Maybe it was growing on her but it tasted great.

"Then that's what we'll do. Breakfast at the café, then we'll drive around the Preserve and look at colors. If we find something we like, we'll take a picture of it and show it to Rob. He can figure out what the colors are."

"That sounds easy enough. After that, are we going to a movie?"

"I think we should. See how the theater is. Maybe look in some of the shops after. As long as we aren't too tired." He gave her a look before setting his coffee aside again. "From what comes next, that is."

She giggled and put her cup on her nightstand.

An hour later, they were at the café. They hadn't relied on an Uber, like they usually did. Instead, Miguel had driven them in his car. He'd confessed that he preferred being driven, but as long as they were home before it got dark, he'd be fine. She couldn't imagine they'd be out that late.

At the moment, they were seated at a nice table, and waiting for their breakfasts to arrive, new cups of coffee before them.

Willie felt like she'd reached a whole new level of happiness. "Every day should be like this."

Miguel nodded. "I agree."

She leaned in like she had a secret to tell him. "I love being married to you. I can't wait until we're in our new house."

He grinned, eyes gleaming. "That will be heaven." He reached across the table to take her hand.

They stayed that way until their breakfast arrived.

The food was great, as Willie expected it would be. They'd both ordered eggs benedict. Hers had crabmeat instead of Canadian bacon. Miguel's had slices of filet mignon. They shared bites with each other.

Willie laughed. "This feels wrong."

The lines on Miguel's brow deepened. "What does?"

"This! I feel like I'm still on vacation. Like the honeymoon never ended."

He chuckled. "It does feel that way." He let out a

contented sigh. "I didn't know life could be this way. It's very good."

They finished their breakfast and headed out to drive through the Preserves and look at house colors. They headed to their lot first to doublecheck the colors of the houses on either side. They knew they couldn't duplicate those.

Willie gasped as they approached. "Miguel, look! They really have broken ground." Rob had told them that but seeing it made it all so real.

Miguel parked along the curb and they got out to have a better look. The lot was staked with little orange survey flags.

"Oh," he said. "This is very exciting."

Willie stood by one of the flags. "Take my picture."

"Okay." He got his phone out and squinted at the screen. "All right, I think I got it."

"Now set the timer so we can both be in it."

He shook his head. "I don't know how to do that."

"I do. On my phone, anyway. Here, you come stand where I am and I'll set it up." She took her phone out of her purse as they traded places. She tried a few spots on the car and found that if she was careful, she could rest the phone along the little edge where the window went down into the door.

She positioned it with the front facing camera on to be sure she had Miguel in the frame, set the timer, then moved as quickly as she could to get into position next to him. The timer gave her five seconds. She just made it.

She retrieved her phone, tucking it away in her purse. "Let's have a little look around before we go."

"All right."

They walked around the flags, being careful not to step on anything that looked important or purposeful. They made it all the way to the water's edge. It was pretty in the morning. Very peaceful. And very sparkly with the reflected sun.

"This will be a wonderful spot to have our coffee," Miguel said.

"I agree." She took his hand as they stood there, looking down the canal. "And I can't wait."

After a few more minutes, they went back to the car. Willie dutifully snapped photos of the houses on either side so they wouldn't repeat those colors, then Miguel carefully drove them around. It was the first time they'd really been through the rest of the Preserves. The houses were gorgeous.

Willie saw all sorts of things she liked. She

pointed at one house. "Look at that house with all of the white trim. I like that a lot."

He nodded and slowed. "It's very...old Florida."

"Does that mean you don't like it?"

"No, I do. Take a photo."

She did. They drove on. They went about two more blocks before Willie let out a gasp. "Stop the car, Miguel. That's what I want. Right there."

He pulled alongside the curb and put the car in Park. "It's very nice. Looks happy."

Willie smiled. "It does give off a happy feeling, doesn't it? It makes me happy just looking at it."

The house was a gorgeous sea green with accents of white in most places, like the trim around the windows, the railings, the front porch. But the shutters and the front door were a soft, welcoming turquoise. The combination reminded Willie of the most beautiful parts of the Gulf when the sun hit it just right.

She took numerous pictures. "I've got it. Let's go show Rob what we want."

Chapter Thirty-one

*E*veryone was finally back in the studio and Jules was thrilled about it. The goal today was to record *Folsom Prison Blues*, then move on to learning and rehearsing the next song. This time it would be Sierra's contribution, *Bayou Moon*.

Jules felt it made a nice companion piece to the much more raucous *Dixie's Got Her Boots On*, and if interest in that song kept up, *Bayou Moon* would be the next one she'd release. She knew sending a slower, more emotional ballad out after a rolling, fast-paced danceable tune was a risk, but she wanted to show all her new fans how much range she had.

And how much range the new album was going to have. Hopefully, that would be seen as a welcome thing.

She also wanted to put something out that her core audience would feel more comfortable with, just in case *Dixie* had made them think Jules had abandoned her roots. She definitely hadn't, and *Bayou Moon* would show them that.

With its emotional lyrics, slow melody, and nostalgic themes, *Bayou Moon* reminded Jules of something she would have written herself at the beginning of her career. That part of it made her extra happy.

"How we doing in there?" Jesse asked.

He was back in the control booth even though they still had a couple of hours of rehearsal in front of them to make sure the song was as good as it could be. She wasn't complaining about his presence. She loved having him around. She just didn't want him to get bored. Or feel like he should be doing something else, like taking care of his own business.

Except she was very much aware that he considered this part of his business now, too. She was okay with that. He might not be playing an instrument or singing, but he was working hard on her behalf all the same. He'd proved that with the video people.

"We're good," Jules said.

Cash nodded as he checked a few of his guitar strings. "Just about there."

"Okay," Jesse said, leaning in to speak through

the microphone. "I assume you're going to run through it a few more times before you're ready to record?"

Jules nodded. "We are." She looked around. Everyone else was nodding. "You know how it goes," she said. "Practice makes perfect."

"Then in that case, I'm going to run out and make a few phone calls, but if you're ready before I get back, just text me."

"Will do," Jules said.

As he headed out, she checked with her crew. They all looked poised to go. She counted them down. "One...two...and..."

Sound filled the studio. The addition of Rita on the slide guitar and Frankie on his banjo rounded out the song, giving it some additional layers of richness. Even for the first full run-through, they all sounded great together, which was saying something, since Jules already thought they sounded amazing.

As the song came to a close, she strummed the last note and stood up to face the rest of the group. "That was perfect. I'm not sure we need another run-through, but we should probably do it anyway. Frankie and Rita, you both sounded so good.

Anyone listening would have thought you guys had been here for the first rehearsal."

Frankie laughed. "It's *Folsom Prison Blues*." He shrugged. "Been playing that song for a long time."

"Plus," Rita added with a smile and a glance toward the other side of the studio. "Bobby gave us some notes."

Bobby had a big grin on his face.

Jules chuckled. "Nicely done, Bobby." He'd really stepped up since the last rehearsal, giving some great comments and directions. She loved working with seasoned musicians. She never failed to learn something from them.

Which wasn't to say Cash and Sierra weren't welcome. Young blood had its place, too. Especially on this album.

"All right, once more." Just then, her phone vibrated in her pocket. She wondered if Jesse was checking in on them already. "Hang on." She dug it out and looked at the screen. Lars. She sighed. "I'm going to step out for a second. You all go on without me."

She didn't want to talk to her ex but if she didn't, he'd probably keep calling. He could be relentless. Better to get it over with.

She kept a smile on her face until she was out of

the studio and in the hall. She called him back, expecting...well, she really didn't know what. Sober Lars was very different from non-sober Lars.

She had no idea which one would be answering.

"Jules?"

Hard to tell from one word which one she was dealing with. She braced herself, prepared for the worst. "Yep, it's me. What's up?"

He cleared his throat. "I, uh, just wanted to say that I'm sorry for...you know. I screwed up. We have one more gig tonight, then I'm flying back to L.A. and going directly into rehab to get straight again."

Softly, she exhaled in relief. "Good for you, Lars. I'm proud of you. I know that can't have been an easy decision."

"Actually, it was. Well, maybe not easy but necessary. I don't like who I am when I'm not sober. I know you certainly don't. Neither do the boys. My band's not thrilled with me, either. I messed up. I'm sorry."

"You're forgiven. You might want to let Cash know."

"Yeah, I'm going to call him next."

"Good."

"Congratulations, by the way. Your new song is

fire. I can't get away from it online, which is a good thing. Different sound for you, huh?"

"A bit, yes, but it was time for something new." She smiled. *Dixie* was her rebirth. Billy, her agent, had texted her just this morning to say sales of her backlist were up. Always a good sign. "Thank you."

"If there's anything I can do to help, just let me know. Be happy to."

"I will." She couldn't think of anything she'd need him for, but it was kind of him to offer.

He sighed. "I know there were other issues besides my sobriety when we were married, but I wish things had gone differently."

She wasn't sure she felt the same way. Not with where she was at now. "Things work out the way they're supposed to. I don't think you were ever meant to be married, Lars."

"Hey, we did all right."

"*You* did all right." She wasn't in the mood to pretend about the past. She had too many scars to do that. "I had my heart broken every time you slept with another woman." Or disappeared into a bottle.

"We had Fen and Cash."

"Yes, we did. And they were the two best things that ever came out of that marriage." She paused, but realized she was done catching up. Maybe it was fun for him, but she didn't feel the same way. And she had work to do. "I should really get back to rehearsal before the band thinks I've quit. I'll let Cash know you're going to call."

"Okay. I'm really glad he's with you and doing well. Sorry again, Jules."

"Thanks. Good luck in rehab." She hung up and turned around to find Jesse coming toward her. She stuffed her phone in her pocket.

His brows pulled together as he focused on her face. He had some paperwork in his hand. "You okay?"

She nodded and crossed her arms over her chest. "Lars called to apologize and tell me he was headed to rehab as soon as he gets back to L.A."

"That's good."

"It is." She nodded, a melancholy feeling lingering. Where that had come from, she wasn't sure. Probably thinking about the past and all the ways it had gone wrong.

"But?"

She smiled at him. This was her present. And there was nothing melancholy about *it*. "But nothing."

"No regrets?"

"Concerning him?" She laughed. "No. I am very

happy with how my life is going. Especially the part where you're in it."

He grinned and held up the paperwork. "Good, because I just got the designs for your new T-shirts from the graphics people. As soon as you approve them, they'll send images to put on your website and we can get your store up and running."

She shook her head. "How did you know I needed T-shirts? And a store?"

He grinned. "Your business manager and I have been talking. Cash is a smart guy. He's got great ideas."

"He does. But you're amazing, too."

Jesse put his hands on her shoulders and brushed a soft kiss across her mouth. "The feeling is mutual."

Chapter Thirty-two

*R*oxie was happy to be back at work with Ethan today. She was helping him drywall the office area for the photography studio, which he'd finished framing out yesterday. Drywall was something she'd never done and never thought she'd be doing. But she liked working with him. Learning something new was always good.

"You sure you want to do this?" Ethan asked. "You might break a nail."

She shrugged. The manicure she'd gotten for the wedding was already chipped. "This is my family business now. Might as well pitch in. Plus, I know Thomas needs to move his business as soon as he can, since he's losing his current location. I also know things are a little nuts with trying to get all four units ready."

He nodded. "That much is true. Although the

salon and bakery are both nearly done. Putting the extra crew of guys on the salon made a huge difference."

Roxie laughed. "Yeah, my mom didn't spare any expense with that. It scares me to think how spoiled Trina might be if my mom had come into money sooner in her life."

Ethan grinned. "I have a hard time imagining Trina as spoiled."

"Same here."

Ethan handed her a pair of safety glasses. "Not your usual accessory, I know, but I'd like you to wear them all the same."

She put the clear plastic glasses on. "How do they look?"

"Like you should be modeling safety glasses." He winked at her. "All right, I'll bring the first sheet over and then you can hold it there while I screw it in place. Then we'll keep going until the walls are covered inside and out."

"I'm ready," Roxie said. "If I'm not doing something right, just tell me. You won't hurt my feelings."

They got to work. Ethan carried a sheet of drywall over, put it in place, then Roxie kept it there. He used a drill to screw the sheet in at regular intervals, making it look easy. She was pretty sure it wasn't.

"Why don't you use nails?" She asked.

"Because screws are more secure and less likely to pop out. Nails are cheaper, but cheaper isn't always a good thing."

She nodded. "I agree."

Ethan worked fast. Surprisingly fast, but then again, this wasn't his first attempt. As the day rolled toward noon, he paused. "You okay to keep going? Or do you want to stop for a break?"

"Let's get it done. There's only a few more sheets to go."

He looked pleased with that decision. "All right."

Three more full sheets and two smaller strips at the end of one wall and they were done. Ethan had obviously done the hardest parts, like carrying the drywall up the ladder for the top sections. She'd then gone up on another ladder right next to his to hold the drywall in place as he screwed it down.

They worked well together and he was so patient. She brushed a streak of white off her jeans. She felt like she'd learned something new today, although when she'd put her new knowledge of drywalling to use again, she had no idea.

"Let's eat," he said. "I'm starved. Gino's?"

Gino's was a pizza joint nearby. Roxie didn't think she'd ever been there. She looked down at herself. She'd worn grubby clothes today, because she knew she'd be doing hard, dirty work. And it had been. "Like this?"

Ethan laughed. "No one at Gino's is going to care how you look. Which is beautiful, by the way. You're the hottest construction worker I've ever had on my team."

She snorted. "Fine. Gino's it is. Although being sweet and saying nice things doesn't change the fact that I look like a bum." At least she'd put makeup on.

"Come on," he said. "You're not going to see anyone you know anyway."

"True." She took her safety glasses off and set them by Ethan's on the top of a large, sealed bucket, then grabbed her purse.

He drove, but Gino's was literally down the road about four minutes. Inside, they grabbed a table, which were already in high demand. Gino's was mostly a takeout place, with four large booths on one side, and four small tables on the other. A steady stream of people picking up to-go orders, lots of them blue-collar guys, filled the middle. Garlic and spices scented the air as pizzas cooked in the big ovens.

"What do you want?" Ethan asked.

She looked up at the menu, which hung over the counter and register area. "I worked too hard to eat a salad. How about the small Italian sub with everything on it?"

He nodded. "Excellent choice. Gino's makes a good one. And all the subs come with fries."

"Okay."

"What do you want to drink?"

"Diet cola."

"Be right back." He got in line to order.

Thankfully, the line moved fast, and the kitchen crew cranked the food out in remarkable time. Cold food, like their subs, took hardly any time at all.

Ethan soon returned with a red tray loaded with their lunches. He put the tray down, then her food in front of her. A red basket lined with a sheet of waxed paper held her sub and a pile of fries. He set her drink next to her sub, then put his order on his side, and returned the tray to the counter.

As soon as he sat, he took a long drink, clearly very thirsty.

She picked up her sub. His was twice the size of hers. "Did you get the same thing?"

He nodded as he squirted ketchup from the

bottle on the table into one corner of his basket by the fries. "Yes. The Italian sub is my favorite."

She took a bite and immediately realized the bread was toasted, giving it a nice crunch. The sub was delicious and for a few minutes, neither of them did anything but eat. Hard work made a person very hungry.

After a while, Ethan wiped his mouth with a paper napkin and laughed. "I was going to ask you how you like it but I think I can tell."

She grinned. She'd eaten more than half of her sub already. "It's really good. And I was really hungry."

"Wishing you'd gotten the large?"

"No, I'm all right with this. I still have fries." She'd barely touched those. They looked good, but French fries and a trim figure generally didn't go hand in hand.

Ethan, however, didn't seem to be one bit bothered by that. His were half gone.

"You come here a lot?"

He shrugged one shoulder. "It's good for a quick lunch or dinner. They have good pizza, too. If I'm over this way, yeah, I swing by."

"You've never brought me here."

He snorted. "This isn't exactly the kind of place

that reeks of romance. And besides, you're...you know."

She really didn't. "I'm what?"

He looked perplexed that he had to explain himself. He picked up a fry. "You know, fancy."

She stared at him, highly amused. "I'm fancy?"

"Well, you are. You're always dressed nice, and your hair is done and you're made up pretty. I don't see this as being your kind of place."

She could only smile. "Just because I'm fancy on the outside doesn't mean I'm fancy on the inside." She ate a fry. "I look the way I do because... I grew up poor and my mom always stressed that appearance was important when you were poor so that people didn't realize just how poor you really were."

He nodded. "Makes sense. Willie certainly takes a lot of pride in her appearance. Trina, too. But you're not poor anymore."

"No, but I'm not exactly rolling in it, either."

He took another bite of his sub and nodded. "Who is?" He swallowed his food. "I see you didn't wear your ring today."

"Because I didn't want to take a chance that something might happen to it." She reached under the neck of her T-shirt and pulled out the chain she had on to show him the ring dangling there. "But it's still close to my heart."

He smiled. "I'm going to marry you one of these days."

A little breathless ripple of joy went through her. She smiled, her brows lifting slightly. "Is that right?"

"Yep." He sat back, eyes narrowing. "And when I do, *that* ring is going to make the one on that chain look like it came from a gumball machine."

Chapter Thirty-three

*T*rina's first stop of the day was Lady M's Boutique. Her plan was to go to as many of the shops downtown as she could, handing out flyers and business cards for the salon. A lot of those shops catered to tourists, but they were owned by locals.

Walter was home by himself, so she didn't plan on being out too long. She wasn't sure how many hours he could manage before needing to go out and she didn't want him to have an accident in the house.

Once inside Lady M's, she went up to the counter to see if Lisa, the woman who'd helped Mimi find her wedding dress, was there.

She was behind the counter but on the phone. Trina stood a ways back, letting her have some privacy to finish her call.

She looked through the nearest rack of tops.

They were all pretty. And all expensive. Someday, when the shop was well established and she'd paid back her grandmother, Trina was going to shop here all the time.

"Trina, right?"

She looked up. "Yes. How did you remember me?"

Lisa smiled. "Your grandmother is a hard woman to forget. How was the wedding?"

"It was great," Trina said. "You want to see a picture? I have some on my phone."

"I'd love to."

Trina had her flyers and business cards in a tote bag slung over her shoulder, which left her hands free. She got her phone out of her purse and pulled up her photos, finding a good one to show Lisa. She turned the phone around. "Here you go. That's my Mimi and her new husband, Miguel."

Lisa smiled and nodded. "They look so good together and so happy. And your grandmother's dress was a great choice. She looks beautiful."

"She really did. Thanks for your help with all of that."

Lisa touched her heart. "It was my pleasure. Is there something else I can help you with today? I'd be happy to."

"You mentioned that you wouldn't mind knowing when my salon was open and we're really close. I have some flyers and business cards, if you think you might know anyone who'd be interested in checking us out."

"Did you do your grandmother's hair for the wedding?"

Trina nodded. "I did. And my mom's." She quickly found a photo of her mom's updo. "This was her."

Lisa leaned closer. "That's a great look."

"Thanks. My mom doesn't usually wear her hair up, but she wanted something different."

"You're good, Trina." Lisa held out her hand. "I will definitely take a flyer and you can give me a stack of business cards. I have women in here all the time who could use a new stylist. Takes some tact, but I'd be happy to steer them your way."

"Really?"

"I mean it. Good stylists are hard to come by. I might come see you myself."

"I will take such good care of you!" Trina dug in her tote bag and pulled out a flyer and a small bunch of business cards. "We should be open in a couple of weeks, if not sooner. I can call you, if you like."

"I'd love that. Have you joined the WBA?"

Trina shook her head. "I don't even know what that is."

"The Women's Business Association. It's a little like the Chamber of Commerce but not quite as big or active. Mostly we do a once-a-month luncheon and get to know one another so we can support each other's businesses. I'd be happy to have you as my guest for the next one, if you'd like to check it out."

"I'd love that. Thank you." Trina handed over the flyer and cards. "My number's right on there. Let me know when it is and I'll be there."

"Perfect." Lisa set the stack of cards near the register. "I'll be in touch."

"Great. Thanks." Trina headed out. "See you soon."

"See you soon," Lisa said.

With that success under her belt, Trina made her way down Main Street. She stopped in every single shop, even the ones she wasn't sure would welcome her flyers. It was a little intimidating to talk to all those people she didn't know, but she was more afraid of the salon failing than she was of being embarrassed.

Besides, she had Walter to think about now. She realized he wasn't the same as having a child, but he still needed taking care of and looking after. She had to provide his food and shelter, and with Mimi eventually moving into her new house, that would just leave Trina and Roxie to pay the bills.

Which they'd do. No problem. But Roxie would be working at the salon, too. Which meant it *really* had to be successful.

Around lunchtime, Trina stopped at Pepper's, a little sandwich place a block off of Main. She ordered grilled ham and cheese with fruit instead of chips, got a bottle of water, and took a seat at a table by the wall to wait for it to be ready.

So far, the day had gone all right. People had been mostly receptive, although some had been obviously uninterested. Besides Lisa, she'd had one other woman get really excited about the new salon.

But it was a little tiring to sell yourself like that. She could feel her energy was lower than usual. Maybe she just needed to eat. All she'd had for breakfast had been some toast and scrambled eggs.

Weirdly, part of her mood was because she missed Walter. Which was crazy, she realized that, but all the same, she missed his company. She'd thought about bringing him, but not everyone would appreciate a dog in their store. And he might have gotten tired out by so much walking.

What would she have done with him then? She couldn't leave him in the car. No, keeping him at home had been the right move.

"Number thirty-one," the guy behind the counter called out.

That was her. She got up and got her food. Before she ate, she said a little prayer that her afternoon would be even better. She took a bite of her sandwich. As she chewed, she looked up and saw a bulletin board on the wall across from her.

There were a few business cards and For Sale ads tacked to it. Also ads for a pet sitter and a seamstress.

When she finished her lunch, she went back to the counter and asked if she could put a flyer on the bulletin board. The guy said sure.

Now she was extra happy she'd stopped at Pepper's for lunch. She put a flyer up, then tacked a couple of business cards under it. She gave the guy a wave. "Thanks again. Great sandwich!"

He waved back. "Thank you."

She headed out to visit all the shops on the other side of Main Street.

By the time she got home, her feet hurt but her flyers were gone. She'd handed out quite a few business cards, too. All in all, a good day. No telling what would come of it, but at least three people besides Lisa had mentioned wanting to check the salon out.

She let herself into the beach house. "Walter, I'm home."

He came running from the living room. She scooped him up and kissed his face. "Hi, baby. Did you miss me?" From the amount of licking he was doing, she guessed yes. Laughing, she carried him back to the living room and collapsed on the couch.

She couldn't stay there, though. Walter needed to go out. And after being home by himself for so long, he deserved a walk.

"All right, Walter. Give me a second to change, then we'll hit the beach." She went to her room with Walter following her and changed into shorts, a T-shirt and flipflops. She put her sunglasses on, attached his leash, and down they went.

He lifted his leg to pee as soon as he hit grass.

"Better?" Trina asked. "Sorry I had to leave you alone for so long." Although she'd thought her mom and grandmother would be back by now. Well, maybe not her mom, but Mimi at least.

She looked toward Miguel's house. Maybe her grandmother was back, but just at Miguel's. Trina wasn't sure.

Walter was sniffing around but seemed to be

done with whatever business he had to do, so Trina called to him as she backed toward the water. "Come on, baby. Let's go down to the beach and you can really stretch your legs."

At the sound of her voice, he looked up from the rock he was smelling and came after her.

She wasn't sure how long of a walk they were going on, but she knew he needed it. She figured she'd go as long as he seemed interested.

That took them quite a ways down the beach. On the way back to the house, she spotted two familiar figures coming toward them. She grinned. "Hi, Jules and Toby!"

Toby was already tugging at the leash to get closer. Jules waved as she broke into a little run. "Hi, Trina. Hi, Walter."

The two dogs hadn't met yet, so Trina kept a careful grip on the leash, just in case. She didn't think either dog would react badly, but she didn't want to take any chances, either. Fortunately, they seemed to like each other. Trina shook her head. "That's an awful lot of butt sniffing."

Jules laughed. "It's the handshake of the dog world."

Trina chuckled. "I'm just learning all of this."

"How's he doing? Settled in?"

Trina nodded. "He's doing great. He's got his spot on the couch where he likes to sleep. At night, he's on the bed with me."

"Same as Toby," Jules said. "Spoiled. Which is exactly what all dogs should be."

Trina looked at Walter. "I couldn't agree more."

Chapter Thirty-four

*K*at got to Alex's about twenty minutes after she'd left her office. She was tired, but also energized knowing she was going to hang out with him. It was a weird combination. At least they wouldn't be doing anything stressful. At most, after dinner they might head to the beach for a walk, but more likely, they'd just hang out and watch a movie.

She was good with either plan, though sitting on the couch sounded pretty good. She laughed at her unmotivated self. A walk on the beach would be better for both of them. Chances were good Alex hadn't gotten a lot of exercise today.

She'd managed fifteen minutes on the treadmill at the office before she'd eaten her lunch. Eloise was right about it helping to manage the stress of the job.

Kat could see time on the treadmill becoming a necessary part of her day.

She pulled into the parking lot of Alex's apartment complex and found a spot near his building. She grabbed her bag from her backseat, which contained the clothes she'd brought to change into, and went to his door.

He opened it as she arrived, letting her know he'd been waiting. He was in his standard outfit these days of gym shorts and no shirt, just the sling holding his arm in place so his shoulder could heal. Not a lot of guys could pull that look off, but Alex did. And he did it well.

She was so happy to see him. "Hiya. How was your day?"

"Hiya," he said back. "It was good. Guess what?"

"I have no idea." She couldn't imagine.

"I'm making dinner." He stepped out of the way to let her in.

"You are? I thought I was supposed to be doing the cooking." She walked in, the aromas in the apartment teasing her senses. She honestly had no idea what his capabilities were in the kitchen. At the very least, it would be interesting.

"I got bored so I went grocery shopping and got the idea."

"Smells good. What are you making?"

He smiled proudly. "Honey-soy glazed salmon with steamed broccoli and sesame rice."

She blinked at him. "Really?"

He laughed. "Yes, really. I can cook."

"I can't believe you went to the store. You're supposed to be resting."

He shot her a look. "I've done plenty of that."

"Well, I'm impressed."

"I hope you still feel that way after you taste it."

She did, too, but even if it wasn't good, she wasn't going to tell him that. He'd obviously gone to a lot of effort. "What can I do to help?"

"Nothing. I've had all day to get ready, so there really isn't anything for you to do."

"Then I'll go change out of my work clothes."

"See you at the table."

She went into the bathroom and swapped her white denim skirt, lavender print blouse, and white sandals for heather gray capri leggings, a Chauncey's Surf Shop T-shirt, and flipflops. Much more comfortable. She folded her work clothes and tucked them into the bag with her sandals, then rejoined Alex.

He was putting a plate down on the table. It looked *good*. Like practically restaurant good. The salmon filet had a gorgeous shiny glaze, the broccoli was bright green, and the rice was flecked with seasonings and black sesame seeds.

"Wow."

His smile returned. "Be right back with my plate, then we can see if it's really worth that."

She sat down. There was a glass of water with ice at both places and paper towels folded in half for napkins under the silverware.

He came back and set his plate in front of his chair, then took his seat.

"It looks fantastic."

"Well, dig in and tell me what you think."

She started with the salmon. It was perfectly cooked so that it flaked away when she dug her fork in. The glaze was the right mix of sweet and savory and complimented the fish beautifully. "It's delicious."

She tried the rice next. The seasonings were just right. Even the broccoli tasted good. Not overdone or mushy the way steamed veggies could get. "You have really been hiding your light under a bushel. I had no idea you could cook like this."

A coy expression came over his face. "It wasn't that much work."

She found that hard to believe. "It was *some* work."

"Publix helped." He sipped his water. "The rice came in a box, the broccoli in a microwavable bag, and the salmon was from the grab-and-go ready-to-cook section. The sauce was included. All I had to do was cook everything according to the directions."

"But you did it. And you did it really well. And you went to a lot of work to do this. I mean, you still did it all with one arm in a sling." She pointed at his arm with her fork. "I'm no less impressed because Publix helped. This is a great meal."

"Thanks."

"How was the rest of your day?"

"Pretty good. I'm really glad you're here. I am so bored of being by myself. I went over to the firehouse last night to hang out and see everyone. Trina brought her new dog over, so that was nice. But a half hour after she left, the alarm went off and everyone had to dispatch." He sighed. "I went home. No point hanging out by myself."

"I'm sorry. I know having to rest is driving you nuts. Even if it is for your own good. Do you want to walk to the beach and hang out there when we're done?"

He shook his head. "No, that's okay. Seeing the

water and not being able to go in kind of sucks. I'm all right just to hang around here and watch some TV."

She felt for him. He was such an active guy. "Maybe we can find a movie."

He smiled, nodding. "I'm just glad to have company. You especially. I don't really want to snuggle on the couch with Miles."

She laughed louder than she'd intended. "I'm sure Trina would be glad to hear that."

He snorted.

"Hey. What if we went out for ice cream after this? I'll drive. It would be something to do. After that, we can come back and watch a movie."

"Yeah, that would be all right. You'll have to help me get a shirt on."

"I can do that."

He asked about her job while they ate, so she filled him in. When they finished dinner, Kat made Alex sit while she cleaned up. She figured he'd done enough. Once that was all taken care of, she drove them to Beach Freeze, the little ice cream shack that wasn't too far from the library. There was quite a line, but they had nothing else to do anyway.

When they finally got their cones, Alex had rocky road while Kat went with peach cobbler. They sat at one of the picnic tables, both of them on one side, and people-watched while they ate their dessert.

It was interesting to see what flavors people picked. A lot had soft serve, which Kat liked, too, but Beach Freeze offered more varieties in the hard-packed ice cream. And the lure of peach cobbler had been too great to pass up.

"This is really good. Maybe the best ice cream I've ever had," Kat said, cutting her eyes at him. "Better than yours."

He laughed. "You don't know that."

"Yes, I do. Nothing could be better than this."

He lifted his chin. "Lemme see."

She held out her cone for him to take a bite.

He did, then nodded. "It is really good. Totally tastes like peach cobbler. But definitely not as good as rocky road. The chocolate chunks and marsh-mallow pieces alone make mine better."

"Doubtful."

He snorted and offered his cone to her. "Try it."

She took a bite. It was delicious, but she wasn't about to admit that. "Okay, it's good. But the peach cobbler is still better. I mean, it tastes like fresh peaches. And you can actually taste the cobbler part.

Sorry, my choice is superior." She laughed even as she said it.

He was grinning and she was so glad. She'd needed this. He probably had, too, but her heart was light just from being near him, the weight of her job forgotten.

He nudged her with his elbow. "Thanks."

"For what?"

"Coming over. Making me get out of the house. Forcing me to eat ice cream."

"Forcing?"

He winked. "I love you, Kat Thompson."

"You'd better," she said, nudging him back. "I'm wearing your ring."

Chapter Thirty-five

Claire inhaled the sharp tang of bitter orange that lingered in the air from all the zesting and juicing she'd done. It was a beautiful smell. It surprised her that no one had turned it into a candle yet.

She'd made six dozen fat chocolate chip cookies, most of which had gone into the freezer as dough, and eight sour orange pies. Not a lot of pies, considering how many she could have made, but she didn't want to overdo it.

Her main goal had been to make enough to fill part of the cold case so that when the *Gulf Gazette* came to get pictures, she'd have something for them to photograph. And taste. She knew Conrad had had the pie already, because she'd made him one. But the photographer wouldn't have.

The way she figured it, the more people who tried the pie and could spread the word about how good it was, the better.

Once the photos were done, the seven remaining whole pies would go to Jesse at the Dolphin Club so he could start offering them to his customers. It was a little nerve-wracking to know her food would soon be available for the public to taste. Even before the bakery was officially open.

Her fingers were crossed that the pies did well for Jesse. It pleased her to know that the bakery's first official sale, to him, was something she was responsible for.

Technically, Jules was truly responsible for it. She'd taken the pie to the club for Jesse to try. But Claire was taking some of the credit for making the pie.

It was a good feeling to know that she'd contributed in that way.

She wiped the last counter down and took a look to see if there was anything else that needed to be cleaned before she left.

Danny came into the kitchen. "It smells so good in here. I can't imagine what it's going to be like when we're actually open."

She smiled. "We'll probably get used to it after a while. Which is a mixed blessing. There's nothing like the smell of fresh baked goods, but I'll be less tempted once the smell doesn't affect me as much."

"True." He raked a hand through his hair. He looked a little tired. "You done for the day? Say yes, because otherwise you're doing too much."

"Yes, I'm done." At least she thought she was. "I was just making sure I'd cleaned everything that needed to be cleaned. I don't have a routine for this kitchen yet, the way I do for the one at the beach house."

"You'll get there."

"Are you finished out front?"

He nodded. "We are basically good to go. At this point, we just need our final inspection and we're ready."

"When is that happening?"

"Next week." He grinned. "Then we can do our soft opening and before you know it, we'll be celebrating our one-year anniversary."

That made her laugh. "I hope it doesn't go by quite that fast."

"We start interviews tomorrow. I've got ten of them lined up."

"Ten?" Claire stared at him. That seemed like a

lot. "Seriously?"

"Yep. You ready? Because four of them are for bakers, so those will be up to you. If we can get two good bakers and three counter people, we should be in good shape. At least to start with. Hopefully, we get busy and need to hire more."

"I'm ready. I'm glad I had a chance to work here today. Gives me a real sense of what's required to produce in a kitchen like this."

"Excellent. Now, how about we go home?"

"I might be too tired to eat. Not really, but I might eat lying down."

He laughed. "I was thinking about eating pizza in the hot tub. I'm not even kidding. I could use the relaxation."

She let out a little groan as she put her hands on her lower back and stretched. "That actually sounds pretty good, considering how I feel. Which reminds me—you know what I realized we need in here today?"

He looked around. "What's that?"

"Anti-fatigue mats." She moved her hands to her hips. "Standing on this hard concrete all day is not going to work."

He slapped his hand against his forehead. "That's on me. Sorry. I completely forgot to order them. Which I will do tonight, I promise. In the meantime, I think we have some extras at one of the shops. I'll text Ivelisse. She'll know. If so, I can run over and get them in the morning."

"That would be great." Claire headed toward the office to get her purse. She grabbed it, then flipped the light off and came back out. "So...pizza at your place?"

The twinkle in his eyes warmed her insides. "Only if we're eating it in the hot tub."

"I'm in. So long as the pizza is thin crust and includes at least one veggie. That isn't onions."

"Mushroom and sausage okay?"

"Perfect. See you in half an hour?"

He nodded. "I'll try to still be awake."

"Yeah, I know what you mean." She chuckled as they walked out together, their cars parked side by side.

"Thanks for all your hard work today. And the day before and the day before that and you know."

"You're welcome. And thank you. You made this happen."

"*We* made this happen." He kissed her before opening her car door for her. "See you in half an hour."

She nodded. "Don't forget the pizza."

She actually made it to his place in twenty-eight minutes, not that she was counting. She wore her favorite blue flowered tankini with a white coverup over it. Her stomach was rumbling and while pizza wasn't carb free, she was past caring. She'd burned some serious calories in that kitchen today.

In the last couple of days, really. They'd both been working like dogs. Well, not dogs like Toby. She smiled. That lazy thing did nothing but lay around and look cute, which he was very good at.

Instead of going to Danny's front door, Claire cut across the property line and took a seat by his pool, which the hot tub was connected to. The lights and jets were already on, bubbling away. The lights under the house were on, too, giving everything a romantic glow.

Not that she thought anything too romantic was about to happen. They were both tired from the day and ready to eat. The only thing she'd brought with her was her phone and a twenty-dollar bill, which she planned to give him as her contribution to their dinner.

I'm here, she texted him.

On my way down, he answered. *Water or diet ginger beer?*

DGB She grinned at her abbreviation.

He responded with a thumbs-up.

A couple of minutes later, he came out of the house and down the back steps. "Pizza should be here in another ten or fifteen minutes." He had swim trunks on with an unbuttoned shirt and a little cooler in one hand. She knew that held the ginger beer.

He took the chair beside her and set the cooler on his lap so he could open it. He took the top off the first bottle and handed it to her.

She took the bottle. "Thanks. Are your dad and Willie here? Do they want to join us? I don't mind." She really didn't. They were both good company.

"No, they're at Willie's tonight." He opened a ginger beer for himself. "Do you want to get in now or wait until the pizza arrives?"

"Up to you. You're the one who'll have to get out to get the pizza."

"Then I'm getting in. My old bones need to soak as long as possible."

She reached into the pocket of her coverup and got the twenty-dollar bill out. "Before I forget."

He made a face. "What's that for?"

"My half of dinner."

He rolled his eyes like she was being silly. "Put that away."

She laughed softly and pushed it toward him. "Danny, you can't always buy."

"Sure I can." He ignored the proffered bill, stood up, and took his shirt off.

Which almost made her forget about the money. She cleared her throat and made herself focus. "Come on, take it."

"Nope."

"So stubborn," she muttered. Maybe she could stick it in the front pocket of his shirt when he went to get the pizza. Unless he put it back on.

"I heard that." He went down the steps of the hot tub, eyes closing as he sank into the water.

She shed her coverup and joined him. The water was *hot* but felt really good as she got used to it. She eased in, and sat next to him, both of them facing the beach. The sun was close to setting, the sky streaked with pink and orange. "This is heavenly."

He nodded and lifted one dripping arm to put it around her and draw her closer. "Yes, it is."

The pizza arrived not long after. Danny stood up and waved at the guy when he parked and got out of his car. "Hey! We're over here!"

The guy walked underneath the house to reach them at the pool. "Evening, folks. One sausage and mushroom?"

"Evening. That's us." Danny climbed out, gave the man a couple of bills to cover the food and the tip, then, pizza box in hand, walked back down the steps. He stayed standing, setting the box on the decking that surrounded the hot tub.

Claire got up and helped herself to a slice after he opened the box. The savory aroma and the sight of the melted cheese made her stomach rumble again. "I am starving and this smells incredible."

They both sat back down with their slices and ate in silence. The pizza tasted like the best Claire had ever had. Probably because she was so hungry, but good was good. Before long, they were each on slice number two.

Claire stopped there, although she could have had another. Danny did. While he ate, she drank her ginger beer. "I'm a little nervous about the interviews tomorrow, but I think I'll be all right. Are you sure you don't want to do them with me?"

"Do you want me to?"

"Yes and no." She laughed. "How's that for helpful?" She sighed. "I've never interviewed anyone before."

He smiled and ate another bite of his quickly disappearing third slice. "It's not that hard. You have to like the person. You're the one who's going to be working with them on a daily basis. You're going to be their boss. Same for the front of the house people, but I figured I could handle that. Ideally, you'd be a part of all the interviews."

"I'm sure whoever you hire will be great. You staffed the popcorn stores without a problem."

"Ivelisse did some of that hiring." He looked over at her. "I promise, you'll do fine. Remember, you're the boss. If anyone should be intimidated by the process, it's the interviewee, not you. Plus, I have a list of questions you can ask."

She smiled. "Those will help, but you're right. I do need to remember that. I've never been a boss before. That's kind of amazing."

"You've earned it." He ate the last of his pizza, crust and all. "That was good. I could eat another slice but I'd regret it later. If only I had the same metabolism I had at twenty."

"Must have been nice." She frowned, thinking about her figure at twenty. "I'm not sure mine was ever that great. I could have had a third piece, too, but same thing. I knew I'd be unhappy about it afterwards."

He sighed. "Getting old is not for the faint-hearted, is it?"

"No, it is not." She moved closer to him, causing

a ripple in the water. It quickly disappeared into the froth and foam of the bubbles. "Helps to have someone to get old with, though."

He kissed her temple. "Yes, it does."

Chapter Thirty-six

*A*fter waking up, Willie and Miguel had come out to the couch. She yawned as she sat next to him. When they were at her house, they'd start taking the couch so they could sit side by side. That meant Trina had to sit in Willie's usual spot, which was the first chair, and Roxie was in the second chair where she normally sat all the time.

At least Trina and Roxie would have been in the chairs, if they'd been in the house. Both of them had gone out for a walk after starting the coffee. Which was what Willie and Miguel were currently waiting on. They had the television turned to the local morning show. As usual, it was mostly nonsense.

Willie glanced toward the beach. Trina had taken Walter with her, so Willie imagined she'd be back sooner than Roxie, who did a whole workout thing besides the walking.

As the weather report ended, Miguel patted Willie's leg. "Today's the day."

"For what?"

"The results of the test."

"Oh, that. I know." Willie gave herself a little shake. "I hope it's good news."

"Which would be what?"

She pursed her lips. "I don't know." The coffee machine dripped out the last few drops and exhaled a sigh of steam. "Coffee's done. I'll get it."

"Thank you, my love."

She fixed two cups and brought them back over. As she was sitting down, Trina came in through the sliders, Walter in her arms. "He needs rinsing off, since he ran into the water before I could stop him. The crazy thing. He's all sandy." She laughed and kissed his head. "Aren't you, you naughty boy?"

Walter, tongue out, looked rather pleased with his adventure.

Miguel got up. "I'll close the doors for you."

"Thanks." Trina headed to her room. "I guess he's getting a bath before I get my coffee."

"Don't worry, there's plenty," Willie said.

Trina stopped at the entrance to the reading nook that connected the living area with the bedrooms and foyer. "I hope human shampoo is okay to use on dogs. I didn't buy any for him. I'll have to get some."

"I'm sure it'll be all right one time," Willie said. How different could dog hair be from human hair?

The morning show was on its last guest when Trina came back out, Walter wrapped in a beach towel and looking less happy than when they'd returned from the walk.

Trina put Walter down in the towel on Willie's chair, then fixed herself a cup of coffee and came back. She settled in next to him, with Walter half on her lap and half on the chair cushion. She'd scooched over so they could share.

"You all right like that, my girl?" Willie asked.

Trina nodded. "We're good, Mimi. But I'm going to need some breakfast soon. Have you guys eaten?"

Willie shook her head. "Not yet."

Miguel looked over. "What would you like? An omelet? I can do that. I'm good at omelets."

Trina shook her head. "I can make my own breakfast, you don't have to do that."

Miguel got up and bowed slightly. "I want to. I would be happy to. Please, let me." He looked at Willie. "What kind of omelet for you? Chorizo with a little Jack cheese?"

"Mmm," Willie said. "Sounds good."

"Do we have chorizo?" Trina asked.

Miguel smiled. "We do, since your grandmother and I went grocery shopping. How about you? Want to try one?"

"Sure," Trina said. "Thank you. It's very kind."

Miguel went straight to the kitchen and got breakfast underway, pulling things from the fridge and getting pans out.

He made Willie proud with the way he wanted to take care of them. He was such a sweet, wonderful man. "You want me to get the toast started?"

"No, I can do it," he said. "You just drink your coffee and relax." He started cracking eggs into a bowl. Once that was done, he got the bread out and filled the toaster slots, but didn't push the bread down yet.

Roxie came in, a sheen of sweat covering her skin. "Morning, all." She looked toward the kitchen. "Is there coffee left?"

"There is," Miguel answered her. "And once you get yours, I'll start another pot."

"Be warned," Willie said. "He makes it strong."

Roxie smiled. "I don't mind strong coffee, but I won't be ready for another cup until I've finished my workout and had my shower." She got herself a cup and made her coffee the way she liked it. "Smells good, whatever you're making."

"Chorizo omelets. Would you like one?"

She shook her head. "I'm going to have a protein shake later."

Trina glanced at Roxie. "Ma, you could have that for lunch. When do you get anyone offering to make you a fancy omelet?"

Roxie sipped her coffee. "I suppose that's true." She looked at what Miguel was doing. "It's a lot of work to make omelets for this many people."

"Nonsense," he said as he whipped the eggs in the bowl. "I'll have it ready for you by the time you're out of the shower."

"Yeah?"

"I will." He nodded, adding the eggs to the first frying pan.

"All right, you talked me into it. Back in a bit!"

Coffee in hand, she headed for the bedroom.

Miguel pushed the lever to lower the bread into the toaster and got a second frying pan out, then he quickly cracked some more eggs into the bowl.

Willie smiled. She loved all this family around her, all the activity. It would be a lot quieter when it was just her and Miguel at their new house, but that would be all right, too. They'd have slow, leisurely mornings together, sitting by the water, maybe watching the dolphins, and enjoying each other's company.

Nothing wrong with that.

"You okay, Mimi?" Trina asked. "You looked far away for a second there."

She laughed. "Old age does that to you, my girl. Just thinking about what mornings will be like at the new house. Quieter, that's for sure."

Trina smiled. "Not on the mornings that Walter and I stop by for coffee. Maybe even breakfast if we get there early enough."

"That would be fantastic." Willie meant it, too. Seeing her granddaughter any time of the week would be good. "Tell you what. You let me know what kind of dog food he likes, and I'll keep some on hand for him. Then he can have breakfast with us."

Trina smiled. "That's nice of you." She ruffled the fur on Walter's head. He closed his eyes. "I'm glad it won't be for a while yet. That you're moving out, I mean. I like having you and Miguel around."

Still working on omelets, Miguel smiled. Willie nodded. "We like being around."

"Yes, we do." Miguel tipped the first omelet onto a plate. "Who wants the first one?"

"You take it, Trina," Willie said. "Miguel and I

will eat last so we can eat together. Besides, you and your mom have work to get to."

"Okay," Trina said. "I do plan to go out and visit more businesses today to tell them about the salon."

Miguel brought her the omelet along with a slice of buttered toast. "Here you go."

"Thank you, that looks great," Trina said. Walter seemed to think so, too.

Willie's phone went off. She glanced at the number and quickly got up. "I'll take this out on the porch. Be right back."

She stepped outside. "Hello?"

"Mrs. Rojas?"

"Yes."

"Good morning. This is Gabe Rodriguez. I have the results of the lab tests you ordered."

"Good morning." She sucked in air, her chest oddly tight. She took a seat on the couch, her gaze focused on the bands of blue sky and darker blue water before her, but she wasn't really seeing them. "Go ahead. I'm listening."

"As you know, we ran the half-sibling DNA test on the samples you provided. There are enough markers present to indicate the two samples are paternally related. In layman's terms, they have the same father."

She exhaled. "Okay. That's what I wanted to know. Thank you."

"I'll be mailing you the paperwork that confirms this, but Miguel said you'd want to know immediately, so that's why I called."

"And I appreciate it. Thanks again."

"You're welcome. Please let me know if there's anything else I can do for you. Have a good day."

"You, too." Willie hung up and rested her phone on her lap. Her gaze stayed straight ahead.

Bryan really was Nico's father. That was that. And there was no need to tell anyone anything about it.

Chapter Thirty-seven

*M*argo had no idea what to expect from Dinah, but Conrad had told her in an early text that it was fine to work at his house this morning.

Margo had eaten a leisurely breakfast of scrambled eggs, fruit, and toast, taking her time in case he texted back to say they needed to go to the library instead. No such text had come in, however, so she'd gotten herself ready, packed up her things, and driven over.

Dinah's car was still in the driveway. Margo frowned. That didn't seem like a good sign.

She knocked on the door and Conrad answered shortly, a curious smile on his face. "Good morning. Come in."

"Morning." She accepted his kiss on her cheek. "What's going on?"

"What makes you think something's going on?" But there was a hitch in his voice that told her she'd guessed correctly.

"You're a terrible liar."

"I haven't lied about anything."

"Then I'd say you're terrible at pretending everything's fine, but I really have no idea what you're up to."

"*I'm* not up to anything." He gestured toward the kitchen. "Coffee?"

"Yes, please."

He led the way. Dinah was at the table, drinking coffee and eating a bowl of cereal. "Morning, Margo."

Margo did her best to stay positive. "Morning, Dinah. How are you?"

"I'm really good. Have a seat."

The woman sounded oddly pleasant. Margo wasn't sure she trusted that. Dinah was too much of a game player. Too liable to shift into harpy mode at the drop of a hat. Cautiously, Margo sat on the other side of the table and waited for the other shoe to drop.

Conrad brought her a cup of coffee. "Can I get you anything else?"

"No, this is fine. Thank you." Margo set her purse and laptop down on the other chair, then took a sip. "Good coffee."

"Thanks." Conrad got himself a cup of coffee and joined them, taking the seat between the two women.

An odd sense of the unknown thickened the air like smoke. Margo sipped her coffee as Dinah ate the last bite of her breakfast.

She put her spoon down in her bowl and looked at Margo. "I'm sorry for everything I've done to you and Conrad since I've been here. Neither of you deserved it. And it was all born out of my own insecurities."

Margo blinked but said nothing.

Dinah stared into the small puddle of milk left in her bowl. "I haven't had an easy life. I don't mean that to be an excuse. More of an explanation, really." She glanced at her brother. "I know Connie told you about it some."

"He did," Margo said softly, sensing real honesty in Dinah.

Dinah pushed the bowl away. "I thought a lot about what you said yesterday. About second chances and increasing my circle of friends. I don't have a lot of those. As you probably guessed." Her mouth bent in a quick, uncertain smile, then flattened out again.

"You sacrificed a lot of your life to take care of your father," Margo said. "I'm sure that didn't leave you much time for socializing."

Dinah nodded, still without making eye contact. "I didn't have to give him as much of my time and attention as I did, but I was...scared of life. And taking care of him was an easy way to avoid it." She exhaled and seemed on the verge of tears. Not a breakdown, exactly, but the kind of resolved unhappiness that came with the self-realization that her life was exactly what she'd made it.

"I did a lot of that, too, after my second husband died," Margo confessed. "Life seemed completely unjust and full of sorrow. I didn't want anything to do with it, so I retreated into my grief. I let it define me."

Dinah finally looked up. "How did you get out of it?"

"Willie helped me." Margo laughed. "Now there is a woman who lives life by her own rules."

"She's the one who just got married? The wedding we went to."

"That's her. And that's a perfect example of what I mean. She does what she wants, doesn't let anything, including her age, hold her back. She seems perpetually happy, and I think she truly is. She helped me understand that happiness is a choice, and that life is meant to be lived."

Dinah shook her head. "I don't know how to do that. But I'd like to learn. I want to be happy."

"That's great." Margo wasn't sure what that meant for Dinah, but she was thrilled that Conrad's sister had made such a big decision.

"I'm going to do what you said. I'm going to move here."

Margo blinked in surprise. "You are?"

"Yes," Dinah said. "I'm going to put my house up for sale when I get back and while that's happening, I'm going to get rid of whatever I don't need so that my move here is as easy as it can be."

Conrad, who'd said nothing until now, finally spoke. "She's going to stay here with me if she can't find a condo right away."

"But I won't be a problem," Dinah quickly added. "I want you two to be happy. You're good for my brother, Margo. I know that. I knew it before I got here. I think that was why I was so bothered by it." She closed her eyes for a moment. "I'm over that, I promise."

Margo smiled at Conrad as he picked up his coffee. "He's very good for me, too."

He winked at her while he took a sip.

With a smile, Dinah patted Conrad's hand. "You really should just ask her to marry you and get on with it."

He almost spit his coffee out. "Dinah."

"What?" she said. She looked at Margo. "You just used Willie and her marriage as an example. What's holding you two back?"

"I..." Margo thought hard for the right words. "We're still in the very early stages of our relationship."

Dinah's brow furrowed. "Had Willie been seeing Miguel for that much longer?"

"No, but—"

Conrad cleared his throat and interrupted. "Margo's not ready for that level of commitment and that's fine."

Margo looked at him. "*I'm* not ready?"

He seemed confused by her words. "Is that not right?"

"Are you saying you *are* ready?" She didn't believe that was true.

He made his usual thinking face, brows pulled

together, eyes narrowed slightly as he appeared to study the question and her at the same time. "I'd marry you tomorrow if that's what you wanted."

"Do you mean that?" Margo studied him right back. That was not the answer she'd expected.

Dinah grinned and clapped her hands. "Does that mean—"

Margo put her hand up, palm flat toward Dinah. "Hold your horses." She addressed Conrad again. "Are you serious?"

He nodded. "As much as I've ever been about anything." A pensive light filled his gaze. "You want to get hitched?"

Dinah sucked in an audible breath, but didn't say anything, her fists in front of her mouth.

Margo stared at him. "'Hitched' is not a word I would use."

"No, it's not, is it?" One side of Conrad's mouth quirked up. "Margo Bloom, would you do me the honor of becoming my wife?"

A smirk bent her mouth, giving away nothing of her elevated pulse or the flutter in her stomach. "Well, since you put it that way...All right."

Chapter Thirty-eight

*T*oday was taping and mudding of the drywall, something Roxie couldn't really help Ethan with, so she'd moved on to the storefront that was going to be the dog groomers. It needed a *lot* of cleaning out before the remodeling could begin.

Previously, it had housed a touristy knickknack, T-shirt, and jewelry shop. An odd combination, but maybe they'd done whatever they could to make ends meet. Whatever the situation, the tenants had defaulted on their rent and gotten out fast. That was all according to what Ethan had told her.

They'd left the place a mess of boxes, broken merchandise, dangling shelves, and partially dismantled racks. On one side there was a long counter area that had once been glass on top and in the front, probably where they'd displayed the jewelry, she imagined. The glass was fractured, and the pale blue velvet lining was covered in a layer of dust. A couple of old tags remained, along with a tray that would have held rings.

Sad, really.

Just as sad as the junk littering the shop everywhere she looked. Ethan had said it was too much work for her, and she understood why he'd think that, but she disagreed. This was right up her alley. She liked cleaning and didn't mind getting dirty, especially when the job needed doing, like this one.

Dressed in jeans, an old T-shirt, her hair pulled back through a ballcap, and the safety glasses that Ethan insisted she wear in place, she stood in the middle of what had once been the main retail area and took a look around, trying to figure out where to start.

There was a slight mustiness to the air. Enough that it tickled her nose. She propped the front door open, then went to the back door and did the same to get fresh air flowing through. She'd need the back door open anyway to make getting to the dumpster easier.

She found a big empty box and decided to use it as her trashcan. She pulled on the gloves that Ethan had also insisted she wear. As she slipped her hands into them, she smiled. She'd expected them to be big on her, thinking they were an extra pair of his.

Instead, they fit great. They were a little stiff, too. Because they were new. He'd bought them for her. That had to be what he'd done. She shook her head. That man.

She decided to start at the front of the store and work her way around. That was the plan, anyway. She began by filling the box with old copies of some of the tourist guides available for free around town. These were in a pile by the front door, like they'd been dumped off the rack they'd been on. Even if they'd been pristine, which they weren't, there was no point in saving them. They were old and out of date.

Crumpled newspaper, probably once used to wrap fragile items, went in the box, too. She hadn't made it a quarter of the way through the front of the right side before the box was full. She hefted it and carried it out to the dumpster.

She made that trip over and over, carrying box after box of what was basically garbage the previous tenants hadn't bothered to throw away. Damaged knickknacks. Ripped or stained T-shirts. Cracked sunglasses. Expired bottles of suntan lotion. Diamond Beach snow globes with no water in them.

Or no globe. Faded postcards. Sticky, melted lip balms, bathing suits with rotted elastic, broken souvenir mugs and shot glasses.

More junk than any tourist could ever want.

Roxie was glad a dog groomer was moving in and not another shop like what had been here. Shops like this only cheapened the place and there were already several of them closer to the beach.

She hoped they stayed there.

Already sweating, she took a break, wishing she'd brought a drink with her. She hadn't been thinking about it when she'd left the house this morning. It would have been easy to fill a travel bottle with ice water, but it hadn't occurred to her.

She left her trash box and went to see what the rest of the shop looked like. There was an office, a bathroom, and a small storeroom.

The office held a rickety metal desk and a rolling chair that was missing two wheels. Stacks of paper littered the desk, as did an old phone book, a handful of corroded batteries, and a small box filled with more papers.

Two shelves lined the wall across from the door. More tourist guides and a big pile of old T-shirts. She wondered if they'd be useful for dusting. She grabbed the pile to have a look and knocked loose a small box with a few yellowed envelopes in it.

She dropped the T-shirts on the desk to retrieve the box. There were three envelopes in it. The front of each envelope, which were roughly three by five inches, was printed with a form that had the shop's name and address, then a place for a customer's name and address, then a description of work to be done.

The forms were all filled out, but the information was hard to read, because at some point, they'd gotten wet, causing the ink to bleed and distort the letters.

All three of the envelopes had some bulk to them. Meaning they had something inside. She sat in the wobbly chair and opened the first envelope. The flap wasn't sealed, just tucked into the envelope.

She dumped the contents onto the desk. A chain of gold links, one of them broken. Looked like real gold, too. She turned the envelope over to study what had been written on it. As best she could tell, the single word written in the Work To Be Done section said "repair" in hastily scrawled writing.

Most of the name and address of the customer weren't readable but she was able to pick out the abbreviation for Georgia and the name Darla or

Darcy. Had she been on vacation in Diamond Beach, broken her necklace and brought it here to be repaired? If so, that hadn't worked out very well for her.

The phone number was still legible. Roxie called it, but the number was no longer in service. Didn't mean she couldn't try to track the person down, but it would take a little more work.

She moved on to the second envelope. This one contained a pretty little amethyst and diamond ring, not to be repaired but to be resized. She tried it on her pinky. It was cute. No doubt whoever dropped it off would want it back. She would, if it had belonged to her.

The last envelope had a little more weight to it. She opened it, then emptied the contents into her palm. A strand of lustrous white pearls slipped out, along with one single pearl. Each one was about the size of a pea. The necklace had a gold clasp with a tiny diamond set in it, but the silk knotted between the pearls was dirty and frayed in a few places, but worse, the strand was broken near the center. Obviously where the single pearl had come from.

She turned the envelope over. The repair instructions simply read "restring."

Who on Earth would have left such a necklace

here? Roxie wasn't an expert on pearls, but these looked old and genuine. Like something that might even be a family heirloom. She couldn't imagine entrusting such a thing to this shop, but someone had. Probably a tourist, hoping to get the necklace fixed before they went home.

She studied the name and address. They were almost impossible to make out. She put the pearls back in the envelope and then returned the envelope to the box with the other two. She had to find a way to get these things back to their original owners if at all possible.

She didn't want to leave them here. She supposed technically these things now belonged to Willie, since she'd bought the property lock, stock, and barrel. Roxie made a mental note to ask Ethan about that. Even if that was true, Roxie knew her mom. She'd want the jewelry returned to its rightful owners.

Roxie got her keys and took the envelopes out to her car, where she put them in the glove box for safekeeping. She didn't know how she was going to track the owners down, but she was definitely going to give it a shot.

Chapter Thirty-nine

*A*nother long day of rehearsing and recording behind them, and Jules was once again happy with how things had gone. Every single member of her new band was hardworking and dedicated, and genuinely interested in making this album the best it could be.

She was so grateful for that attitude and that level of professionalism.

In keeping with that, after her chat with Lars and the continued influx of notifications from being tagged in social media posts, she'd put her phone on silent. All that social media attention was fantastic, but she did *not* want to be distracted from what really mattered. The music.

"Great job today, everyone," Jules said. Jesse opened the door from the control room and leaned against it, listening as she continued, "Really outstanding. Rita and Frankie, not only was that good work today on the new song, but the input was spot on and much appreciated."

Sierra nodded, eyes shining with pride. "I can't believe how good you made it sound with those minor changes. I mean, everyone did an awesome job, but the slide guitar and banjo really did something special to it. You gave it soul."

Rita smiled as she put her guitar in its case. "It's a great song, kid. Something to be proud of for sure, but the soul was already there. We just gave it more of a voice."

"Well, I'm grateful for that voice. Thank you," Sierra said. She looked at Jules. "Thank you, too. I feel blessed to have it included on this album."

"So do I," Jules said. "Always good to discover new talent. Although that credit probably should go to Cash."

He winked at Sierra before answering his mom. "I'll take that credit. Now I'm going to go home and get to work getting the shop up and running on your website."

Jules gave him an odd look and shook her head. "I have a website designer. You don't have to do that."

"I know, but I've got to organize everything for the shop. Graphics, descriptions, pricing. Then she can just input it. But I need you to email her, and make sure she knows I'm authorized to order these changes."

"Already done," Jules said. "I did it this morning while I was having my coffee." She held a hand up. "Just realized there's something I meant to tell everyone."

They all stopped what they were doing to pay attention to her.

"I'm partnering with Future Florida to donate a portion of this album's profits to help battered and abused women. Kat, my niece, works for Future Florida and they're going to be sending out a press release in the next day or so. Just wanted you to know if you saw it that it's all legit."

Bobby put his hand on his heart. "That's real good, Jules. Future Florida is a terrific organization. They helped rebuild the little library in my hometown after it was destroyed by a hurricane."

Jesse applauded. "That's fantastic, Jules. Not just smart marketing but a very worthwhile cause, too. Great idea."

"It was Kat's. And I agree. I love the idea of giving back."

"Hey," Cash said. "That's got me thinking. What if we offered some signed merchandise on the website? We could do a poster based on the new T-shirt designs and have everyone sign it."

"I love that idea," Jules said. "Might as well capitalize on the song's popularity." She looked at the other musicians. "Everyone okay to do some autographing?"

Sierra was all smiles. Everyone was.

Rita shook her head. "Never thought I'd see the day someone would want my autograph. It's just fine with me."

"Great," Jules said. She looked at Cash. "Add that to your list of things to do."

"You got it." He pointed at Jesse. "Since you're the guy with the graphics connection, add that to your list of things to do."

They all laughed and went back to packing up. Jules took her phone out of her pocket and had a look at it. More notifications than she could count, which was good.

But she'd also missed two calls from her agent, which wasn't good.

She looked up at Jesse. "Can I use your office to make a phone call?"

"Of course. Come on, I'll unlock it for you." He waved to the rest of them. "Have a good night, all. See you tomorrow."

"Yes," Jules said. "Have a great evening. Cash, I'll meet you at the Jeep?"

"Sierra and I are going to Burger Barn." He glanced at Sierra. "We are, right?"

She nodded. "Heck, yes. I'm starving. Anyone else who wants to come is welcome, too. They have great milkshakes."

As the crew discussed that, Jesse and Jules walked to his office. He got his key out. "Everything all right?"

"I hope so. I missed two calls from Billy."

They reached the office, and he unlocked the door and pushed it open. "I'm sure it's good news. I'll leave you alone."

"No, stay. Please." She gave him a quick smile. "I'm going to tell you what he says anyway."

He held the door for her. "All right. Thanks."

She went in ahead of him and turned the light on. As he closed the door, she called Billy back. Jesse settled into the chair behind his desk and sorted through a few bits of paperwork laying on the blotter.

Billy answered after one ring. "Jules, there you are. In the studio today?"

"I was, which was why I missed your calls." She

took a few steps toward the door, then stopped and turned. "Sorry about that."

"Nothing to be sorry for! You get into that studio as much as you can. The sooner we can get that album out, the better. Listen, good things are happening. For one thing, *Rebel Yell* has reached out to me."

"They want an interview, right?" She smiled. "I had a feeling that might happen, since all the social media stuff started to blow up."

"Jules, this is more than an interview. They want to *feature* you. They want to put you on the front cover. This is major press. Major."

Her mouth fell open. She'd never dreamed their interest would turn into anything more than a review of the new album. "Are you serious?"

"As a heart attack. Not only that, *Wake Up, America* wants to book you as soon as possible for a segment. They want you to play *Dixie* live as part of their spring concert series. They'll fly you and the band to Manhattan and put you up. We just need to find a date that works."

The thumping in her ears was her own heart beating faster. "This is crazy and amazing, and I don't know what to say."

"Say you'll do it!" He laughed. "This is it, Jules.

This is what you've been working for your entire career. Congratulations! Sales of *Dixie* are through the roof. You're number two on Spotify and iTunes and I suspect that will be number one by the end of the day."

She swallowed and sat down on the couch, feeling a little faint. "I can't believe it. I just...wow."

Jesse was smiling at her, even though he obviously didn't know what Billy was telling her. She got up and went over to his desk and sat on the edge so she could reach out to him. She needed something strong to hold onto. She took his hand.

He held it in both of his, patiently waiting for her to fill him in.

"Listen," Billy went on. "I know it's a lot to absorb. Get me an answer on the morning show thing as soon as you can. The *Rebel Yell* interview can be done whenever, because they'll come to you. Although I know they don't want to wait too long."

"Okay, I'll talk to the band tomorrow morning, first thing. As far as the magazine, um, I'm pretty open."

"Next week?"

"Sure," she said, not expecting it to be that soon. "Just give me the dates and I'll make them work."

"You got it." There was a brief pause and when

he spoke again, he almost seemed a little choked up. "I'm proud of you, Jules. We've been together a long time. I know how hard you work. You deserve this."

"Thanks, Billy. Thanks for never giving up on me, either." There'd been a few times when she'd wondered if he'd let her go as a client. She wouldn't have blamed him. She'd done all right, but never anything like this.

He laughed. "Not in a million years. Talk soon."

As he hung up, she put the phone down and let out a long breath. She hung onto Jesse's hand and shifted slightly to see him better. "Wait until you hear this."

Chapter Forty

*T*rina had spent another day visiting businesses and handing out flyers and business cards. It was a good day, but again, long. She'd had great comments, and a few women who'd said they'd stop by.

It wasn't until she was at Happy Pets, getting shampoo for Walter, that her phone rang. She didn't recognize the number, but she answered anyway. "Hello?"

"Is this A Cut Above?"

"No, but this is Trina Thompson, the owner of the salon. How can I help you?"

"Oh. I was trying to see if I could make an appointment."

"We won't be open for a few more weeks. I could call you back then."

"Hmm. I really need my hair done now. I know it's late notice, but it's kind of an emergency."

Trina nodded. She totally understood. "What's going on? Special event?"

"Not exactly." The woman sighed. "I sort of colored my hair myself because I couldn't get in to my regular girl, and it didn't come out well. I don't really want to tell her what I did, either."

Trina stifled a laugh. If she had a dollar for all the times she'd run into this before, she'd have more than enough to pay for Walter's shampoo. And some for herself. "I get it, I really do. Tell you what—I don't usually make house calls, but—"

"*Please.* I will pay you double. My hair is orange in some spots and slightly green in others. I cannot go out this way. Lisa at Lady M's Boutique said you might be able to help me. I am desperate."

Trina could tell just by the sound of the woman's voice that she was sincere. "I'll need to see your hair and assess it before I can do anything. Do you live in town?"

"I live on Shell Seeker Lane. Do you know it?"

"No, but I can find it. Text me your address and I'll be on my way."

"Thank you. You're a lifesaver. Texting you right now."

Trina headed for the register. "Sounds good. See you soon."

Her phone chimed with the incoming text as she hung up. She got directions for the address. Ten minutes away.

She texted her grandmother first. *Can you let Walter out? Hair emergency that I need to take care of.*

Her grandmother answered right away. *Miguel and I will take him for a little walk. He's in good hands.*

I know he is, thank you. Love you. Relieved, Trina added a happy face with hearts for eyes. She paid for the shampoo, then jumped in her car and followed the GPS directions to 1022 Shell Seeker Lane.

The house was big enough to be impressive, but not so large that it looked like there'd be staff. Trina parked at the curb and went up the driveway, then followed the sidewalk to the door. She rang the bell.

A woman a few years younger than her mom answered the door, her hair twisted up into a messy bun that was indeed several shades of orange, blond, and, sadly, green. "Are you Trina?"

"I am."

"I'm Rebecca Tate. Thank you so much for coming." Her expression crinkled into one of plain unhappiness as her eyes rolled toward her hair. "It's bad, isn't it?"

Trina bit her lip. "Let's take it down and let me look at it under some good light."

"Come into the kitchen," Rebecca said.

"Beautiful house, by the way." Trina looked around. The place was all white and cream, with touches of deeper shades of sand and marina blue. There was lots of glass and modern art. The whole thing looked like it was straight out of a magazine.

"Thank you. I'm having a dinner party tomorrow night, so getting my hair right is important. I cannot believe I thought I could do it myself. I have no idea what happened."

"Box hair dye is tricky," Trina said. "Do you swim a lot?"

"I do." Rebecca flipped on the kitchen lights and pulled the elastic out of her hair so that it came tumbling down. She turned so Trina could see her hair better. "I know it's bad."

It wasn't good. But Trina wasn't intimidated. She'd dealt with worse. She lifted a few strands, looked at the roots, felt the hair. Despite what had been done to it, it seemed healthy and in good condition. Well taken care of otherwise. "I can fix this. I'll need to get my tools and the right supplies, of course. Might take more than one process, though."

Rebecca exhaled. "Whatever you need to do." She turned around, her palms together in front of her like she was praying. "Thank you. How soon can you do it?"

As much as Trina wanted to go home and hang out with Walter, she smiled and said, "I can start tonight, if you like."

"Yes, please. That would be amazing."

Trina checked the time. "Give me an hour or so to get what I need, and I'll be back."

"You're a lifesaver. I mean it." Rebecca headed toward the far end of the kitchen counter. "Let me give you some money now. Like a down payment."

"You can wait until I finish tonight."

"No, no. If you have to buy products, that shouldn't be on you." She got out her wallet and handed Trina two fifty-dollar bills. "To get you started."

Trina took the money. "Okay. I have to go to the beauty supply store, then back to my house to get my things. Besides the color correction, you could use a trim. Unless you don't want me to—"

"No, I do! Please, whatever it needs to look good again."

Trina nodded. "I can do that. No worries. See you soon."

Rebecca walked her out. "Thanks again."

"You're welcome," Trina said.

She went to the beauty supply store first, since it was on the way, and stocked up on everything she knew she'd need. Box hair dye was no joke. This would take all of her knowledge and experience to fix.

From there, she went back to the beach house to get all of her tools. Mixing bowls, application brushes, developer, bleach powder, cape, foils, everything she thought she might possibly need. She stepped into the house, the cool air washing over her. It was quiet. "Mimi? I'm home. Walter? Mama's here."

But there was no answer and no patter of little feet. Mimi and Miguel must have taken Walter out already. She smiled, although the feeling was bittersweet. She'd hoped to see him before she headed out again.

She put all of her supplies into her hard-sided kit with the handle, then changed into black capris and a black blouse. Standard salon wear for her. If she was going to get chemicals on her clothes, it would be better that they be something already intended for work than clothes she really cared about.

She went to the sliding doors and looked out,

just to see if she could spot Mimi, Miguel, and Walter on their way back. There was no sign of them. With a sigh, she went out the front door, locked it behind her, and down to her car.

She arrived back at Rebecca's, collected her things from the car, and went to the front door.

Rebecca opened it as Trina stepped onto the front porch. "Hi again."

"Hi. Ready to go?" Trina walked in.

"So ready. Where do you want to do this?"

"Whatever room you're most comfortable in. Kitchen. Bathroom. Doesn't matter to me."

"Let's do it in the kitchen." Rebecca led her through, stopping by the table. "Can I get you something to drink?"

"Um, sure. Just water would be fine. I've got to mix up a few things, so I'm going to get set up and do that now. Do you have a placemat or something to put down on the table? I don't plan to spill anything, but just in case."

"Sure." Rebecca opened a cabinet and came back with a vinyl tablecloth that had elastic around the edges. "This'll do, won't it?"

"That's perfect," Trina answered.

Rebecca smiled as she put the tablecloth on. "This is what we use whenever we have a shrimp boil. My husband's from Louisiana, so we have to have one every now and then." She snapped it into place. "All right, let me get us a couple bottles of water, then you just tell me where you want me and I'm there."

Trina tapped the back of one kitchen chair. "Right here will be fine."

Then she pulled on some protective gloves and got to work mixing up her bleach wash. "The good news," Trina said. "Is that not all of your hair was affected. I'm going to work on the worst sections individually, so that's why I'm using foils. To keep those areas isolated. Once that's done, I'll reassess and see what needs to be done next."

Rebecca settled into the chair and took out her phone, ready to occupy herself while Trina did her thing. "Sounds good to me."

Trina knew Rebecca probably only cared about the end result, but she liked to educate her clients about what she was doing. And she really hoped that if she did a good job, Rebecca might consider becoming a new client.

As she worked, saturating each section, she glanced up at some of the photos on the wall in the living room, which was right next to the kitchen in the open-plan design. There was one in particular that caught her eye. "Is that your husband in the photos with you where you're all dressed up?"

Rebecca looked over and nodded. "Yep. That was us on inauguration night."

"Inauguration night?"

Rebecca went back to her phone. "Mm-hmm. My husband is Griffin Tate. He's the mayor of Diamond Beach."

Chapter Forty-one

Kat was glad Alex was going to hang at the firehouse this evening. Not that she didn't love time with him, but being around the crew would be good for him, too.

When she left work, she made a stop at the grocery store to pick up a few odds and ends that her mom had texted her about needing. More half-and-half for the coffee, some zucchini, and a pack of ground beef.

Dinner tonight was zucchini lasagna, a recipe that was basically regular lasagna but with slices of zucchini instead of noodles. It was one of Kat's favorites and something her mom had come up with when Kat was a kid.

It had come about because Kat had grown zucchini for a school project, and they'd had a bumper crop. Way more than either of them had thought possible. After giving away as much as they could, her mom had made zucchini into everything else she could think of. Muffins, bread, pancakes, and...lasagna.

Kat smiled just thinking about it. Funny how certain things were attached to distinct memories.

She picked out plenty of nice zucchini, and grabbed a big package of ground beef, because her mom was making two trays of it in order to feed all of them. Conrad was coming over and bringing his sister, who, according to Kat's grandmother, had had a big change of attitude.

Kat would believe that when she saw it for herself.

While she was still in produce and near the deli, she picked up a chopped chicken salad and a small bottle of iced tea to take to work with her the next day for lunch. Then she headed for the dairy section to get the half-and-half. She passed a Buy One, Get One display of dog treats and grabbed two boxes.

One, she planned on taking down to Trina for her new dog, Walter. He was so cute it made Kat think about adopting a dog herself, but she worked too much right now. Besides, she had Toby if she needed a dog fix.

That was the best she could do right now. Unlike

Trina, Kat wouldn't be able to take a dog to work with her. At least, she didn't think she'd be able to. No one else brought a dog there. She didn't even know if they had dogs, just that Eloise had a cat. A cat who probably wouldn't want to come to work anyway.

She got the half-and-half, then looped around to the registers. After putting her items on the conveyor belt, she added a pack of mints. Those would be good to keep in her desk drawer. She paid, picked up her bags, and went out to the parking lot.

At home, she stepped off the elevator to a full house. Well, a mostly full house. She saw her mom in the kitchen, and her grandmother, Conrad, Dinah, and Aunt Jules with Toby at her feet in the living room, but no Cash.

Her mom was the first one to greet her, as the rest of them were in conversation. "Hi, honey."

"Got everything you asked for. Need help? I can slice the zucchini. Or cook the ground beef. Whatever you want me to do."

"That would be great. The zucchini, I think. Nice and thin. You know how to do it."

"I do. Let me just go change and I'll be right back." Kat set the bags on the counter. "One of those boxes of dog treats I'm taking down to Trina."

Her mom smiled. "I'll set them over here on the counter for you."

"Thanks." Kat changed and quickly came back out.

Aunt Jules called out to her as she returned. "How was work, Kat?"

"Good. How was your day in the studio?"

Aunt Jules broke into a big smile. "It was good. The whole day was good. Guess who's going to be on the cover of *Rebel Yell*?"

Kat shook her head. "I don't know. Uncle Lars?"

Her aunt laughed. "No! Me, silly!"

"What?" *Rebel Yell* was a big deal. It was one of the few magazines she still saw in the grocery store checkout aisle. "That's amazing! Congratulations!"

"Thanks. They're coming next week to interview me and do the photo shoot."

"That is so cool. Hey, do you think you'll get a chance to mention the partnership with Future Florida? That might really earn me some brownie points at work."

Her aunt nodded. "I'm definitely going to bring it up."

"Thank you." Kat grinned. "It's pretty cool having an aunt who's a famous musician." And getting more famous by the day, apparently. She figured she'd talk to Aunt Jules about the Fourth of July fundraiser after dinner. "By the way, I got Toby some dog treats. I hope that was okay."

Toby immediately stood up and started wagging his tail.

Aunt Jules laughed. "It's fine and you'd better give him one now."

"Come on, Tobes," Kat said. "Come get a cookie."

He trotted right over. She picked him up and kissed his head as she carried him to the counter where the box of treats was. "You're such a good boy." She put him back down on the floor, where he immediately sat and stared up at her in anticipation.

She got a treat out. It looked like a nugget of bacon. Kind of smelled like one, too. "Here you go."

She held it out to him. He took it carefully from her hand, then trotted over to his bed and ate it there. So cute.

After closing the box up, she took the other box and went downstairs with it. "Anybody home?"

"Just us seniors," Willie called out. "Come on in."

Kat laughed as she came around the corner from the foyer. "I got a box of treats for Walter. I was going to give them to Trina."

"She's not here, honey," Willie said. "Hair emergency. But that was real sweet of you. If you want to leave them, I'll make sure she knows they're from you."

"Okay. Thanks. Hi, Miguel. Hi, Walter."

"Hi," Miguel said.

Walter, who was sitting between Miguel and Willie on the couch, moved his ears but not much more. She didn't blame him. He was being petted by two people. Treats were good, but not *that* good.

Kat set the box on the breakfast bar and headed for the stairs. "Have a good night."

"You, too," Willie called out.

Back in the kitchen, she got to work on the zucchini, washing it first, then slicing it into thin circles on a cutting board. Her mom had started browning the ground beef with some finely chopped onions and seasonings in a big skillet.

"Where's Cash?" she asked her mom.

"Out with his girlfriend, according to Jules. They were going to Burger Barn."

"He's missing out," Kat said.

"I don't think he knew we were having zucchini lasagna."

"How was your day at the bakery?"

Her mom smiled. "Really good. I did my first real

baking there today. Chocolate chip cookies and sour orange pies. Conrad and a photographer from the *Gulf Gazette* are coming over tomorrow to take pictures and taste the pies. I did the interview with him when he got here tonight."

"That's pretty exciting. Should be great press."

"I think so, too." Her mom stirred the ground beef. "Once the pictures are done, the rest of the pies are going to the Dolphin Club to be sold as one of their desserts. Jesse said he'd come pick them up. I just have to text him and let him know they're ready to go."

"Exciting, huh?" Kat asked. "People eating your food, I mean."

Her mom nodded. "It is. Of course, if they don't sell—"

"Mom, there is no way that will happen. That pie is amazing. People might be reluctant to try it because it's not something they're familiar with, but once they do, word is going to spread. You'll see."

"I hope you're right."

"I know I am." Kat sliced the last zucchini. "What do you want me to do next?"

"You can get the mozzarella, the parmesan and the ricotta out of the refrigerator."

"Okay." Kat did that as her mom drained the ground beef.

There were two aluminum lasagna pans on the counter. They'd be building the lasagnas in those pans. That made for easy cleanup when the food was gone.

"What about the oven?" Kat asked.

Her mom nodded. "I completely forgot. Yes, turn it to four hundred. By the time we've got these put together, it should be ready."

Kat got the oven going, then turned back to watch her mom add the pasta sauce to the ground beef. Once that was mixed in, she took the skillet off the heat.

She then got out a big bowl. "I need two eggs."

Kat grabbed those from the fridge.

"Go ahead and crack them into the bowl."

Kat tapped them on the counter and broke them into the bowl that her mom had already put the ricotta into. Her mom then added some parmesan, some salt and pepper, and a good sprinkling of dried parsley and stirred it all up.

She pointed to the two aluminum pans. "Add a thin layer of sauce to each one."

"On it," Kat said. She used the big mixing spoon

in the pan to scoop sauce and meat into each pan. She spread it thin. "Zucchini next, right?"

"Right. Slightly overlapping in nice straight lines."

Before long, they had both lasagnas built, using up almost all of the zucchini slices. As Kat was sprinkling shredded mozzarella on the last one, the oven timer went off to let her know it was hot enough.

"Cookie sheets," her mom said. "Those are full. They might bubble over. And I do not want to clean the oven."

"Neither do I." Kat got the cookie sheets out.

Her mom got the tinfoil, putting a layer of it down on each cookie sheet. The lasagna pans went on top, and both of them went in the oven. Her mom set a timer for fifty minutes.

"Thanks for the help," she said. "I really appreciate it. I thought you might be too tired after work."

"If you're not too tired, neither am I," Kat answered. "And actually, now that I'm a few days in, I'm finding my rhythm and I don't feel nearly as wiped out as I did those first couple of days."

"Good." Her mom took a sip from her glass of water. "I hope I can get that way at the bakery."

"Are you baking again tomorrow?"

"No." Her mom's expression changed into one

that looked slightly nervous. "Tomorrow, we do interviews. And, hopefully, some hiring."

"Good luck with that," Kat said. She meant it, too. Her mom needed good, reliable help or she'd end up doing more than she should. Kat understood her mom was excited about the bakery, and rightfully so, but Kat didn't want her wearing herself out over there, either.

Chapter Forty-two

Dinner had been a resounding success. An odd thought to have upon waking up, Claire realized, but maybe that was because she was worried about handling the interviews today and her subconscious knew she needed a positive thought to hold on to.

Whatever the reason, she'd take it. Although pleasing her family wasn't that hard. Pleasing Dinah, however, was a very different task, but she'd actually asked Claire for the lasagna recipe.

A win was a win. Even if Dinah had only asked out of politeness. Hadn't seemed that way to Claire, though.

Even Cash, who'd arrived home at the end of the meal, had had a piece of the zucchini lasagna. Not as much of a win. That boy rarely turned down any kind of food.

She got up and stared at her closet. Whatever she wore today needed to be professional, but also something she wouldn't mind being photographed in. She wondered if the photographer would want her in one of the Mrs. Butter's Bakery aprons?

If so, her outfit needed to go with that, too.

No stripes. Might be too busy. And the photo would be in black and white in the *Gazette*, so...

Ugh. This was hard.

She ended up with a butter yellow and white polka dot blouse with white capris and white sandals. She hoped that was all right. It looked nice together and the black apron would provide good contrast.

With that settled, she changed from her nightgown into her walking clothes and went out to the kitchen to start the coffee.

Kat showed up as Claire hit the Brew button. "Ready to walk?"

Claire nodded. "I am now."

They did a fast-paced thirty minutes, returning home sweaty and ready for coffee. Both of them took a cup into the bedroom with them so they could shower and get ready.

After a much-too-short shower, Claire spent extra time on her hair and makeup. She also packed a small bag with her powder, blush, concealer, and lipstick so she could do a touchup before she had her photo taken. Vanity, she supposed, but she didn't care.

She wanted to look good so the bakery would look good.

Danny texted that he was walking out the door ten minutes before she was ready. She let him know that, then hustled to brush her teeth, get her shoes on, and make sure she had everything she needed.

She made it downstairs in eight minutes. He'd pulled his truck into her driveway, so she didn't have to walk over.

"Morning," he said as she got in. "You look nice."

"Morning. Thanks. So do you." He was in khaki pants and a turquoise polo shirt, which was an amazing color on him. "Ready to hire some people?"

"I am. I hope they're as good in person as they are on paper."

He pulled out of the driveway. "I take it that means you read over the applications and resumes I emailed you?"

"I did. Last night before bed."

"Who do you like the best so far?"

"Rosemary and Raul are my top two picks for bakers. Jasmine seems ideal for the retail side."

"I'd agree with that. I like Amy for retail, too."

"Yes, she looked good. Young, though."

"Could mean she has a lot of energy."

"Agreed. I'm just hoping it doesn't also mean she's got green hair and is covered with tattoos and piercings."

He laughed. "Yeah, probably not politically correct to say so, but that's not a great look for someone working in our kind of retail. We don't want to scare people off. Some people don't care, but the truth is, some do."

"The crazy-colored hair isn't so bad. On some people it's actually cute. But the rest... Maybe they'll be the kind of tattoos and piercings you don't really see." She shook her head. "I guess we're old, huh?"

"Age is relative, but I suppose we are. For me, there's just something about all that body modification that doesn't mesh well with food service. Which is essentially what we are. If that's antiquated thinking, so be it."

"I agree with you and I'm sure other people do, too. Better not to risk alienating any customers. Not when we're a brand-new business." She snorted. "Even if that does make us fuddy-duddies."

They arrived at the shopping center, Danny parked, and they went in. Claire immediately noticed the sharp scent of fresh paint had been replaced by a more subtle aroma. Fresh baked goods from her work yesterday. It was a nice change.

The sour orange pie display looked great with all the pies in it. It would have looked better with more pies, though, and now she was second-guessing her decision to only make eight.

"What's wrong?" Danny asked.

"I should have made more pies. Filled up the case more."

He stood next to her and studied the display. "How about we move the pies from the bottom shelf up to fill in the middle shelves more? Then we'll see if we can get the photographer to frame the picture so it doesn't include the empty part of the case."

"Good idea."

"You could also fill some empty pie tins with whipped cream, put them in boxes, and use them to make the shelves look completely loaded. In a black and white photograph, I doubt anyone would be able to tell the difference."

She grinned at him. "Two great ideas in under thirty seconds? You definitely had your coffee this morning."

He laughed. "Yes, I did, but I'd still like some

more." He glanced at his watch. "We have about forty-five minutes before the *Gazette* folks show up. You want me to start filling pie tins? If so, how many?"

"I'd say six would be enough. We don't need to go crazy. While you do that, I'm going to see if I can get the coffee machine going. I cleaned all the parts the other day, so it's ready. I hope the directions are easy to understand."

"So do I. And not just because I really want coffee."

He was so funny. She nodded. "Same here. I'm going to drop my purse in the office, then I'm going to give it my best shot."

"Call me if you need me. Coffee beans should be in the walk-in."

"They are. I put them away myself." She put her purse in the office, then grabbed a bag of beans from the walk-in and went to tackle the coffee machine. The whole bag of beans went into a reservoir so only what was needed was ground each time a pot of coffee was made.

She loved that idea. Not only did it mean the coffee would be as fresh as possible, but it also meant the aroma of the beans would perfume the bakery whenever it happened. Even people who didn't like to drink coffee often enjoyed the smell of it.

The instructions for the machine were relatively easy to follow. She read them all the way through, just to get a good understanding of what needed to be done.

Beans went in, the water tank was filled, the carafe put in place, then she had to select the grind and strength and press Start. Not that hard.

She picked the settings based on both of them liking strong coffee, and tapped the button to start the process. She was rewarded with the sound of the grinder starting up. She stepped back, hands pressed together.

"Sounds like you did it," Danny said.

"I think so. We'll know soon."

The aroma she'd been expecting started to waft out of the machine. It was a good smell. She got mugs out and set them on the counter next to the machine, ready to go. Underneath the machine was a small fridge to store creamer and extra bags of beans in.

They'd also be offering the additions of three different syrups, vanilla, caramel, and chocolate. They weren't a coffee shop and had no intention of competing with those kinds of places, but a shot of syrup wasn't a big deal.

While she waited for the coffee to brew, she put on an apron and went to look at herself in the bathroom mirror. She decided to wear it for the photos, but she'd take it off for the interviews. Apron still on, she went back to see how Danny was doing with the pie tins.

She found him in the walk-in, looking at the shelves.

He shook his head. "Where's the whipped cream?"

She pointed to the containers of heavy whipping cream. "Right there. It has to be made."

"Made?"

She nodded, amused by his reaction. "Were you expecting to find giant cans of Reddi-wip?"

He shot her a look. "Sort of."

She pursed her lips. "First of all, that's not really whipped cream. Secondly, we are not that kind of bakery."

He grinned. "I'm good with that."

She grabbed a jug of heavy whipping cream. "Come on. I'll show you how to do it."

A few minutes later, the cream had become

whipped cream, with the addition of some powdered sugar. She filled two large pastry bags, both with fat star tips on the end, then handed him one. "These have the same piping tips on them that I use for the meringue, so it'll match what's already out there."

"Good." He didn't look too confident.

"Watch me. It's pretty easy." She filled the pie tin in front of her, doing a quick layer to provide a base, then a more careful layer on top of that to make it look pretty. "There. Think you can do that?"

"I have no idea but I'm going to try."

"We'll do it together."

But he didn't make any motion toward filling the pie tin. "How about I fill the bottom and you do the fancy top layer? These are going to be in pictures. They need to look right."

She took the piping bag from him. "How about you go get us two cups of coffee and I'll knock these out?" She could have had them both done already. And she didn't want him to feel like he'd messed anything up.

He smiled. "Good to know I'm not the only one with great ideas around here."

She laughed and started piping.

Chapter Forty-three

Margo didn't mind that they were looking at condos again today, because this time, things were going to be different. She pulled out of the driveway of the Double Diamond and headed for Conrad's house.

Dinah was serious about the move now. Not only was she serious, but she seemed eager to make the change.

It was amazing how much her attitude had transformed since Margo had been completely upfront and honest with her. She'd been like a different person at dinner last night. Actually enjoyable to be around. Margo gave Dinah a lot of credit for her apology and admitting she'd been wrong.

That wasn't easy to do. Sometimes it felt like the older Margo got, the harder that kind of confession was. Dinah was to be commended for not backing away or getting angry. It was a big part of why Margo planned to do her best to befriend the woman.

After all, Dinah *was* Conrad's sister. She was also his only living family, outside of a few distant nieces and nephews. Once Dinah moved to Diamond Beach, she'd be part of Margo and Conrad's life together.

Margo wasn't sure if she and Dinah would ever become particularly close, but Margo would endeavor to create a friendship with Dinah that made the woman feel included and welcome.

There were a lot of times in Margo's life when such a relationship would have been welcome, but never came about. She supposed that was her own fault for putting walls up and allowing herself to wallow in grief.

At least Dinah didn't have that hurdle to get over.

As for Margo agreeing to marry Conrad...she and Conrad had decided that wouldn't happen until Dinah moved to Diamond Beach. They weren't setting a date. Didn't mean they weren't committed to each other. They were.

She turned toward his neighborhood.

The thing was, Margo had another commitment to consider. One to Sal and Mirna Clarke to buy their house. She couldn't very well back out of that, could she? She thought about it for a moment. She probably could, but it wouldn't feel right.

She also didn't want to. What did that mean? She sighed. She knew what it meant. She didn't want to move into Conrad's house. It was lovely, but it was very...him. Very masculine. And that was just as it should be. It was *his* house.

Buying the Clarkes' house, for all the work it needed, meant she'd have a blank slate to put her own touches on. A place that would be exactly the way she wanted it. She loved that idea. At least she did now that she'd gotten past the realization of how much work would have to be done.

Would Conrad want to move into that house with her? It did have a nicer pool and a bigger backyard. That might not be enough of a draw. Not when he'd lived in his place for so long.

All she knew was that she needed to talk to him, preferably alone. She didn't want Dinah to think she'd had a change of heart about her moving to Diamond Beach. That wasn't the case at all. But marrying Conrad hadn't been in Margo's plans. Not this soon, anyway.

She arrived at his house and parked at the curb. Dinah's car was on the right-hand side of the drive-way, leaving the left side open so that Conrad could get his car out of the garage. Important, since he'd be driving today. She went to the door and knocked.

Dinah answered, smiling with genuine pleasure at Margo's arrival. Still an odd thing to see. "Morning. I really appreciate you coming with us today."

Margo came inside. "I'm looking forward to it."

"That's kind of you. Especially since I know it means giving up a lot of time that you and Connie could spend writing."

"There will be plenty of time for that later." Margo meant it, too. As much as she loved writing with Conrad, there was a thing called balance. Life happened and it couldn't be ignored.

They walked into the kitchen where Conrad was setting the dishwasher to run. "Hi, there. Ready to go?"

Margo smiled and held a finger up. "Could I have a word with you alone for just a moment?"

She half expected Dinah to whine, but the woman just smiled. "I'll just go freshen up. Call me when you're ready."

She left and Conrad's brows lifted. "What's up? Everything okay?"

Margo wished she'd rehearsed this conversation in the car. "It's about the whole wedding thing and—"

"I know. It's happening fast. But we already decided not to do anything until Dinah's moved down. And you're moved into your place."

"That's just the thing. How much sense does that make? Why would I move into the new house only to then, what...move again?" She sighed. "There's more to it than that. I have to be honest with you, Conrad. I really want the Clarkes' house. I want to remodel it and make it into my perfect vision of a place. Your house is lovely, but..."

He nodded in what seemed to be understanding. "But it's my house. Always has been. And you don't see yourself here, do you?"

She felt apologetic that this conversation even needed to take place. "No, I don't. I'm sorry. But there's no point in pretending otherwise. We agreed to be honest with each other, so that's what I'm doing."

"I'm glad you are. But there's an easy fix."

"There is?"

"Sure. I'll move into the new house with you. If that's what you want. Do you?"

She stared at him, astounded by his quick decision. "You'd do that?"

"For you? For us? Absolutely. On one condition."

"What's that?"

"That we turn the medium-sized bedroom into the office so there's room enough for both of us to work in there together." He put his hands on his hips. "I know you were going to use the smaller room for that purpose, but I don't want us to feel cramped. We need enough room that we can both have our own workspaces."

She smiled. "That's not a problem. The small bedroom can become the guest room. It's unlikely it'll ever get used anyway." She looked around. "You won't mind selling this place? You've been here a while."

"Who says I'm going to sell it?" He looked toward the sliding glass doors that led out to the pool and backyard. "I think I'll rent it." He grinned. "And I already have a renter in mind. Dinah! Come in here."

Dinah appeared a few moments later, her purse on her arm. "Ready to go?"

"We might not have to. How would you feel about staying here instead of buying your own place? Could you live here? In this house?"

She blinked and shook her head. "I...that's a lovely offer but I don't want to be underfoot. Especially once you and Margo are married." She bit her lip. "I just couldn't. Especially not for free."

"First of all, I'm talking about you renting the place. A nominal amount, which we can work out. I'm more interested in covering the utilities, the insurance, and such. Secondly, you'd be here by yourself," Conrad said.

Her eyes narrowed. "Where would you and Margo go?"

"My house," Margo answered. "I'm buying one in this neighborhood. Needs to be remodeled, but once that's done, I'm moving in."

"What do you say?" Conrad asked.

Dinah looked around like she was seeing the place for the first time. "I'd have the whole house to myself?"

"The whole house," Conrad said. "And your own pool and your own backyard and garage and you'd be within walking distance of us. Plus, you'd be in a safe neighborhood, which I know is one of your concerns."

Dinah put her hand over her mouth as her eyes welled up. She regained her composure. "You'd do that for me? After how awful I was?"

"Water under the bridge," Conrad said. "You've always been there for me. Now it's time for me to be there for you."

She sniffed, then hugged him. "Thank you. Thank you so much."

"You're welcome." He hugged her back, laughing softly. "Does that mean we're not going condo shopping today?"

She backed away, nodding as she looked at him and Margo. "That's exactly what it means. It also means I'm packing my stuff and going home so I can start to organize my belongings and get ready to sell my house."

Dinah reached out and took Margo's hand. "Thank you, too. I know you had a part in this. Whatever it was, I appreciate it."

Impulsively, and against her usual instincts, Margo hugged Dinah. She'd never imagined today would go this way, but just like that, everything had worked itself out.

Chapter Forty-four

Willie sat on the couch on the back deck with Miguel, staring out at the water and drinking her coffee, which was exactly what he was doing, too. The morning was peaceful and calm, the skies blue, the breeze gentle. A perfect day in Diamond Beach.

They had no major plans. Maybe a leisurely walk on the beach after breakfast. Maybe a trip into town later to do a little window shopping and have some lunch. If so, they might swing by the shopping center and see how things were coming along at the salon and the other shops. Laundry at some point. But nothing too strenuous.

She smiled. "How about that Trina? Fixing the mayor's wife's hair. Trina said that woman has promised to tell everyone she knows about the salon. Isn't that something?"

Miguel smiled and nodded. "It definitely is. Very proud of that girl. Everyone who's anyone will be coming to see her."

"I think so, too," Willie said. "And not another word from that Liz. Very happy about that."

"So am I." He glanced over at her, his mug in his hand, his expression becoming more serious. "Are you going to tell Trina about the DNA test?"

She exhaled and shook her head. "No. No reason to. She already believes Nico is her brother. Why tell her what she already knows? Besides, she might get bothered that I had the test done in the first place." Willie didn't think she could stand her granddaughter being upset with her.

He nodded solemnly.

"You don't think I should have done it at all, do you?"

"I think you did what you thought was right. What you thought was necessary to protect your family. I would have done the same thing."

She looked at him. "You're not just saying that to make me feel better? You really would have?"

"Of course." He set his coffee down so he could gesture with his hands the way he always did. "What else do we have but family? Who is going to protect them if not us? We're the elders. It's our job."

She smiled. He always knew what to say. She drank the last of her coffee. "You want some breakfast?"

"I could eat. Nothing too much, though."

"Oatmeal? With raisins and brown sugar?"

He smiled. "I like it better with bits of dried mango and honey."

"I've never had it that way. And I don't have either of those things in the pantry."

"Brown sugar and raisins is fine."

She picked up her empty cup. "After we eat, I'm going to take my shower. Then I think I'd like to go over to the shopping center. See how things are going."

"We should. I haven't been to the bakery in a while, and I ought to at least show my face."

"Then that's our plan. Breakfast in a few minutes." She went inside and got the oatmeal started in a pot on the stove. She didn't like microwaved oatmeal. Never tasted right to her, but she didn't complain when Roxie made it for her. Willie understood that sometimes convenience meant sacrificing something else.

Roxie was already out, doing her morning walk, and Trina had taken Walter out to walk as well, although they weren't going as far as Roxie did.

Willie only knew that because she'd heard them talking while she and Miguel were still in bed.

Thankfully, Roxie had made coffee before she'd headed out.

Willie smiled. She was going to miss that when she moved to Dunes West. She'd miss more than just the coffee, though. The mornings with her family were so nice. She glanced toward the back porch. Being with Miguel would make up for some of that.

She knew they'd visit. Once again, she considered the idea of her and Miguel getting a little dog of their own. Might be nice. Might not be as much work as she thought. They'd taken Walter out for a walk, and it hadn't been hard.

She got the raisins and brown sugar down from the cabinet and made the oatmeal as good as she could. She even added a sprinkling of cinnamon to make it fancy. When it was done, she served it up in two dishes, added spoons to them, and carried them out.

Miguel met her at the sliders, opening them for her. "Looks good."

"I hope it tastes good."

"I'm sure it will."

Steam wafted off the bowls, so they let them sit

and went back in for more coffee. Soon, they were able to dig in.

"This is very good," Miguel said. "We should have this once a week."

"Yeah?" Willie was proud of herself. "We can try it your way. With the honey and mangos."

He nodded. "It's good for us, too. Maybe not the sugar, but the oatmeal." He grinned. "Although if you wanted to turn this into oatmeal cookies, I'd be all right with that."

She laughed. "Cookies for breakfast?"

He shrugged. "At our age, we should be able to do what we want."

"I agree with that."

Trina and Walter returned from their walk first, coming up the back steps. Trina used an old towel to clean the sand off Walter's feet, then took him inside to let him eat while she got ready for the day.

Roxie was next. She looked at their bowls. "Oatmeal?"

Willie nodded. "With brown sugar and raisins."

"Nice, Ma. Is Trina back?"

"She is. Probably in the shower already."

"That's where I'm going to be soon," Roxie said. "I need to get over to the shopping center. Ethan and I are working on finding the owners of that jewelry I uncovered yesterday, if at all possible. Which it might not be."

"Good luck with that. Miguel and I will be over later this morning. I want to see how it's all coming along."

Roxie nodded. "You're going to be amazed." She smiled at them both as she went in.

They finished up their food and coffee, then Willie went to take her shower. She could hear Trina's blow dryer going. Walter wasn't around. Probably in Trina's room. He loved being close to her.

Miguel showered after Willie, while she got dressed and did her makeup. By the time they were ready to go, Trina, Walter, and Roxie had already left. Willie and Miguel weren't too far behind them. Soon, they, too, were off to the shopping center with Miguel behind the wheel.

She liked him driving. He was very careful. And driving his own car meant he wasn't spending money on an Uber. Those were nice, but she had no doubt all those trips added up. Had to be more than what gas cost.

"I'm excited to see the progress that's been made," Willie said.

"So am I."

"Do you want to start at the salon first or the bakery?"

Miguel thought a moment. "Let's start at the bakery. Then, if Claire's made some goodies, maybe we can take something to Trina."

"Okay," Willie said. "Good idea."

He parked in the middle of the parking lot when they arrived and they walked to the bakery. Miguel opened the door for her.

Willie sucked in a breath. "Wow. This place looks great. So different."

Danny, who was behind the big glass display case adjusting the racks, straightened and smiled. "Hey, there."

"Son." Miguel gave him a nod. "Just wanted to stop by. See how things were going. I love everything you've done with it."

"Thanks." Danny looked proud, and he should, Willie thought. The place really did look fantastic.

Danny tipped his head toward the back. "Let me just tell Claire you're here."

He went through the door into the kitchen and returned with Claire. She was in a black bakery apron that had a smudge of flour across the middle of the logo.

"Hi, there! What a nice surprise." She brushed at

the flour. "I was making a batch of cookies. Hey, would you like a cup of coffee and a chocolate chip cookie? You can be our practice customers."

Willie was never going to turn down either of those things. "Sounds good to me." She looked at Miguel.

He nodded and pulled out a chair for Willie at the closest table. "Thank you. Very kind of you to offer."

"Coming up," Claire said as she disappeared into the back.

Danny rubbed his hands together. "Would you like a little something in your coffee? We have vanilla, caramel, or chocolate syrup."

"Chocolate," Willie answered as she settled into the chair. She didn't need to think about that. "And creamer. If you have it."

"We do," Danny said.

"Just plain for me," Miguel said. He took his seat as his son went to fix their coffees. Miguel looked at her. "Nice in here, huh?"

"Very. You're going to do a great business, honey."

He smiled.

Danny was still working on the coffees when

Claire returned with two white plates, each one bearing a large, *thick* chocolate chip cookie.

"Those are huge," Willie said as Claire set them down on the table.

Claire grinned. "That's kind of our thing. Big cookies. We have to do something to compete with Publix. Everyone knows how good their bakery is."

Miguel nodded. "True. But they won't have the sorts of things you'll have here. Especially not the Puerto Rican treats."

"Something else that will set us apart," Claire said.

Danny brought their coffee out. Willie's had a swirl of whipped cream that had been drizzled with chocolate syrup.

"Now that," she said, "is my idea of a coffee." She took a sip and nodded. "Very good. How's it going with everything else? Pretty close to opening?"

Claire nodded as she stood beside Danny. "The interview with the *Gazette* will be out in two weeks and we might actually be open by then."

"Just waiting on our final inspection," Danny said. "Plus, Claire's got about three thousand hours of baking ahead of her to get this place stocked."

Claire laughed. "Not quite, but close. We hired

some great people yesterday, though. They'll help us get going. Two of them will be working with me in the kitchen, so I won't be doing all that baking on my own."

Miguel had broken his cookie in half to take a bite. "This is outstanding. How do you get it so chewy in the middle?"

"You can't ask that," Willie said. "It's probably a secret."

Claire smiled. "I don't mind telling you. It's a combination of things, but a lot of it's the brown sugar. Really gives the cookie moisture."

Miguel looked at Willie. "Brown sugar seems to be the secret ingredient of the day." He glanced up at his son. "Could we get one of these to go? For Trina?"

"Not one for Roxie?"

Willie shook her head. "She's off carbs right now."

"I understand that. I'll package it right up," Claire said. She went back toward the kitchen. "Just give me a minute."

"Thank you," Willie called after her.

The bakery was beautiful and there was no way it wouldn't be successful with Claire's talents in the kitchen and Danny's business savvy.

Willie got a lump in her throat, but it was all good. She was just overwhelmed with how incredible her life was, with the blessing of her new husband, his amazing family, and Zippy's tremendously generous gift that had provided a future for her and her family.

Life in Diamond Beach had become a dream come true. What could be better than that?

Chapter Forty-five

 hat a nightmare. Roxie stood in the middle of the dumpster, knee deep in trash. So much trash. To say she felt a little defeated would be an understatement.

Last night, she'd told Ethan all about the work she'd accomplished cleaning out the last storefront, saving the part about discovering the jewelry for last.

He'd been surprised she'd found something of value, but not *that* surprised, telling her again about how quickly the owners had pulled out. He'd known they'd owed back rent, but hadn't thought too much of it, because the previous owners of the shopping center hadn't exactly kept the place up the way they should have.

But forgetting valuable jewelry only seemed to underscore just how eager the tenants had been to leave the premises. That and the state of how they'd left things, like a bomb had gone off.

Her real concern, and the thing she'd told Ethan about, was how she really wanted to get the jewelry back to its rightful owners.

He'd then told her there might very well be a logbook or copies of the job orders somewhere in all the paperwork that had also been left behind. He'd had the shop repair a necklace for his mom, and not only had they written it up on one of the repair envelopes, but they'd put it in a ledger, too.

The problem was she'd already cleaned out the office and thrown all the stuff she'd found there away, not realizing it might be important. Sure, she'd looked for more jewelry envelopes, but anything that was paper had been dumped.

"Dumb move," she sighed out. "Dumb. Move."

Ethan had offered to do the digging through the dumpster, searching through everything she'd already tossed, but she'd done it, so she felt like she should be the one to get her hands dirty. Literally.

Besides, he still had a lot of work to get done so the photographer would be able to move into his new studio space before the lease ran out on his current location. That was important. It was one of the big reasons he'd signed the lease with them.

Roxie had told him it would be possible, and it would be, if Ethan kept working.

Which meant she was on dumpster duty.

She was hot and sweaty and not really sure why she'd bothered to shower this morning. At least the dumpster hadn't been used for much more than cleaning out the storefronts and scraps of construction material. There was no rotting food or hair sweepings like there would be in a couple of weeks.

She went through every bag and every bit of paper she found, analyzing it for anything that might be a customer record from Bits and Baubles, the shop in question.

Nothing. Not yet, anyway. She kept going, working her way from one end of the dumpster to the other.

After sifting through the contents of the big metal container, she still came up emptyhanded. Frustrated, she climbed out and brushed herself off, but she felt grimy and gross all the same. At least she'd be able to wash up at the salon, since there was plenty of running water, soap, and towels there.

First, she was going back into the store to finish the cleaning out. No sense in washing up before that. She'd only have to do it again.

She went inside and took a look around. She'd

only managed half the store yesterday and that had felt like a monumental task. Could she really get the rest of this done today? After spending a solid hour and a half in the dumpster?

She supposed she could. If she worked hard enough. At least today she'd remembered to bring a big bottle of ice water. She unscrewed the top and downed a couple of gulps, instantly feeling better.

There was a knock at the front door. She turned and saw her mom and Miguel peering in through the glass. She went to unlock it, propping it open now that she was back inside. Fresh air was always a welcome thing when the weather was this nice. "Hi, guys."

Her mom gave Roxie an odd look, her gaze shifting to her daughter's forehead. "What happened to you?"

"Why?"

Her mom reached up and picked a scrap of something out of her hair.

"Oh, that," Roxie said. She felt through her hair to see if anything else was stuck in there. "I was just in the dumpster."

Willie grimaced. "The dumpster? Where the trash goes? What in the Sam Hill were you doing in there?"

"Trying to find some old customer records." Roxie explained to them about how Ethan thought there might be a second recording of the jewelry repairs the shop had taken in. "He once had a necklace repaired for his mom and said they'd written it down in a ledger as well as on the envelope."

Miguel took a long look around and nodded. "Could still be here. There's certainly a lot to look through."

Roxie nodded. "There is. But I figured any records would have been in the office, which I cleaned out yesterday. The rest of this stuff is just junk that needs to be tossed."

Miguel's gaze narrowed slightly. "Are you sure about that?"

"No, not really, but most of it has been so far." Roxie sighed. "Don't worry, I'm going to keep looking. It's just going to slow down the cleanout. This is where the dog grooming place is going to be, obviously, and it needs a lot of work to get ready."

"We'll help you," Miguel said.

Willie nudged Miguel. "Good idea. We can sort through papers as good as anybody else. Besides, I'm hopped up on caffeine and sugar." She rubbed her hands together. "Might as well put that energy to use."

Miguel laughed.

Roxie hadn't been expecting them to offer. "That's sweet of you, but you don't have to do that. This is dirty, sweaty business."

Her mom lifted her chin and cut her eyes at Roxie. "It's also *my* business. I can help if I want to."

Roxie smiled and held her hands up in surrender. "If you want to, I'm happy for the help. Let's do it. This whole side clearly still needs to be gone through, so start wherever you like. I'm going to the front and working my way back."

Miguel and Willie went to the old jewelry counter. Willie set her purse on a stack of boxes as she prepared to look.

Roxie didn't think there was much chance of them finding anything over there, but the fact that they wanted to help was really all that mattered. It was sweet and kind, and it made her feel less alone.

She used the same trash box from the day before, filling it with big stuff like newspaper that had been used for wrapping and any large items such as hangers or broken pieces of fixtures that were clearly not what she was looking for.

She had the box pretty close to full and was about to pick it up and haul it to the dumpster when Miguel called her name.

"Roxie? Can you come take a look at this?"

She straightened and brushed a little hair out of her eyes as she walked over. He and Willie were still behind the counter and Miguel was holding up a faded blue ledger. On the outside, in black Sharpie, was written, "Repairs." Roxie let out a little gasp, but she was reluctant to hope too much until she looked inside it.

Willie was smiling proudly.

He handed Roxie the book. "Found it in the drawer under the cash register, which was locked."

Roxie looked at him. "If it was locked, how did you get it open?"

He held up a bent paperclip and smiled.

She laughed. "You're amazing. I really hope this is it." She held her breath as she opened the ledger and took a look inside. Pages and pages of names, phone numbers, dates, job numbers, and brief descriptions of the items to be repaired.

"You did it." She leaned across the counter and kissed Miguel on the cheek. "I was so sure I'd thrown away any chance of finding those customers. Thank you."

"That's it?" Willie asked. "That's what you were looking for?"

Roxie nodded. "Ethan said the work was

recorded in a ledger. This is it. If I can match up the names with the description of the item dropped off, I should be able to find the customers. Even if the phone numbers aren't still active, I might be able to track them down on social media."

Willie hugged Miguel. "My husband, the hero.

Smiling broadly, Miguel brushed his hands off like it was no big deal. "Just helping out."

"You're going to make three people very happy," Roxie said. "And me, too. I don't know why, but getting that jewelry returned felt really important to me."

"Might be sentimental," Willie said.

Roxie nodded. "Might be. Thank you both." She smiled at Miguel. "I'm really glad you're part of our family."

He bent his head slightly, his eyes dampening. He reached across the counter and placed his hand over Roxie's. "Thank you. I am very glad to be a part of it. My life has ..." He swallowed and cleared his throat. "It's gotten better than I could have imagined it to be. And it was already pretty good."

Roxie got a little choked up herself. "All of our lives have gotten better by coming here and meeting you and your family. Same with us meeting Claire and her family, and I never thought I'd say that."

Willie sniffed.

Roxie swallowed, her emotions near the surface. "But I'm especially glad that you and Ma found each other. You give me hope." She glanced at the commitment ring on her finger. "But then, I have a lot of things to be hopeful about these days."

Chapter Forty-six

*J*ules sat on the edge of the couch in
Jesse's office. Sierra and Cash were in
there with them, too.

As she'd already told the three of them, she was
in the mood to celebrate. There was no other way to
describe what she was feeling. After another great
day in the recording studio, and with the incredible
news she'd gotten from her agent, she wanted to
share all of that happiness with family and friends.

She crafted an impromptu text to her mom, Kat,
and Claire but included Willie and Miguel on it as
well so they could bring their families. Jules wanted
to throw a party, and she wanted everyone to have
their special someone with them.

Jesse would be with her. He was going to let his
new hire take over for a few hours while he came to

the celebration. In fact, he was helping her put the whole thing together.

Hello, friends and family! Life has been very good to me lately. I want to celebrate and I want to do it with all of you. Dinner is on me this evening! Meet me under the house at 7pm for a fried chicken picnic. And meet my new band! Please bring your favorite person and a folding chair. Dogs welcome!

She hit Send, smiling to herself, then got to her feet as she looked over at Jesse, Cash, and Sierra. "Sent. Time to go shopping for me and Jesse. You two are on setup, so you know what to do. After you get the ice and fill the coolers."

Cash nodded, all smooth confidence. "We'll handle it."

Sierra smiled, looking very much like she was happy to be included. "We'll make sure Toby gets taken out, too."

"I appreciate that very much," Jules said. "All right. Battle stations."

Jesse snorted. He grabbed his keys and stood. "You're making this sound more like a military maneuver than an impromptu dinner party."

She shrugged. "Maybe a small military maneuver. We're talking about, what? Twenty-five people and four dogs? If everyone shows up with a friend, that is. Which I hope they do." She'd included her new bandmates, telling them to bring their significant others, as well.

Rita was bringing more than just her husband. She was also bringing her dog, Patsy.

Cash and Sierra were out the door. He gave his mom a wave. "See you at the house. We'll probably be done with our stuff by the time you get there, so we can help unload the car."

"Even better. See you then," Jules said.

She and Jesse walked out after them. He turned off the lights and locked the door, then gave her a smile and a quick kiss. "I'll be right behind you."

"Get your own cart when we get there. I think we're going to need two."

"You got it."

Since he had his own car, he followed her to Publix, where they each got a cart and headed in to get everything they'd need. She'd called ahead to let them know she needed a big batch of fried chicken. She figured with twenty-five people and maybe three pieces of chicken each, that was a minimum of seventy-five pieces.

But that didn't take into account the big eaters, like Cash, Alex, and Miles. She wasn't sure about Bobby and Frankie, either.

To be on the safe side, she'd ordered the one-hundred-piece fried chicken platter. Publix claimed that fed about forty people, but again, they hadn't met Cash.

Jesse rolled his cart alongside hers as they headed for the deli. "What do you want me to get?"

"The chicken order is in my name, so I have to handle that, but I figure we'll pick that up last, since I have to do it over at customer service." She looked at the quick list she'd scribbled down. "Can you grab two flats of bottled water? The ones with twenty-four bottles."

"Consider it done. But I can do more than get water."

"Think you can handle the paper plates, napkins, cups, and utensils? Oh, and some disposable tablecloths. That'll make for easy cleanup."

He nodded. "I can absolutely get all that. Any particulars?"

"Get the good stuff. Nothing flimsy. Get the biggest tablecloths they have. Better them be too big than too small."

He smiled. "I'm on it."

Her phone went off. "I'd better answer that." Might be someone needing details. Or offering to bring something.

"Text me if you think of something else."

"Okay." She dug her phone from her pocket and answered, seeing her sister's name on the screen. "Hi, Claire."

"Are you seriously doing a dinner party for everyone with five minutes' notice?"

Jules laughed. "I know, I'm crazy. But I'm in such a good mood that I need to share it and we've all been going in different directions. Just felt like a good excuse to get everyone together. And for you guys to meet my new band."

"I think it's great. And, yes, you are crazy, but in the best possible way. How about I bring chocolate chip cookies for dessert? It just happens that I have a lot of them made."

"That would be perfect. Thank you."

"Anything else I can do?"

"Not really. Cash and Sierra are getting ice then heading to the house to set up tables and chairs. Although we could probably use another table. Or two."

"Danny's got some. I'll take care of it. Let me know if there's anything else I can do."

"I will. Thanks. Love you."

"Love you, too, little sister." With a happy chuckle, Claire hung up.

Jules approached the cold case that housed all the ready-to-go sides the deli offered. Different varieties of potato salad and coleslaw, as well as macaroni salad. There were all kinds of salads, really, but she was most interested in the ones that went best with fried chicken.

When she'd called, she'd asked how many servings the large salad was. She'd been told eight. Seemed reasonable to her. Factoring in the big eaters, she put five potato salads in her cart, along with four containers of coleslaw and four of the macaroni. She also got five of the smaller broccoli salads.

She grabbed three packages of sweet Hawaiian rolls, four jugs of Publix lemonade and four of Publix sweet iced tea from the refrigerated section in the deli.

With the waters Jesse was getting, they should be good on drinks. She did not want anyone going hungry or thirsty.

Next, she hit the pickle aisle and got two jars of bread and butter pickles. She was putting the last one in the cart when her phone chimed. A text from Jesse.

Where are you?

Pickles, she answered.

He found her shortly. "Did I get enough of everything?"

She looked into his cart and glanced over the things he'd selected. The two flats of bottled water she'd asked for were on the bottom, everything else was in the cart. "Looks good to me. Claire's bringing chocolate chip cookies for dessert."

He nodded. "That's nice of her. Anything else we need?"

"Just the chicken."

"Customer service it is."

There was one other person in line ahead of them, but they quickly got their chicken order, paid for everything, and headed to the cars. All the bags and the big trays of chicken went into her Jeep, because Jesse was headed back to his place to get Shiloh.

He glanced at her, car keys in his hand. "If we forgot anything, text me and I'll pick it up."

She nodded. "You got it. See you soon."

When she arrived at the beach house, Cash, Sierra, and Danny were all there. Tables and chairs had been set up and arranged and the three of them were standing around chatting. When she parked, they came over to help her unload.

She got out. "Looks like you guys have been

busy." She nodded at Danny. "Thanks for lending us the tables."

He smiled. "Thanks for inviting us."

Cash reached for a few bags in the back of Jules's Jeep. "He brought four chairs over, too."

"Even better," Jules said.

Sierra grabbed a few bags as well. "I took Toby out. He's such a cutie."

"Yes, he is. The bags with the plates and napkins and stuff can stay down here." Jules started to heft one of the two big aluminum containers that held the chicken, but Danny stepped in to help, picking them both up together.

"I can get that," he said. "Where do you want it?"

"Upstairs. I'm going to put them both in the oven on the warm setting until everyone gets here."

"Good plan."

Jules took two jugs of drinks and carried them to the cooler that should already have ice in it. Thankfully, it did. She nestled the jugs into the ice and went back for more.

Danny and Cash got on the elevator. Sierra brought more jugs of lemonade and tea over. They weren't all going to fit, but they managed three of each in the big cooler.

"You want me to take the other two upstairs and put them in the fridge?"

Jules nodded. "That would be great."

As Sierra waited for the elevator, Kat arrived home. She jumped out of her car. "Hey, I picked up a couple bags of ice just in case you might need them. Was that okay?"

"That was actually perfect. I'm going to put them in the other cooler and fill that one with bottles of water."

Kat went around and got the bags out of her trunk. "This is pretty cool of you to do, Aunt Jules. Perfect timing, too, because Alex told me Miles is off today. He's going to pick Alex up on his way over and Alex said they'd bring a watermelon."

"That's awesome. Your mom is providing chocolate chip cookies."

"Yum!" Kat brought the bags of ice over. Jules opened the second cooler and Kat dumped them in. She smiled at her aunt. "You're pretty awesome, too, Aunt Jules. My new bosses are so impressed with you donating a portion of your profits. And now that you've agreed to perform at the July Fourth fundraiser, they are seriously in love with you."

Jules laughed. "I'm happy to do it. But I'm sure they're pretty impressed with you, too."

Kat shrugged. "Maybe a little." She grinned and hugged Jules. "I love you. I probably don't say that enough, but I do."

"I love you, too, Kat." Emotions tugged at Jules.

Gravel crunched as Jesse's vehicle pulled into the driveway.

Kat glanced at his car, gave him a little wave, then headed for the elevator. "I'll change and come back down to help."

"Thanks." Jules wiped at her eyes.

Jesse got out, freeing Shiloh from the back seat but keeping her on a leash. "You okay?"

She nodded. "Just full of appreciation for my wonderful life. And my wonderful new boyfriend."

He smiled at her as he encircled her with his free arm. He held her tight and kissed the top of her head. "'Wonderful' is a great word."

Chapter Forty-seven

*T*rina loved people and she loved parties. Jules suddenly deciding to host one and saying dogs were welcome was about the best thing ever. After working at the salon, where she'd finished shelving all the retail products that had arrived, Trina had stopped by Happy Pets on the way home. This time she'd bought Walter a festive bandana to wear.

The bandana was white with a pattern of watermelon slices, blue sunglasses, and yellow suns. Very happy and summery. She'd bought him a red, white, and blue one, too, since they were on sale and July Fourth was coming.

On the way home, she'd heard from Miles. He was picking up Alex on the way over and they were going to bring a watermelon. Trina felt like she ought to be contributing something, but her mom had said not to worry about it before she'd gone in to take a shower. Now her mom was lying down for a few minutes, so Trina was being quiet.

Her mom had also said Ethan was picking up some sangria, and Mimi and Miguel were making rum punch.

Trina had taken a quick shower, too. After that, she'd touched up her makeup, then put on some frayed jean shorts and a cute tee that tied at the waist. It was short enough to show a hint of her stomach but not so short that it was indecent.

Now, she sat on the couch giving Walter a brushing before tying on his new bandana. She fixed it so it lay flat over his shoulders. He looked even more handsome than usual, which she would have thought impossible. "You are the cutest thing ever, Walter baby."

He sat and smiled up at her, making her heart melt at the sight of him for about the hundredth time today. She kissed his nose.

She attached his leash, stuck her sunglasses on her head and her phone in her back pocket. "Let's go down and see if we can help, okay? And maybe we'll get you a quick walk, too."

Trina decided her contribution would be whatever Jules needed her to do. She closed the door softly and they took the steps. Walter wanted to barrel down, but Trina was afraid he'd trip and hurt himself. She kept a tight grip on the leash, but he made it down just fine.

"Hi, there," she said as she walked out into party central. The tables all had tablecloths on them and a line of old-fashioned citronella candles in colored glass jars ran down the center of each one. It was simple, but pretty and with the lights on overhead, just about perfect.

"Hi, Trina," Jules said. She crouched to greet Walter. "Look at this cute face! I love your bandana, Walter. Always nice to see a gentleman dressed up."

Trina grinned. Toby was over by the couches, his leash secured under one of the table legs. There was a much bigger dog, a golden retriever, sitting on the ground near him. "Thanks. What can I do to help?"

Jules looked around and shrugged. "There's really nothing left to do. It's nice of you to offer, though."

"I could take Toby for a walk with Walter. If you want. I was going to try to wear him out a little before the party starts. Not sure I could handle the big dog, too, though."

"That's Jesse's dog, Shiloh. And he actually just took them for a walk. He's upstairs at the moment, trying to find clips to hold down the tablecloths. Maybe you could take Walter over and see how they like each other. Shiloh's a sweetheart, I promise. She can be rambunctious, but she and Toby love each other."

"Okay. But if you need help with anything, just give me a yell."

"I will. Oh! I might actually need some help next week. There's a magazine coming to take some pictures of me. Would you be available to do my hair?"

"Really?" Trina blinked once, then smiled. "I would love to do that for you. Yes, I'll be available. Just let me know where and when and I'll be there."

"That's great," Jules said. "I'll make sure you get credited in the magazine." Jules broke out in a big grin. "It's *Rebel Yell*, so not too shabby a publication."

"Seriously? I thought doing the mayor's wife's hair was cool, but this is even better!"

"You did the mayor's wife's hair?"

Trina nodded. "She called out of the blue. She tried to do it herself because she couldn't get in to see her regular girl, and it didn't go so hot. I fixed it for her. She was *very* happy. Paid me really well. And said she's going to tell all her friends about the salon."

"That's great," Jules said. "Good for you."

"Thanks." Trina looked down at Walter. "Ready to go make a new friend?"

She took him over to Toby and Shiloh. "Hi, Shiloh. What a pretty girl you are. Hi, Toby. Remember Walter?"

Walter's tail was wagging so fast his little butt was shaking. Shiloh came over and Toby hopped down off the couch. Much sniffing and more tail wagging happened. Shiloh stretched out her front legs and woofed softly at Walter. He barked in reply, his happy, friendly bark. That seemed good.

She decided to let Walter play with the dogs instead of taking him away to walk. Shiloh and Toby would wear him out just as well.

It took about twenty minutes of them chasing each other and being silly before all three were on the big wraparound couch, sprawled out and looking like old friends. Trina snapped a few pictures because it was just too cute.

She'd just posted the best photo to her Instagram when Miles and Alex arrived. Miles brought the watermelon over and greeted Trina with a kiss. "Hey, babe. I see Walter made some friends."

"He sure did. They just played like maniacs and

now they're pooped. Thanks for bringing Alex. And the watermelon. That was nice of you."

"Sure. Where should I put it?"

Trina glanced at Jules. She was straightening out a tablecloth that the breeze was trying to dislodge. "Maybe on one of the coolers for now?"

"Okay."

The elevator doors opened, and Jesse and Kat came out, each loaded down with party supplies. At the same time, Danny, Miguel and Willie came walking across from the Rojas's house. Danny was carrying a big drink dispenser full of what looked like rum punch. Trina smiled. Things were getting underway.

Before long, new people arrived that Jules introduced as her bandmates, who then introduced their spouses. One lady, Rita, brought her dog, too. Then Claire came down with Margo, Conrad, and his sister. Trina couldn't remember her name. Something with a D, but not Diana.

Cash and Sierra came down next with the big containers of chicken. Miles went up to help bring more stuff down. By the time they returned, Ethan had arrived with the sangria.

The next thing Trina knew, people were taking seats and the food was being passed around. She sat next to Miles with Kat on the other side of her.

Jules stood a few feet from the tables and raised her hands. "I just wanted to say a big thanks to everyone for coming on such short notice. I'm especially glad to have my new bandmates here along with their spouses. I'm so happy for them to meet all the rest of the people who are important to me."

Lots of smiles all around.

"There's no one reason for this celebration other than I feel so blessed and very much wanted to share that with all of you. Some of you know this already, but *Rebel Yell* magazine is coming next week to do a photo shoot and interview with me." She smiled. "What most of you *don't* know is that two weeks after that, me and my band are flying up to Manhattan to perform my new song as part of the spring concert series for *Wake Up, America.*"

Trina gasped. "That's amazing. Congratulations, Jules!"

"Thanks." Jules's eyes seemed to shine with happiness. Happy tears, Trina realized.

That made her well up a little, too. But then, it didn't take much for her to cry sometimes. Miles put his arm around her.

Jesse stood up and started clapping. In a matter

of seconds, they were all on their feet and joining him in the applause.

"All right, all right," Jules said, looking a little embarrassed. "That's enough of that. Let's eat some chicken."

Laughter and cheers announced everyone's agreement.

Miles leaned closer to Trina. "When dinner is over, you want to take a walk on the beach with me? We can bring Walter."

She nodded. "I'd like that."

He smiled. "Cool."

There was lots of fun conversation and delicious fried chicken. Trina tried all three of the salads and drank two glasses of lemonade. She also had a small glass of her grandmother's rum punch, although she suspected Miguel was really the mixologist behind it.

It was good but strong, and one small glass was more than enough.

As dinner wound down, two of Jules's bandmates, Frankie and Bobby, got out their instruments and played a few songs. The music was incredible. Soon, Rita and Cash joined them on their instruments and Sierra sang some songs.

Trina glanced at Miles. "We can't leave while

they're playing. It would be rude. And I don't want to."

He shook his head. "Neither do I. So I'll just give you this now." He put a small black velvet box in front of her. "Just a little something so you know how I feel about you."

"Miles, you shouldn't have."

"Yeah, I should." He winked at her. "Open it. I hope you like it."

She opened the box and found a silver ring inside with a smoothly polished luminous stone set between two faceted teardrop-shaped stones that were the perfect pale blue. "It's beautiful."

"That's a moonstone in the center. I chose it because moonstones seem to hold their own light. You're just like that, T. Full of light, no matter what. And the blue stones, those are topaz. I liked them because they reminded me of the blue water the day we went surfing."

"I love it. And the reasons you picked these stones." She slipped the ring onto her finger and kissed him. "Thank you."

He just smiled and put his arm around her again. "This is forever, you know. You and me. I mean it."

Trina nodded, too emotional for words. She held her hand in her lap and looked at the ring. It really was beautiful. And very special. Just like the man next to her. The man she was going to spend the rest of her life with.

She glanced at him, knowing if she looked at him too much right now, she'd cry. Happy tears, of course, because life couldn't get any better.

Chapter Forty-eight

*K*at helped her mom and aunt clean up after dinner, although there wasn't much food left to put away. They'd eaten a surprising amount of it. Trina pitched in on cleaning, too, along with Sierra.

When that was done, her mom started making up a plate of chocolate chip cookies to take down for dessert while Jules sliced up the watermelon and arranged it on a large platter.

Kat grabbed a slice as she headed back down in the elevator with Trina. The watermelon was sweet and delicious, and she was definitely having another piece. Or three.

"So..." Trina stuck her hand out. A silver ring caught the light. "Miles just gave me this tonight."

"Wow, it's beautiful," Kat said. She used the back

of her hand to wipe watermelon juice off her chin, then examined the ring more closely. "He did good."

"Thanks. I think so, too." Trina turned her hand back and forth to show off the ring some more. The center stone gleamed with blue light. "You think he got the idea from Alex and the ring he gave you?"

"Maybe," Kat said. "But it's very different from mine. It really is pretty."

"I love it," Trina said. She looked over at Kat. "We ended up with some good guys, didn't we?"

"We totally did."

The doors opened and they got off the elevator. Jules's bandmates were still playing. Kat tossed the watermelon rind in the big trash can that had been set up.

Trina gave Kat a little wave. "See you later. Miles and I are going for a walk on the beach with Walter."

"Great idea," Kat said. "Maybe I'll see if Alex wants to go for one, too. We'll go in the other direction, though, so you don't feel like you're being followed."

Trina laughed. "Okay. Have fun."

She went to meet Miles while Kat joined Alex, who'd left his spot at the table to sit closer to the music. She sat next to him. The elevator doors opened again, and her mom and aunt came out with the desserts. "You want a cookie? Or a slice of watermelon?"

"Did your mom make the cookies?"

"She did."

"Cookie."

Kat got up and grabbed him one, plus another slice of watermelon for herself. They sat and ate, listening to the music. Alex finished his cookie before her watermelon was gone. She got up to toss the rind and came back.

She sat again, but this time only on the edge of the cushion. "You feel like going for a walk or would you rather stay and listen?"

"I'm happy to walk if you want to. Probably should burn a few calories, considering everything I ate."

She snorted. "I was going to say we didn't have to go far, but maybe we will. Whatever you want to do. I just need a little alone time with you."

He smiled. "Yeah?"

She nodded. Being with him around all these people was great, but being alone with him was a different kind of wonderful. "Yeah."

They got up, left their flipflops by the couch, and

walked past the pool and out to the beach. Kat liked the feel of the soft sand between her toes. It was good to be back on the beach. Miles, Trina, and Walter were about ten yards ahead of them and headed right.

Kat and Alex went left.

He went down all the way to the waterline, getting his bare feet wet. "I have a checkup with the doctor tomorrow."

"That's good."

"I've been following his instructions to the letter, so I hope he tells me I'm on track to go back to work soon."

"Me, too. I know you miss it."

"Man, do I." He took her hand. "It's made me realize how important it is for me to be busy. Which probably sounds odd, because a lot of what we do at the firehouse is really just sitting around, waiting."

"No, I get it. Being there and being ready to help is a lot different than sitting on your couch with no plans to do anything else."

He nodded. "I like being useful."

"So do I. I wouldn't have understood that need before, but I do now. Being part of something bigger than yourself is just so much more fulfilling. It's no wonder I was so unsatisfied with my old job but working at Future Florida has made me see so many things in a new light."

"That's great."

"It really is. Although your job is more immediate. You're out there on the front lines of life. Saving lives. That's big." She squeezed his hand. "Makes me so proud of you. I probably haven't said that enough, but I am really proud of you."

"Thanks."

"Which isn't to say that your job doesn't scare me. It does. And I know we've talked about this, but I understand that...caring about you means accepting that risk. It's part of who you are. I'm not going to try to change that part of you, either."

He stopped walking to pull her in as best he could with one arm. "I'm so glad I found you, Kat. When I first talked to you on the beach, I had no idea you were the woman I'd been hoping for, but I know it now. And I never want to lose you."

She cupped his face in her hands. "You're not going to. And not just because you gave me a ring. I can't imagine my life without you, Alex. You've done so much for me in such a short amount of time that I feel like I'm indebted to you."

He laughed. "You don't owe me a thing."

"I feel like I do. But it's more than that. I'm..." She

was almost afraid of what she wanted to say next. Not because she thought she'd scare him off but because talking about their future when they didn't have a firm plan yet felt like taking a risk, in a way.

"You're what? It's okay to say it. To say anything. No judgment here."

She took a breath. "I was going to say that I'm excited for the future. To see where it takes us. And I know this is a long way off and I'm talking about stuff that hasn't happened yet and might not, but I'm excited to see all sorts of things."

"Like?"

She hesitated, but what was the point of holding back? He either felt the same way she did, or he didn't. "Like what our life will be a few years from now. Where we'll be with our jobs. What kind of kids we might have. Things like that."

For a moment, he did nothing but stare into her eyes, the setting sun painting him in shades of gold and orange. Then he smiled. "I think about that, too."

"You do?" That shouldn't surprise her, but it did. "You think about us having kids?"

"I do." He nodded. "I'll go one better. I've even thought about names."

She laughed, the sound catching in her throat

because of all the emotions coursing through her. "I love you, Alex."

"I love you, too, Kat." He reached up to cup her cheek and kissed her.

She kissed him back. As they came apart, she asked, "Do you ever imagine a dog in our future?"

He smiled. "A dog would be great. Did Walter make you want one?"

She shrugged. "He was definitely an influence. He is pretty cute. But I love Toby, too. I don't think it would be fair for me to get a dog now. I'm at work all day. He'd end up being someone else's responsibility. But in the future..."

"When we're married and living in the same house?" He nodded. "That's totally different."

She smiled, her heart and her soul light with joy. "Totally different." She kissed him again, a quick press of her mouth to his. "You know that house will be the beach house. I own half of it, and I see no reason not to live here."

His grin went wide. "If you think I'm going to argue about living on the beach in a big, beautiful house, then maybe you need to get to know me better."

She laughed. "I definitely plan on doing that, but

I was pretty sure you weren't going to complain about it, either."

He let out a contented sigh. "We're going to have a great life together."

"We are. We already do," Kat said as they started to walk again. "It's just going to get better."

Chapter Forty-nine

*C*laire ate a slice of watermelon while Danny sat next to her, demolishing a cookie.

He held it up, a big half-moon missing from where he'd taken a bite. "These are really something. You've made a lot of outstanding things in the last couple of weeks, but this is, I mean, it's a chocolate chip cookie. A basic thing to most people. To make something so familiar taste so much better than all the other versions out there..." He shrugged. "I don't know how you do it."

She smiled, flattered by his praise. "I use the best ingredients I can get. That helps. Really good chocolate is key. I also use different quantities of things than what's standard. And I know it's a cliché, but I really do make them with love."

"Is that what it is? Love?" Eyes full of amusement, he took another bite and chewed. "I thought it was witchcraft."

She laughed, louder than she'd intended, but no one noticed. He could be so funny sometimes, whether he realized it or not. "Nope. I promise you, there's no eye of bat or tail of newt in there."

"Good to know." He broke a piece of the remaining cookie off and popped it in his mouth. "Health Department might frown on the bat bits. Not sure what the regulations are on newt parts, either."

She shook her head at his silliness, chuckling softly.

Conrad came over and sat across from them. "Claire, I just had to tell you that the *Gazette* photographer was really impressed with that pie of yours. I know he told you he liked it, but I wanted you to know he meant it and wasn't just saying that to be kind."

"That's nice to hear."

Conrad nodded. "He talked that pie up so much in the office that I've been asked to bring one in." He raised his brows. "I know you're not officially open, but what are the chances I could buy one anyway?"

"We'll get you one, on the house," Danny said.

Then he glanced at Claire. "As long as that's all right with you."

"It's fine. I'll be happy to make one for the *Gazette* folks. Maybe I should check with Jesse and see how his are selling. If they aren't, you could always get one from him." She hoped that wasn't the case, obviously. She waved Jesse over.

He came when she beckoned. "Yes, ma'am. You want me?"

"I do. Just wanted to know how the sour orange pies are doing."

He put the palm of his hand to his head. "The pies! I'm so glad you brought them up. I've been meaning to talk to you about them. I think we should up the order to nine of them a week. I could take delivery anytime, really."

Claire's mouth came open. "Nine? And you want them soon?"

He nodded. "I had a group of twelve last night and nine of them ordered it. Then other people in the dining room saw the pie, wanted to know what it was and just like that I only have two pies left. How soon can I get more?"

Claire swallowed in disbelief and looked at Danny. "I guess I know what I'm doing tomorrow."

He grinned. "We'll get the pies to you day after

tomorrow." He looked in Claire's direction. "Right? Because they need to chill?"

He paid attention, which was one of the many things she loved about him. "That's right." She returned her attention to Jesse. "We'll bring them over as soon as they're ready to travel. Nine of them." She smiled at Conrad. "And one for the *Gazette* office."

"That pie is going to buy you a bigger catamaran, Danny," Jesse said. "When that article comes out, it's going to be standing room only at the bakery." Then he paused and asked Claire, "Hey, did you mention in the article that the Dolphin Club is the only place outside of the bakery to get the pie?"

"No, but that's not a bad idea," Claire said. If people could taste the pie before the bakery opened, they might actually end up with a line. Wouldn't that be something? "Conrad, can you slip that in somewhere?"

Conrad nodded. "It hasn't gone to print yet, so I'll make it happen. It's the least I can do in exchange for a pie." He got up. "Better get back to the girls. Thanks, Claire."

"You're welcome." She loved that he called Margo and his sister "the girls." Even more, she loved that he and Margo had made peace with Dinah. Families should be together.

Jesse waved his goodbye and returned to his spot closer to the band.

Danny ate the last piece of cookie while Claire basked in the praise she'd just received. It felt good to know that such an old recipe, something that had been in her family for years, might actually get some recognition. The money they'd make off of it was just the icing on the cake, really. Or the meringue on the pie, such as the case might be.

Pun intended.

Danny wiped a smudge of chocolate off his fingers. "I don't really have any plans to buy a bigger catamaran, you know."

"I'm okay with that." She tapped her foot to the music. The band was so talented. And Jules was about to become a superstar. She smiled at all the goodness filling their lives. "I like that little boat of yours. It's a lot of fun. Although I suppose it'll be a while before we get to go out on it again."

"We might fit one more trip in before we're officially open."

"I'd like that."

A few moments of silence passed between them,

then he spoke again. "Don't you want to know what I *was* thinking about spending my money on?"

She looked over at him. "Sure, if you want to tell me."

He gazed into her eyes for a second. "I was thinking about buying a diamond."

She made a face as curiosity got the best of her. "A diamond?"

He nodded. "A nice-sized one. At least two carats. Set in gold. Maybe with a few smaller diamonds around it."

She blinked. "You're getting yourself a ring?"

He rolled his eyes and laughed. "Not for *me*." Then the humor drained off his face. "Or is this your way of telling me you wouldn't be interested?"

Her brow furrowed before realization struck her. "Oh. *Oh.* You don't mean..." She touched her throat. Her pulse jumped under her fingers. "Do you?"

"I do mean that. An engagement ring. For you. Eventually. When you're ready." He exhaled and ran a hand through his hair. "That is where we're headed, isn't it? Because I thought—"

She kissed him. He tasted of chocolate and promises. "I thought that was where we were headed, too, but...oh, Danny, I'm nuts about you. You have to know that. I've never known a man like you.

I didn't think men like you even existed." She smiled. "Who'd have thought I'd fall for the boy next door?"

Happiness filled his gaze as he put his arm around her and tugged her close. "I need you in my life, Claire. I thought living next door would be enough. I thought working together would be enough. It's not. I want you around all the time. I want to go to bed with you at night and wake up to you in the morning. I want to discover new things with you and enjoy all the old familiar things, too. I want it all, basically."

She wanted that, too, but all she could manage was a nod as she sniffed and leaned into his strong embrace. Finally, she said, "I want that, too."

He spoke softly into her ear, just loud enough to be heard over the band. "I know it's too soon after Bryan's passing. I know society says there's a certain amount of time that you should be in mourning. I don't know how what Bryan did affects your circumstances or if it even does, but when you're ready, you just say the word and I'll be down on one knee before you finish speaking."

She smiled and sniffed again. She didn't really care what society thought, but she didn't want to do anything that might cast the bakery in a bad light, so she just nodded. "I promise to let you know the day I'm ready."

After Bryan's sudden heart attack, her prospects in life had seemed so bleak and dim. She'd never thought she'd get a chance to start over in a place like Diamond Beach. Never imagined she'd find love again with a man like Danny Rojas, who cared for her like she was the only woman in the world who mattered.

His love was better than anything she'd ever experienced. Real, selfless love that was for her and her alone.

She straightened and looked Danny in the eyes. "I also promise that when you ask, I'll say yes."

He smiled. "I love you, Claire."

"I love you, too, Danny."

The band started playing a slow song.

Danny took her hand, kissed her knuckles and got up from his seat. "Come on. Let's have a dance." He winked at her. "Might as well practice for the wedding."

With a big smile, she got to her feet. "I don't need a reason to dance with you, but that's a pretty good one."

As they swayed to the music, she looked around at her family and Roxie's family and thought about how far they'd all come. About the friendships they'd forged. The romances that had blossomed. The new career paths they'd taken.

The future was so very bright for all of them. And she couldn't wait to see what came next.

Big Batch Chocolate Chip Cookies

Ingredients

1 ½ cup salted butter (3 sticks), room temperature

1 3/4 cup dark brown sugar

1/2 cup white sugar

2 eggs, room temperature

1 ½ tablespoona vanilla paste (or extract)

1 ½ tablespoons cornstarch

2 teaspoons baking soda

½ teaspoon salt

4 cups all-purpose flour

3 cups semi-sweet chocolate chips (or whatever kind of chocolate you prefer)

Instructions

In a stand mixer bowl with the paddle attachment, cream together butter, and the brown and white sugars on medium speed. Beat until light and fluffy (2-3 minutes). Add in eggs and vanilla and incorporate on low speed. Then turn mixer to medium-high and mix for 1 minute.

Scrape down the sides of the bowl, then add the cornstarch, baking soda, and salt. Mix for 30 seconds then begin to add the flour ½ cup at a time. Mix until fully incorporated.

Fold in the chocolate chips by hand.

Chill the dough for at least an hour. Overnight is fine too. Then use a medium size cookie scoop to place dough balls two inches apart on the parchment-lined baking sheets. Top with a few more chocolate chips for a bakery look.

To bake, preheat oven to 350 F. Bake for 8-10 minutes until edges start to crisp. Make sure not to over bake, the cookies will set up as they cool.

Once out of the oven, let cookies cool on the baking sheet for 5 minutes, and then transfer to wire rack to finish cooling.

Want to know when Maggie's next book comes out?
Then don't forget to sign up for her newsletter at her
website!

Also, if you enjoyed the book, please recommend it to a
friend. Even better yet, leave a review and let others
know.

Other Books by Maggie Miller

The Blackbird Beach series:

Gulf Coast Cottage

Gulf Coast Secrets

Gulf Coast Reunion

Gulf Coast Sunsets

Gulf Coast Moonlight

Gulf Coast Promises

Gulf Coast Wedding

Gulf Coast Christmas

The Compass Key series:

The Island

The Secret

The Dream

The Promise

The Escape

Christmas on the Island

The Wedding

About Maggie:

Maggie Miller thinks time off is time best spent at the beach, probably because the beach is her happy place. The sound of the waves is her favorite background music, and the sand between her toes is the best massage she can think of.

When she's not at the beach, she's writing or reading or cooking for her family. All of that stuff called life. She hopes her readers enjoy her books and welcomes them to drop her a line and let her know what they think!

Maggie Online:

www.maggiemillerauthor.com
www.facebook.com/MaggieMillerAuthor

Made in the USA
Middletown, DE
14 January 2024

47853062R00243